A Wedding
in the
Olive Garden

Also by Leah Fleming

The Wedding Dress Maker
Daughter of the Tide
In the Heart of the Garden

The Olive Garden Choir

A Wedding
in the
Olive Garden

Leah Fleming

HEAD
of
ZEUS

First published in the UK in 2020 by Head of Zeus Ltd
This paperback edition first published in 2020 by Head of Zeus Ltd

9 7 5 3 1 2 4 6 8

A catalogue record for this book is available from
the British Library.

ISBN (PB): 9781788548724
ISBN (E): 9781788548694

Typeset by Siliconchips Services Ltd UK

Printed and bound in Great Britain by
CPI Group (UK) Ltd, Croydon CR0 4YY

Head of Zeus Ltd
5–8 Hardwick Street
London EC1R 4RG
www.headofzeus.com

*With thanks to those who shelter and protect
all creatures great and small.*

From *THE PARADISE TOURS TO
THE GREEK ISLANDS*

SANTANIKI

Off the coast of Crete lies the beautiful island of Santaniki, sanctuary for wild flowers, ancient chapels, quaint villages set in a turquoise sea. This summer the Elodie Durrante Foundation Trust is offering a variety of courses. This is your chance to meet other artists and poets, and attend workshops and one-to-one sessions to share your work. There will be evenings to discuss your work and guest speakers to inspire you with their readings in the sunshine.

What better way to study than in the spacious villa, home of the late, best-selling romance writer, Elodie Durrante, set among olive groves overlooking Sunset Bay, plus plenty of time to enjoy the island culture and dance under the stars.

Don't miss this chance to make your passion happen. We can organise the whole package for you; flights from the UK and other European destinations, the short ferry crossing from the lively ports of Chania and Rethymno. Places are limited so book now.

June

1

Sara Loveday sat looking out of the plane window, seeing the island of Crete laid out before her like a map. She felt suddenly lighter, as if floating in a dream. The past week had been an unreal nightmare of confusion; a cocktail of disbelief, disappointment, shock that was turning into an all-consuming fury.

She had drowned her feelings in vodka on that first night alone in the flat until she had passed out into oblivion, waking up next morning with a pounding head and a tongue like cork matting. Everything was a blur but she knew what she must do.

The dress was still where she had flung it off, staring up at her as if to say, *What have you done? Missed the last chance of happiness? It could have worked but you never gave him a chance to explain.* She was not staying a moment longer in Sheffield now that she had booked a last-minute break online, to a tiny Greek island where she could lick her wounded pride.

At least she had left her mark on the once pristine loft apartment with its chrome and white starkness. In the cold light of day, she could see the result of last night's mayhem where she had flung red wine over the walls. The decor was not her choice, serve him right. Why had it taken her so long to realise the place was as empty a shell as the man himself? She couldn't bring herself to say his name.

Sara was due a break but not quite the one they had planned. Her assistant, Karen, was capable of taking care of the events and conference business. She had three weeks ahead of her to sort out her future. If only her mind could rid herself of those images.

Sara's ears hummed as they began the descent into Souda Bay, turning onto the flat airstrip as the plane screeched into landing. She collected her baggage and then out into the arrivals hall where the rep from Paradise Tours was waiting, holding up a flag. She guided a few passengers onto a minivan heading for the port. Sara smiled at the bustle of tourists around her, knowing she had sunshine and sea, wonderful salads and fruits to enjoy. It was far away from Yorkshire grey skies and all the humiliation of the past week. She felt the heat on her arms. This was what she needed, and for the first time she felt herself relax.

They arrived at the ferry just in time for the late afternoon crossing to Santaniki. The water was turquoise and choppy but there was a breeze cooling them. Sara sat staring out over the sea as each nautical mile was taking her far from the past.

A middle-aged man was trying to retch over the side, his face grey with seasickness.

'Are you okay?' she asked, seeing his discomfort.

'It gets me every time.' He tried to smile. 'I should know better.'

'I'll get the rep, she may have some wristbands to settle you. You know the island then?'

'I'm the bad penny that rolls up every season; love the light and the food.'

'You're an artist?' Sara was curious.

'A writer... Don Ford. I take summer courses at the retreat house.'

She recognised that name. 'You're the crime writer? My dad is a great fan, wow...'

'For my sins, but I was a friend of Elodie Durrante, the novelist who left her house as a retreat for artists and new writers. They run summer courses each year. Some of these passengers, I guess, will be my clients, all wanting to know how to write a bestseller. And you?'

'Annual holiday,' she replied, not wanting to explain further.

'You are in for a treat; the beaches, the food, the tavernas. It's a very sociable island. You'll see me most nights in Taverna Irini on the market square with my students. Do join us, there's a band of sorts on Fridays.'

Was he making a pass at her? That was the last thing she wanted so she smiled and drifted away from him to scan the horizon as the island slowly came into view.

Her eyes were searching the layers of multicoloured houses with tiled roofs dotting the shoreline, the little ochre mountain peeking above the town. It hadn't the blue and white sophistication of Santorini, much as she loved to visit there. It was more homely, uneven, higgledy-piggledy with boats bobbing in the harbour and fishing smacks beside a marina full of expensive yachts. She spied the white hotels by the water and the golden beach shimmering in the distance. It looked unspoilt.

As they chugged into the harbour, she spotted a crowd on the street, some with suitcases ready for their journey home. She stepped along the gangplank, dazzled by the sun, and fumbled for her sunglasses.

'I've got a lift coming,' Don Ford said humping his case behind her. 'Do you know where you're heading?'

'I have a map… Ariadne Villa. I don't think it's far.'

'It's uphill on the way to the retreat. You are welcome to hitch a lift in the minibus. There's Spiro, our taxi, plenty of room.'

'I'm fine, thank you. The walk will do me good after all that sitting. Enjoy your courses, Mr Ford.' Give him his due, he was persistent, but she was in no mood to make polite conversation with him or anyone else. As she trudged up the cobbled streets with her case rattling, trying to look cool, she began to regret her stubbornness. It was hot and the map she had was sketchy but if she kept to the shade of the stone houses, it wouldn't be far. It had been an early start, a long flight and ferry ride but this was the last lap. Then she could collapse in Ariadne Villa and shut out the world for three whole weeks. Sara was not in the mood for boozy nights in a taverna with a load of wannabe writers or anyone else.

2

The fan in the taverna kitchen did nothing to cool tempers as Mel Papadaki was giving her husband Spiro an earful. 'Do you call this clean? Look at those stains. Mama will have a fit to see such a mess in here… Can I not leave you five minutes to water the pavement…'

'Enough, woman!' Spiro threw off his apron. 'If you can do better, I'm off. The ferry is due and I have passengers and wine to collect. We need more—'

'So *you* can drink it?' Mel yelled back. She could give as good as she got. The fiery Italian half of her could shout with the best of them. She was in no mood to compromise, with his mother Irini sick, no doubt listening into their arguments with glee. Spiro could do no wrong in her eyes.

She wiped the sweat off her brow as the hairnet scratched her forehead. The Santaniki heatwave was unbearable. Oh, to be cooling in Yorkshire drizzle than trying to cook and clean, up and down stairs at Irini's command while Spiro swanned off to the harbour for a smoke. Yes, she knew he was back on the fags behind her back. It had been a tough winter with storms and little work for a builder. Times were tough for Greece. At least their own house was almost finished but cash was tight. He was at a loose end and touchy. Too many fry-ups thickening his waistline. Much as she loved the bones of him, he was letting himself go.

Mel stared at the pile of fresh tomatoes, peppers, courgettes and onions she had picked from their vegetable garden ready to make a cooling gazpacho. Irini came down to inspect the menus and threw out her suggestion with a wave of her hand. 'That's not Greek food. You cannot serve that.'

'But English customers will love something cool and refreshing like this,' Mel argued.

'We are not serving that today,' Irini muttered and that was that. A Sheffield girl married to a Cretan was never going to be easy but she would bloody well make a batch for her and the boys for lunch later. Loading the dishwasher, she heard her mobile ring. What did he want now? It was a garbled message about a booking but the signal was weak so she stepped outside in the square to catch the details.

There was a young woman trundling her suitcase uphill without a sun hat, pausing to look at her map. 'Can I help?' she shouted but the woman carried on, her eyes focused on her task, not hearing her. Ah well. Mel sighed. She was probably Scandinavian or Dutch with little English, she thought, turning back out of the sun, thinking no more about it. Then Spiro's horn honked as his passengers spilled out of the taxi for a quick snack. There was Don Ford, twice as large and full of his usual sparkle.

'Melodia, *kalispera*, it's good to be back!' He gave her a bear hug. 'Just as beautiful as ever... and Irini? I hear she has been unwell...'

'Come, sit down,' Spiro ordered as the new contingent sat in the shade of the taverna. Now the season was in full swing, the tables full each night, Mel could relax a little. It was always tough but this was when their income was made. Their two boys would soon finish school until September and needed supervision, and she had only Katya to help and some students in the village to wait at tables if needed, but they would manage, they always did – if Spiro pulled his weight and kept his eyes on the job and not on the girls in skimpy shorts and tops.

3

Jolyon de Grifford, warden manager of the Elodie Durrante Arts Foundation retreat house, was busy trying to sort the blockage in the bathroom of one of the guests. Greek plumbing had a will of its own, with narrow pipework that forbade any flushing of paper or wipes. This was written in large letters over the bowl, and he asked guests to be careful, but the Brits were not used to this at first, some complaining about such primitive arrangements until they got used to obeying the order. Some never did.

Griff sighed, holding his breath, getting used to this task on a weekly basis. He was just clearing up when he heard a shout through the open window. Peering out, he saw a bald-headed man floundering in the pool. Dropping everything, he raced downstairs and out to the poolside, jumping in fully clothed to grab the drowning swimmer while one of the other guests flung the lifebelt to him.

Griff pulled the man to the shallow end where they could both stand up. 'Don, how many times have I told you not to drink, stuff yourself with chips and then try to swim?' Don Ford may be a famous crime writer but he was rotund, unfit and almost a non-swimmer.

'Sorry, Griff, but it was so hot I just wanted to cool off.'

'You should be in your room in this heat. It's siesta time so have a cold shower. I thought you were having a heart attack. Please don't go out of your depth and keep off the sauce at midday. It's water for you from now on, especially in this heat,' Griff ordered, his shorts dripping, clinging to his legs.

Tragedy averted, Griff returned to his fetid task. Talk about eyes in the back of your head in this job. Warden was a good name for his constant vigilance. What was it with artists, writers, poets – did they live on another planet? Most of them acted like big kids when they weren't closeted away in the shade working on their creations. Nevertheless, this lot were a great bunch and formed a gang.

He was living a world away from his former work in the City with its routines of gym, dinner parties and business meetings. Santaniki was an escape from his past life, thank God. He had his bike and his gardening to get away from bad memories. The courses were usually two weeks long but some stayed for a month, like Don. He was a regular on the lecture circuits and spent most of the summer writing in Elodie's old study.

'I write away from my desk,' he explained. 'It must be the light here, the slow pace, but it just gets my juices flowing.' Griff knew him well enough to guess that the juices flowing through Don's veins were a lethal combination of village wine and raki, sold on the markets with an unknown level of alcohol. Still, Don was a great raconteur when in or out of his cups and a loyal customer in the tavernas around the harbour and the square.

Griff had been here nearly a year and liked having the winter to repair, decorate and join in village life. The London high life was no longer an option for him but even now rage came over him. He would hike up into the hills to cool off his bad temper. He liked being his own boss here and couldn't believe the happenstance that brought him to this tiny island sanctuary – all because his old school friend Felix MacLeod had a new partner, Alexa Bartlett, whose parents were residents here.

Knowing how down Griff could get, Felix invited him to a small gathering to meet Alexa's mother and father. Simon was a retired editor and Chloë a doting grandmother to Olympia, the child of Alexa's first marriage to Felix and Griff's old school friend, Hugh. It was just a throwaway remark that the retreat house was looking for a new warden as the previous family were returning for their children's education. An impromptu visit to the island for a long weekend clinched his decision. Griff fell in love with the limestone rocks, the trails amongst the hills and the food. Perhaps this was the challenge he needed.

Griff had stood on the terrace of the retreat house looking out over the turquoise bay and up at the peaks, the ochre rocks and silvery foliage, inhaling the scent of herbs, and thought perhaps... just perhaps.

On returning to London he made plans. His stay on Santaniki would just be a sabbatical to soothe his wounded pride and sense of failure. He loved ferries and slow journeys so he would travel leisurely towards this new venture on bike, packing everything into panniers. He was determined to travel light through Europe, cycling over the Alps to Italy, overland to Venice, sailing across to Patras and on to Athens to take the night ferry to Chania. It was a challenge but he felt free of everything for the first time in months. Crossing to the smaller island by ferry, he arrived in time for the annual olive harvest in November where he joined in the olive stripping, enjoying this initiation into Cretan life.

As Griff now sat watching the sun descend over the sea like a ball of flame, he felt the island wrapping itself round all his senses; the slower pace, the heat, the light. His guests were living it up at Irini's taverna and he could hear the noise rising and the music of their jazz ensemble floating up to him in the dusk. Griff smiled, turning to Elodie Durrante's book he had promised to read: *Under the Cretan Sun* was set during the Greek and Turkish wars; a Romeo and Juliet sort of tale.

It was then he thought he felt someone over his shoulder and turned but no one was there. He smiled again, thinking the wine had gone to his head, but no, there was a presence, a scent of attar, of roses, his late mother's favourite perfume. She used to love her roses and it reminded him of racing round the garden to find her on her knees, deadheading her precious blooms. His love of gardening came from her. First though, he must clear that border patch at Ariadne Villa, giving the shrubs a chance to breathe and water to refresh their roots, and later take Don Ford on a hike into the hills. He was a heart attack waiting to happen. It would make a change from unblocking sewage.

4

Sara found Ariadne Villa down a side lane. It was well furnished, clean, but had that empty feeling; someone's home let out but not many bookings, she suspected.

There was a complimentary basket of basic groceries waiting for her: olive oil, eggs, milk, bread, feta cheese, a jar of Cretan honey, coffee and tea bags and instructions for use of the appliances. The beds were made up and stone floors mopped with a pungent cleaner. It was a simple two-bedroom house, shower upstairs with one big kitchen and living room downstairs, brightly furnished. She wondered who had once lived there.

Sara opened the shutters, delighting in a veranda draped with purple bougainvillea with a view to the bay, but surveyed the garden with dismay. The olive trees had been carefully pruned, but the oleander bushes were straying over the path and the last fruits of the sweet orange bush were in need of picking. The borders were overgrown but there was a sun-drenched stone patio that looked out over the garden on a slope facing the bay. This was paradise indeed. She unpacked her case into the spare room, decluttered the kitchen and found out how the cooker worked. After that, she felt she had earned her rest.

There was just enough time to get out the sunlounger and soak up some sun.

Lying half asleep, topless, she heard the side door open. Someone had not used the front doorbell but was slipping in; someone familiar with the layout. She quickly tied her sarong over her bare boobs and stood up to see a man standing in the shadows. Was he coming to rob the place?

'Who are you?' Sara's heart was thumping; she was face to face with a tall stranger.

'I thought this house was empty,' he replied.

'Did you now?' Sara stood her ground when she saw he had implements in his hand; she was trying not to tremble, aware of being half naked. 'If you're after rich pickings, I'm afraid you're in for a disappointment. There is nothing of value here.'

'Sorry?' He looked nonplussed. 'You think I'm a thief?' He laughed. 'I'm Jolyon Grifford, here to keep Ariadne's garden in some shape.' He was wearing a floppy sun hat with frayed edges, khaki shorts on long tanned legs in sandals. 'So... who are you?' he asked, eyeing her disarray with amusement.

'I've booked the villa for three weeks but I didn't expect visitors... Sara Loveday.' She tossed back her blonde curls, dismissing him, refusing to give him any further explanation. 'If you don't mind, I was reading,' she lied. 'And I prefer to do the garden myself, thank you. If I need any help, I'll ask, but I like it as it is…' she said, pointing to the gate. 'In future, if you call, please use the front doorbell.' He was dismissed but not before he had the last word. Turning to her seat in the sun, he paused, smiling, looking to the lounger.

'I wouldn't sit there too long – mosquitos like new flesh and I hope you have the coils burning in the house and outside.'

'Thank you, I do, and cream.'

'Better to buy local stuff here, it's stronger. Do cover up at night or they'll get your ankles and you don't want to get dirty bites.'

'Are you a doctor?' She was curious now.

'No, just warden of the retreat house,' he replied in his upper crust accent.

'Oh, that… I met someone on the ferry who teaches there. I gather it's a place for writers and artists to come on courses or stay to develop their projects.'

'You are well informed,' he replied.

'Well thank you, Mr Grifford.'

'Everyone here calls me Griff, but I'll leave you in peace. Pleased to meet you, sorry for the intrusion. I won't bother you again.' With that he made his exit leaving Sara embarrassed. What right had she to stop him working here if he was responsible for the garden? It was not her house. She was just a guest. Perhaps she ought to have offered him some tea or something but entertaining was not on her agenda. She just wanted to lie in the sun and sulk. This was an idyllic escape and she desperately wanted to make the most of it before she went back to Sheffield.

She left her sunbed to check the time. It was nearly

wine o'clock and there was nothing in the house. Time to walk up to the square and the minimarket to top up her supplies. Conscious of her white legs and arms, she fished out a thin dress. It would be good to stretch her legs and find her bearings.

The minimarket was disappointing except for a box of sticky sweet baklava that took her fancy. It was still hot and she sought shade in the taverna, sinking down with relief as her new expensive sandals were chafing her heels.

'What can I get you?' A dark-haired woman smiled at her.

'Something cold but not beer,' Sara replied.

'Would you like to try Irini's home-made lemon cordial? It's refreshing and very popular.'

Sara looked up in surprise. 'You're not Greek, are you?'

'A Yorkshire tyke from Sheffield,' came the reply.

'So am I... how strange. It's a small world.' They both laughed.

'Do I know you? I saw you arriving and you reminded me of someone from school.'

'I doubt it, they say we all have a doppelganger.' Sara felt a stab of alarm but she didn't recall recognising this woman, even if she was about her own age.

'Mel Duckworth, as was, Papadaki now. How is the old place? I've not been back for years. Once you own a place in the sun, everyone wants to come out here. This your first visit?'

'I've been to Greece many times but not here. It was a last-minute booking, spur of the moment.' That much Sara was happy to reveal but she didn't want to be reminded of Sheffield. 'I'm Sara... Sara Loveday.'

'Where are you staying?'

'Just down the road... Ariadne Villa.'

'Ah, it belongs to Ariadne Blunt but she's been in England for over a year. It makes sense to let it out, I suppose. We miss her. How do you like her garden?'

'Funny you should say that but I had a visit from a guy I thought was a burglar. I gave him short shrift.'

'That must be Griff. Did he explain, he does some garden work but he's the warden at the big house up the hill.'

'So I gather, but the garden will do for now. What's it like living here all year?'

'Very Greek, lots of tourists but the winter is quieter. There's enough expats to make a community. You'll see them around in the evenings along with the crowd from the arts courses. Come and join us on Friday. There's an open mic and a few of us make music; you will be very welcome. But let me get your drink.' Mel dashed off into the back.

It was a typical taverna, wooden chairs with cane seats, blue and white tablecloths, the walls festooned with sepia pictures, geraniums in terracotta pots and a bar at the end by the kitchen from where scents of spicy cooking wafted into the air. Mel came back with a jug of cordial and a plate of cinnamon biscuits.

'You've got yourself a fine place here.'

'Oh, it's not ours, my mother-in-law Irini owns the business. She's not been well lately. Spiro, my husband, helps where he can. We have two little lads so I am rushed off my feet at the moment.'

There was a man sitting in the corner staring at them,

trying to catch their conversation, a scruffy bloke twirling his amber beads. 'Don't mind him, he's part of the furniture, I'm afraid. He comes in for a coffee and would stay all day if we let him. You'd think he had better things to do… a farmer from the tops,' Mel whispered. 'He gives me the creeps. He could do with a good wash. I disinfect his chair in case he leaves fleas. You get all sorts in here but it's not my job to chuck him out. That's right, Stavros, I'm talking about you,' she shouted.

Sara sat ignoring the old man, savouring the biscuits and the lemon squash until her legs were sticking to the chair with the heat. 'I'd better be off and those biscuits were delicious. Thanks.'

'Do come on Friday, it'll be a good night and you'll meet the crowd. Are you sure we haven't met before? I feel I should know you,' Mel added.

Sara nodded and sped down the road, unnerved by Mel's insistence that she knew her. She had come to Santaniki to be anonymous and yet the first person she met was from her home city. What a strange, unsettling coincidence.

In the cool of the late afternoon, he roused the tutor from his usual lie-in and insisted they went for a walk while it was still light. Don groaned, 'Do I have to?'

Griff was in no mood after a sharp encounter with the new occupant of Ariadne Villa and did not mince his words. 'If you're going to be here through the summer, we need to get some of that flab off you. I don't want any more incidents in the pool.' Griff was already packed and ready for the off. He insisted Don wore shorts, a sun hat and decent trainers. He would not overdo the first trek as Don was so unfit but he needed to stretch him a little and the view from the plateau was worth the effort.

Don puffed and panted, wiped the sweat off his brow and demanded to sit down under a carob tree. 'Easy does it, old chap. Give me five minutes to enjoy the view.'

'It'll be better when we get to the top, I promise. It's not far and then we can have a drink.'

Don was having none of it, getting out his cigarettes. 'Here I stay, enough for one session.' He lay back with his hat over his face.

'Watch out… there may be snakes or scorpions waiting to pounce on you,' Griff laughed and Don shot up.

'I'm not going any further. You go on, you slave driver.' It was then they heard a strange sound, a mewing. 'What's that?'

Griff looked round but found nothing. There was a louder whimper. 'It's a sheep or lamb somewhere, I expect. I'll take a look.'

'I'm coming with you. It may need help.' Don rose slowly as Griff climbed ahead.

'Over here!' Griff shouted by the rock. Don puffed his way to join him. 'Look at that!' Griff pointed to a little creature huddled under the shade of the rock, a matted, unrecognisable animal like a tiny lamb, but it was not a lamb but a dog, mangey, hairless, bone-thin, that gazed up at them. It looked close to death. 'My God, the poor thing.' Griff could hardly speak. 'It's trying to wag its tail. Fetch the water. There's a towel in the bottom of the bag.'

Don watched as Griff dribbled water onto its lips and it

drank. 'We must wrap it in the towel and lift it. It may be too late but I'll not have it die alone in this state.' The dog offered no resistance and looked up at them in gratitude through crusted eyes.

They carried it in turn close to their chests, wondering if it would survive the journey. 'How on earth did it land up here? Was it dumped?' Griff said.

'No idea. What can you do?' Don replied. 'Is there a vet on the island?'

'Not that I know of. I'll take him to Dr Makaris. If it's too late he will know what to do. This animal has suffered enough. If it survives the night, I'll take him over to the mainland for treatment. Just look at the state of him.'

'It was a good job I sat down for a breather, otherwise…' Don shook his head.

Griff turned to him and smiled. 'If there's a spark of life left in it, don't worry, you will take the credit, but I wouldn't hold your breath.' They walked down the path in silence while Griff prayed the warmth of his body would keep the little creature alive.

Mel was late as usual for the book club meeting in Dorrie Thorner's house. Membership was thin at the moment as many residents were away. Dorrie would take it as a personal insult if there were only a few in attendance. Mel had not done her homework either and that would be noted and held against her. It wasn't her fault. Irini needed more help, Markos was playing up, Spiro was late and she'd given him an earful. 'I don't often get a night off, even if it is only to listen to Dorrie Thorner waxing lyrical about her latest literary sensation, but I do like meeting up and chatting in English all night.'

She stomped off in a bad mood and almost turned back. Meetings weren't the same without their founder member, Ariadne Blunt. She arrived in time to hear the latest gossip about the new arrival in St Nick's.

'Who's the poor victim this time?' she joked.

'The woman in Ariadne's villa. Have you met her? Is she staying long?'

'Only briefly,' Mel replied. 'And she's from Yorkshire so you can't get better than that.'

'She's on her own then?' Dorrie was prying as usual. 'I was told she arrived on that Don Ford's arm. Perhaps he's brought some company with him to keep him in check.'

'We don't know that,' said Chloë Bartlett who was trying not to look interested.

'Give the poor girl a chance, ladies. I've not seen her with the writing group or Don Ford in the taverna yet. I think it's only a short holiday let.'

'Do you think she would be good book club material? We could do with more temporary guests in the season. They have lots of paperbacks to share.' Trust Dorrie to see a chance.

'Most don't have the sort of books you read, surely.' Mel couldn't help herself. Just because someone was single, there was no need to make assumptions, but she bit her tongue. 'Hadn't we better start?'

'We were waiting for you.' Dorrie looked at the wall clock. 'I hope you've all read my choice.' She was looking in Mel's direction.

'Sorry, I meant to, but every time I picked it up in bed, I fell asleep.'

'You're not the only one,' Chloë added. 'I'm afraid the subject matter didn't hold my interest. You know I only give a book seventy pages but after that… sorry.'

Dorrie shook her lacquered bob with a sigh. 'I see… Am I the only one to have read it then?'

No one spoke. 'Then it's a good job I made some notes.'

Mel sat back in the cane chair resigned to at least a twenty-minute lecture, her eyes drooping in the heat. It had been a long, tiring day and she hoped to be rewarded with some decent wine and a slice of Victoria sponge but, knowing Dorrie, it would be something undrinkable and sensible Cretan biscuits.

5

Spiro Papadakis, Mel's husband, stood watching the ferry boat chugging into the harbour. His pickup truck was waiting for the catering supplies and boxes of provisions for the coming wedding celebrations on Saturday. He took his cigarettes from the glove pocket for a sneaky fag out of Mel's range. She was busy in the kitchen cooking ahead for the wedding feast. His mama was doing her best but struggling, bad tempered, snapping at his little boys, criticising poor Mel and demanding everything was done to family tradition.

Dr Makaris's son, Ari, was marrying Father Mikhalis's daughter, Elefteria, and the whole town was invited to the feast. The town didn't have a wedding centre where hundreds of guests could be seated, but the community hall and its car park turned into overspill with tables and chairs sitting out in the open air and the music and dancing taking place on the square itself. Spiro had a rehearsal tonight to sharpen up the dances that his group would be performing.

His white boots needed cleaning and his traditional costume airing. The young couple wanted as many guests to wear traditional outfits but the custom was dying out. The ladies would be adorned in glittery dresses and, when she had time, Mel was busy adding sequins to her long party dress.

Mel had introduced him to a girl renting Ariadne Villa who came from her home town. She had striking green eyes, a freckled nose and a mane of blonde hair with a smattering of tourist Greek but was not his type. He liked women to be full-bodied, like Grecian vases, not tall and skinny. Old man Stavros Metrakis was eyeing her with interest in her khaki shorts and top. He liked to ogle all the foreign girls and some were a sight for sore eyes. Some waddled round the shops as if they were still on the beach. In the old days such brazen outfits caused outrage, but now no one bothered.

Other restaurateurs were gathering by the ferry as the catering was being shared out so as not to cause offence; some would bake bread and rusks filled with tomatoes and cheese, others would make great vats of *boureki*, *pastistio*, lasagne, souvlaki, chicken, *pilafi* rice and chips. Everyone had their list of ingredients and the minimarket ordered from the cash-and-carry in Chania. Now it was all coming over on the ferry. He caught sight of young Ari Makaris striding off the boat. They hugged a greeting. 'Well, young man… *Ti kaneis?*' How are you?

Ari was a medical student in Heraklion, almost qualified. Ari and Ellie had been sweethearts for years and the wedding would be such a celebration here. Everyone wished them well. Tomorrow the women would go to the priest's house to view all their wedding gifts and he was sure Irini would be first in the queue.

No time to be sentimental when there were boxes and crates to be loaded into the truck. It was thirsty work so Spiro fuelled himself with coffee, resisting the cake on view in the *kafenion*. He needed to fit into his dancing trousers which were still a little tight. His mother indulged him like a baby but it was Mel who ruled over his diet while his mother sniffed.

'English eat like sparrows. A man needs a bellyful of good Greek food. It shows he has money in his purse. Have another slice,' she would say.

He saw the tall, blond figure of Griff, the warden loading his boxes onto a trailer attached to his bike. No self-respecting Cretan would waste time pedalling uphill in this heat but Griff was an odd fellow; friendly, though he kept himself to himself, spoke decent Greek and was a regular customer at their taverna, encouraging his guests to dine with them and sometimes playing for Mel and her group on open mic nights in the season.

'How's the little pup you found? I hear he was lost in the bushes,' Spiro said.

Griff paused in his packing. 'Dumped, more like. He's with the vet in Chania. It was touch and go but he's tough and will survive. They are keeping him in isolation and building him up. Thanks for asking.'

'Then what'll happen – he'll go into the pound?'

'Not if I can help it. He'll be coming back with me. He deserves a decent home after all the mistreatment he endured.' Griff shook his head. 'No one has recognised him yet.'

Spiro hadn't much time for pets, especially dogs. Cats were useful enough but dogs were a nuisance, scavenging around bins and dumping fleas everywhere, but the Brits were soft when it came to homing them. It was none of his business and time to get on.

Once loaded up, Spiro made his way up the hill to the *plateia*, stopping to hang out the window to chat to men sitting in the cafés on the square while trying to let the smoke out of his driving seat.

His next building job after his siesta was to help Yannis the mayor put a new roof over the shepherd's hut. It was a fit habitat for goats or chickens, not humans, but needs must and it needed replastering inside, a basic toilet and a sink to make a very primitive shelter for any itinerant workers. Spiro liked to keep busy. It had taken many months to finish the second storey of his own house but Mel was thrilled to have upstairs bedrooms, a bathroom and a balcony. Now they had private family space with a basement ready to receive his mama should the time come.

It would be all hands to the pump in the next few days if they were to cater for over two hundred and fifty guests. The women would see to the church flowers and table decorations, the men would set up everything else, including a platform for the performers after the feast.

On the big island of Crete there were catering companies who saw to all these arrangements but on Santaniki it was a do-it-yourself job, everybody mucking in, arguing, taking offence, storming off but coming back to get stuck in again.

That was their way and Spiro liked it. Ari and Ellie deserved their special day. A wedding might only be for a few days but real marriage took much longer to bed down, as he well knew. He wouldn't swop his Melodia for anyone else. She was his songbird, bearer of his sons. How could a man not be proud to have such a fine woman in his bed?

Midsummer

6

Irini was trying to create an intricate wedding wreath in bread dough but her fingers were not obeying her, even though she had woven it so many times before. 'What's wrong with me?' she shouted in exasperation.

Mel was busy arranging flowers to decorate the community hall. 'What is it now?' She sighed. Irini shook her head but said nothing. There was so much to do and so little time. Irini was tired and fractious and lagging behind in their preparations. We need more hands, Mel thought. Spiro was up at Yannis's farm preparing the lambs for the feast and he was no use arranging flowers anyway. Then she looked up to see Sara standing in the doorway.

'Do you need a hand?' Sara offered, sensing the atmosphere.

'I'm no flower arranger. It all looks wonky to me and I have the table flowers to put in jars,' Mel replied. 'Are you enjoying your break? We've not seen much of you.'

'Give it here, I've done a few of these in my time for

parties and I gather there's a big wedding tomorrow. Two weeks gone already. I can't believe my time's nearly over here.

'You must watch,' Irini interrupted. 'Our traditional weddings are famous the world over. You must see how Cretans do it.'

'Look, now I'm here, let me do the flowers and anything else you need help with. I need to stay in the shade. Look at my legs... like polka dots. I should have taken that warden's advice and covered up.' Sara lifted her tanned legs, covered in red blotches.

'You met Griff?'

Sara reminded her of their encounter. 'On the first day I arrived. He's a bit of a know-all.'

'He's okay,' Mel replied. 'He takes his job seriously, a bit of an eco-warrior, widening the scope of the activities on offer up at the retreat with walking tours to see the wildflowers and birdwatching in season. He's getting full occupancy. He likes his own company except when Don Ford comes over. He's a best-selling crime writer.' She paused and winked. 'You have to admit he is a looker.'

'Don Ford isn't. I met him on the ferry and once here with his writing students. He likes the ladies though...' Sara smiled, trying not to scratch her bites.

'You will see them all again at the wedding feast. Everyone is invited. Do come. We're doing a bit of a turn between courses and then there'll be Cretan dancing and lyra musicians who will play until dawn. One of the English residents, Dorrie Thorner, has already complained about the noise to the mayor. You'll meet her and her husband,

36

Norris, the church warden and trustee. Norris is fine in small doses but she's a pain in the bum and nosy so watch yourself if she starts pumping you. Give her half a chance and she'll rant on about their own forthcoming wedding of the year. According to her, Daniel, their younger son, is marrying some Russian princess here soon. Not that we're involved in any way, I gather.'

Together, they carried on with preparations. Irini's bread wreath was coming slowly into shape and Sara stood admiring its intricate detail. 'That's beautiful,' she said.

Irini beamed with pride. 'My mama showed me many years ago. It is a tradition... bread and salt, we say, pleasure and sorrow, light and shade and friendships for ever. This young couple will be leaving us.' Irini shook her head. 'All our children leave the island but when Dr Makaris retires, who knows? Perhaps Ari will return to us with a quiver of children and fill the school. We must make it a special wedding.'

'Now, you must join us for lunch,' Mel insisted and they sat down to rusks soaked in olive oil and layered with feta, tomatoes and olives, washed down with a jug of village rosé. The taverna was busy with tourists so, without being asked, Sara washed her hands, put on one of the embroidered pinafores and served tables while Mel and Irini went into the kitchen to see to the *gigantes* – a butter bean stew – prepare mountain greens in oil and lemon juice and a salad of beetroot, garlic and walnuts. Spiro arrived with Yannis for a plate of village sausages, roasted vegetable salad with feta and delicious ice cream plus baklava.

'Time you were off,' Mel ordered, seeing Sara sweating. 'We mustn't impose on you.'

'Nonsense, I've enjoyed it.' She made to go, leaving them to return to the kitchen to sort out the dishwasher and prepare tables for the evening trade, but Mel called her back.

'There's a crowd from the writing course up at the retreat and Griff sends them down for us to give them dinner. Spiro will be grilling and Irini will see to the boys for me. Don will be holding forth and he's worth any comedy act. If you feel sociable, come and join everyone.'

'Sounds good... I've met most of them before but I'll enjoy listening to all those wordsmiths.'

'Don will be here all summer, quite a card, drinks like a fish but full of stories. It should be a lively evening with wedding guests arriving from the mainland – could be a long night.'

Mel watched Sara walking down the hill to Ariadne Blunt's villa. There was a sadness about the way she walked. Mel wondered why she was holidaying alone and why she was a bit cagey when asked anything personal. All she had gleaned was that Sara was some sort of events manager, whatever that entailed. Mel wondered what her own life would have been had she not met Spiro on the harbour in Chania.

Going back to Sheffield and her large family of brothers and sisters was always a treat, with pie and pea suppers, fish and chips, browsing the shops, trips out into the green expanses of the Derbyshire Peaks. But since Maria, her Italian mother, had died, she found returning tinged with sadness. She loved to hear the rasp of local voices in the pubs but this was her home now, even though she'd always be an offcomer. Within the community of foreign residents, she had friendship, camaraderie and a bit of home. She had the best of both worlds.

But anyway, tomorrow was going to be hard. Dare she ask Sara to lend a hand?

7

Taverna Irini was buzzing when Sara arrived. Mel called her over to meet the crowd from the writer's course at the retreat. Don Ford greeted her and stood up to find her a chair.

'Hi, I'm Sara,' she replied, knowing she had not introduced herself to the group before.

'Now where was I?' he continued. The new writers were all hanging on his words and he was enjoying every minute of it. 'Ah, yes, book launches... Terrible things. The last one I attended, the author was so squiffy, he fell asleep over his reading and fell off his chair. Not a good ploy for selling his books.'

Sara had to smile. This was something she knew only too well from the conferences where the speaker was half cut; the party where the birthday girl threw her drink over her best friend, accusing her of chatting up her boyfriend; or the celebration anniversary where couples argued about the menu, the decorations, the venue, and refused to pay up. Nowt so queer as folk with a skinful of ale in their belly.

'Oh... and there was this famous lady author, who shall be nameless, of course, who read on and on until her audience was asleep. I think she was the one who used her uncashed royalty cheques as bookmarks.' Don could hold his audience, Sara thought. 'Then there are book signings, another waste of time unless you are famous. Alas, no one has ever queued around the block for any of my events. You sit for two hours to sign three books, if you are lucky, unless you rent a crowd of friends and relatives to give the place a buzz. Am I cynical, yes, I am. It's all a waste of good writing time. There's such a lot of flummery about the book trade. Look on Twitter and Facebook, all these minor authors flashing their selfies and goods online, trying to call themselves bestsellers when they are not. If you want to write what's on trend in the current market, beware. By the time you are published the market will have moved on to the new best thing. Write from your heart, write what burns inside you, write to please yourself. But enough, let's get down to the real business of the evening. Landlord, pass the flowing ale,' he ordered. 'And look who's here. Griff, old boy – what have you there?'

Griff was carrying a bundle in his arms like a newborn baby.

'So you're back with the latest addition to the retreat.' Don pointed to the bundle.

'This is Spartacus. I owe Don a drink for rescuing this little chap from the scrub. Here, you hold him.'

Don shook his head. 'I can't... I never told you I'm allergic to animal fur, got red eyes and itches and fleas after holding him in my shirt. He's looking much better already.'

'Now he tells me,' Griff laughed and seeing Sara nodded. 'What do you think?'

Sara stroked the little dog. 'What sort is he?'

'Who knows: a mongrel? Once his fur grows back, I think he will be a fluff ball.'

She could see how tenderly he held the pooch. 'I like his name. Spartacus, the rebel slave?'

'Yes, Sparky for short because he held onto life until we found him. Now, what tales has Don been spinning? Don't believe a word of it.'

'Sit down, Griff, and join us. The first round is on me.'

'No, just came to show you him. He's still not able to mix, in case...' With that, Griff walked back uphill but then paused. 'Hope you all watch the procession tomorrow. A real Cretan traditional wedding, should be a spectacle.'

That reminded Sara. She sought out Mel and offered to lend a hand. In the kitchen Mel was looking flustered and shook her head at the offer. 'Do you really mean this? It's your holiday. I can't.'

'I am offering. I can watch the wedding from here and might as well make myself useful. One thing I've learned from my own business is that you must be prepared to do everything yourself to a high standard, especially if your traders let you down. Parties are my speciality and I know how hard catering can be.' Sara hoped that she wasn't stepping on toes in offering her services. 'Tell me where I am needed and I'll be round first thing tomorrow.'

'I can't thank you enough. We are short-handed with Irini getting so tired, and Spiro will be busy with the taxi so I owe you one.'

'Us Yorkshire lasses stick together in a crisis, don't you think?'

Mel gave her a hug. 'Thank you... I can see we're going to get along fine.'

Next morning Sara woke with a thick head after the night's carousing with Don and his gang. She could hear bells ringing out as she jumped into the shower to freshen up. Days of her own company were boring, too much time to brood over things back home, wondering if she had done the right thing. It would be good to be busy and part of a wedding event, if only in the back kitchen.

From the taverna she watched the procession of the bride, her father and family dressed in traditional Cretan costume. The girl wore a long red skirt with a beautiful embroidered apron, a white blouse, a black bolero encrusted with gold embroidery and a chain of golden coins hanging from her neck. She wore long white pantaloons under a red skirt with a cummerbund around her waist. Her headdress of white lace glistened in her Titian hair. Her brothers wore white boots, dark blue *vraka* trousers, white shirts, dark waistcoats and lace bandanas round their heads. Villagers and guests followed them all to the church. It brought tears to Sara's eyes. There was nothing tacky about this ancient procession. It belonged to a different time and another world. The couple had already registered at a brief civil ceremony at the little town hall where the mayor wished them well. The real marriage ceremony was now taking place with all the rituals of the Greek Orthodox Church, candles, chanting, in view of golden icons. For a while the village fell silent as the service continued at length.

'At last, they're coming,' shouted Irini in her new grey spotted crimplene dress from the church steps, admiring the bride and groom pausing for photographs and the doctor's wife Caliope in a gold lame dress with her hair coiled around her head. '*Ela!* Come, boys, and let's join the procession.' No tiredness was going to stop her, and the boys in their finery held her hand to guide her.

From her vantage point Sara could hear the horns tooting greetings. By this time the feast was prepared for the bride and groom. The young waiters began to fill the table with *pilafi*, chicken rice salads and sausages. Sara had never seen so much food at a wedding – it made the formal wedding breakfast in England look meagre – but the festivities would go on into the evening.

After a while, Mel changed into a pretty lilac dress to join her local friends Pippa and Duke to sing a few items. Sara couldn't believe Mel's voice, crooning in a 1940's style while guests chatted loudly in the background. Then the party really began when the bride changed into her party gown. It was frothy layers of silky fabric with a strapless bodice, her hair falling down almost to her waist, encircled in a circlet of flowers. Then Spiro's troupe of traditional dancers began their routines, dancing the *pentozali*, the *syrtos* and *chaniotis*, centuries-old traditional moves, danced by the men ever faster with great leaps in the air.

Sara was busy behind the scenes listening to the cheers, her feet tapping to the music. She was happy to stay in the background with the other helpers. Their Greek dialect was too fast for her to follow but they smiled and welcomed her into the chaos in the kitchen with stacks of plates to be washed.

Still the food kept coming; cream pies, bowls of fruit, nut pastries dripping with honey and those delicate little swirls of crispy meringue that were served at every wedding. The lyra players played on and on and the Tannoy system relayed the music across the island so no one would sleep tonight.

Ari and Ellie danced together and the guests joined in before they made their farewell. A striped red, black and gold sack was passed around until it bulged with envelopes and notes. Mel explained the custom was to donate at least as many euros as to cover the cost of their meal but many gave much more to set the couple up in their new home.

Then the guns were rattling off as the bride and groom were taxied to their bridal room for the night, cars following, honking horns. It was a raucous joyful Cretan celebration that made the discreet disco party back home very tame in comparison.

Later, far into the early hours, Sara sat with Mel watching the night turn into dawn, sipping the dregs of some leftover fizz. 'Where did you learn to sing like that?'

'At my mother's knee, God rest her soul. She was Italian and you know how they love to sing. I had a little training too,' Mel replied. 'Did you enjoy the day?'

'I thought it was wonderful. This is the perfect setting for a wedding, isn't it? If only...' Sara hesitated. 'Wouldn't it be good if British brides could experience a little of this?'

Mel smiled. 'I suppose so but it wouldn't work, not the Cretan way.'

'No, of course not, but if they could come and enjoy the setting, feast under the stars, dance and sing and enjoy a holiday too, wouldn't it be good for tourism? Santaniki is such a fabulous setting.'

Mel was half asleep. 'A dream wedding under the Cretan sun,' she whispered. 'Time to hit the sack.'

Sara rose to walk back as the dawn was rising with a glorious orange lavender light. 'A dream wedding under the Cretan sun...' She fell asleep on the sofa still dressed, dreaming of a jetty with an arch of flowers where a bride in a rose petal dress, and a faceless man in a white shirt and linen shorts, were looking out over the turquoise sea as the waves lapped on the shore.

Sara woke, realising she had been here nearly three weeks. The time was slipping away so quickly and she must turn her mind to home, to her business, to the real world, but that strange dream haunted her, still fresh in her mind's eye, as she rose, stiff, crumpled and sweating.

What if... But it was fanciful, silly, a wine-induced idea scuttling across her mind. All morning she kept seeing that image. It was just a holiday fancy, like most tourists who dream of buying a villa in the sun, and all those TV programmes fuelling it. Escape to Santaniki, living like a Greek god on your own special island. Sara laughed. *Don't be so silly.* Sadly, she thought, it would never work, and yet she could not shake the idea out of her head.

8

After the monthly committee meeting of the trustees of the Elodie Durrante Arts Foundation, Griff made coffee as the committee sat on the veranda. Everything was looking good financially. Norris Thorner, the treasurer, was pleased that the courses were fully booked for September and October, and local resident Simon Bartlett, an ex-editor, suggested they print more copies of the famous novelist's journal and memoir that their founder member, Ariadne Blunt, discovered a few years back. 'I've even managed to get it into the bookshops on the mainland,' he announced. 'It should bring across tourists to visit our little museum of her life.'

When the rest of the committee drifted away Simon stayed put. 'Sorry Chloë couldn't attend but she is in London with our Alexa and little Olympia...' He paused. 'Griff, can I ask you something? It's about your friend, Felix MacLeod, Alexa's new guy. How well do you know him?'

'We were at Harrow together. He's a good chap.'

'That's what I wanted to know… Alexa had a tough time with her first husband. I guess Felix told you the score. He left her for another man when she was pregnant.'

Griff could feel Simon's hesitation and sensed what might be coming next.

'I wouldn't want Alexa to be let down again. Is he serious?'

Griff smiled. 'I saw them briefly in London and they looked happy and well suited and he's good with the little girl. He's had his own troubles too – his wife was ill and she had to be sectioned.'

'So, he's still married then?' Simon looked worried.

'No, she died on a railway track…'

Simon bowed his head. 'How sad. It's just that I gather they're thinking about moving in together. We both liked him but we are anxious as Alexa is our only child, Chloë's daughter from her first marriage, and I know what it's like to bring up someone else's kid. You read such awful things in the newspapers.'

To stop this train of thought, Griff held his hand up. 'Felix was my best mate at school and he was a rock when things went pear-shaped for my business. He'll make a good father. He's great with my brother's brood.'

'Chloë thinks he's going to propose to her and she is already planning her wedding outfit, I fear.'

'I don't know about that,' Griff replied. Since his move to Santaniki they were not in regular contact but FaceTimed occasionally. This was news to him. 'She could do far worse than Felix,' he added.

'You can understand me being protective?' Simon said.

'Of course.' Griff couldn't comment on what he

didn't know. 'I think moving in together is a good test of a relationship.'

'You were married then?' Simon was probing.

'Engaged briefly but both of us were a bit too young and ambitious. We parted amicably enough.' Griff lied but he didn't want to reveal how Felix's cousin, Flissa, had fought over every stick of furniture in the flat when he had to sell up. He didn't want to return to that nightmare.

'Thanks for putting my mind at rest.' Simon stood to leave. 'I'd better get on a flight and see their new abode. Since our grandchild arrived, we seem to spend more and more time in London but they're coming out for a holiday soon. Sorry to bother you.'

'Not at all, I hope I put your mind at rest. Incidentally, when will Ariadne Blunt return? I gather there's a squatter in residence,' he laughed.

'Sara… I met her in the taverna. Dear Ariadne is sorely missed; such a generous soul and it's good her house is aired and lived in. I saw Sara at the wedding helping out backstage.'

'Yes,' Griff replied. He was impressed how she chipped in on her holiday. 'What does she do for a living?'

'Not sure, Mel was so busy last week. I gather they are both from the same place. Chloë is the one who finds out everything. I think she returns home soon. It's only a holiday let.' Simon rose and made for the kitchen with a tray of cups. Griff followed behind.

'I forgot to thank you for getting us Don Ford. Him being in residence has boosted our writing courses no end but he's drinking me dry… no spirits left in the bar,' Griff said.

'I could find someone else, I've still got contacts in the publishing world.'

'No, we're fine, Don is a great tutor and good with the new writers but I wish he wouldn't swim with a skinful of village wine. I've fished him out twice and the guest suite smells like a brewery. I am trying to get him fit without much luck so far; he thinks a hike is twice round our gardens. But, he was the one who found little Sparky.'

Simon laughed. 'You know, you're fitting in well here and it's good to see you on the keyboard joining in with the taverna musicians. They're a nice bunch. Now Chloë is away, I dine most nights with Mel and Spiro. Not much good with the pots and pans so come and join me before I dash off to London. They are delighted with the trade you're bringing in.'

'Thanks,' Griff said, knowing the next contingent of ten guests was not due in until the weekend and he wanted to plan a hike up behind Agios Nikolaos chapel to the caves and the hills beyond. He wanted to test all the tracks to check any loose rocks and to find a good hide for birdwatchers. He would join Simon at the taverna later, owing him big time for giving him this post at the retreat. It was good to be his own boss again and this time no shyster would ruin the success of this venture.

Spartacus was waiting on the veranda in his basket. He was improving day by day and his coat was starting to grow, as suspected, into a smoky grey fluff. Griff always got a wagging tail welcome from the little dog but it was still too risky to walk him in the hills. Just in case he got lost again.

★

'Do you mind if I join you?' Sara said, seeing Mel lying under the straw sunshade as the sun went down. Her two boys were splashing in the water.

'Sit down on the lounger.' Mel beckoned. 'Thanks again for helping us out last week.'

This is the life! Sara smiled, watching a sailing boat bobbing in the waves. It was picture perfect; eyes half closed, the scene changed into the jetty with the rose arch and the couple holding hands.

'I had a funny dream last night,' she said, turning to Mel who put her book down to listen. 'About a wedding, a couple on a jetty over there under an arch full of roses.'

'No wonder you were dreaming, we were half cut last night. Don was dishing out raki as if there was no tomorrow but it was fun,' Mel said, staring out to the water's edge. 'I can't see any jetty,' she said.

'It's just I can't get it out of my mind. I could see wooden decking surrounded by white-covered chairs, a platform strewn with rose petals, a flower girl with a basket, in a white dress with a big pink satin sash. It was so real... the sun, the sea, the bride and groom, except he wore linen shorts.'

'Like Griff, you mean. Good husband material there, I reckon...' Mel said. 'But no one, *no one*, should wed in the full heat of the sun. They'd roast.'

'No, don't be daft, not him... but strangers who come to the island to tie the knot. It got me thinking there's a market for such a venture here.' Sara tried to explain the strange ideas forming as she fell asleep on her sofa.

'You mean bring a wedding planner across here to organise weddings and everything?' Mel was curious.

'Exactly. She links up with local providers, beauticians, hairdressers, caterers – that you must recommend, of course... If you helped create such a huge event as Ari and Ellie's do, why not do it for yourself, feed guests?'

'Hang on,' said Mel. 'Stop right there. I've enough to do as it is. Where would we find a wedding planner on this tiny island?'

'Who says they have to live here? There's texts, online contacts, websites and FaceTime. It could all be arranged in the UK.' Sara was buzzing with ideas.

'It's you we're talking about, isn't it?' Mel turned on her. 'You can't be serious?'

'It's an idea worth chewing over. It's not as if I don't know how to organise events and a wedding is no different.' Sara stopped at that thought. She knew more about wedding planning than she was prepared to share.

'Let's get this straight: if you're going to take this idea seriously, you'd have to be on tap here and do it yourself, not in Sheffield. Who has time here to go around getting forms, visas, finding items, decorating rose arches... dream on.' Mel sat up, her dark eyes flashing in Sara's direction. 'It's a great idea, could be a goer, but you would have to do it yourself. What about your business back home? You can't up sticks and come to live here. That's holiday madness. I've seen it before, so many Brits come and go, full of dreams, but the reality of winter out of season, it can drive some potty.'

'I could return to the UK in winter to attend wedding

fairs and do Christmas parties and all the usual stuff.' Mel was talking sense but she was not ready to hear it out loud.

'Surely I don't need to tell you that you need a sound business plan, costings for accommodation for bride and groom, not in some tin shack on the beach, a set-up fund for advertising. Then there's all the bureaucracy here, the red tape, insurance and contingency plans. It's not like in the UK, things go slowly here, frustratingly slow at times. And you need time to set up your suppliers. I'm always happy to cater for small events but that's all... Think bridal cake, menus with English or Greek flavours, table decorations, favours. You can't just rush into a crazy idea and you'd better learn decent Greek, not just tourist Greek. Not everyone has English here.'

'But it has legs, this idea?' Sara asked. Mel was bursting her inflated balloon.

'It does but *siga, siga*, slowly does it. I think an idea like yours is a bit like baking bread. It has to rise. If you rush, it won't work. Ideas like this take time to rise and rest slowly before you make it happen. Go home and think it over. If it's what you want, go for it. It won't be easy but don't count me in, I've enough on my plate.' Mel added, 'Anything worth doing is never easy.'

'Give me credit for knowing that,' Sara retorted. This Yorkshire woman said it how it was but she liked her honesty. 'I'll see how others do it back home but if I return, I could rent somewhere like Ariadne Villa, if it is still free for a longer let, get a feel for how best to design a package. I see there's even a little English church here so I could ask the vicar, find suitable photographers and locations. I might need you to guide me to the best businesses though.'

'Make a list. Sara, don't go blundering into this,' Mel cautioned. 'It won't be all confetti and cakes but I like the idea.' She stood up and shook off the sand, calling in her boys. 'Now, before you go home, you must see one of our famous rituals when it's dark. It's Midsummer Eve and the feast of John the Baptist, the one who lost his head when Salome did the dance of the seven veils... I think. You've only got a few days left to enjoy yourself. So, up you get and put something decent on. I'll meet you in an hour on the beach. I must make tracks because it will be busy tonight.' Mel threw on a cotton kaftan over her head. 'No rest for the wicked.'

'I'll stay a little longer if you don't mind. My mind is buzzing with ideas.' Sara sat in silence, lost in her thoughts. She could see it all unfolding: the taverna tables with white cloths and candles, chairs covered in linen, bridal colours in the flowers, sparkly champagne flutes, fairy lights strung around and flowers everywhere.

Am I off my head? How can I make that dream a reality? Mel was right: it wasn't the time to make rash decisions. She'd made enough already in fleeing here. Time to return home to test the reality of such a crazy scheme. Celebrations always had balloons and cake and party clothes, speeches and dancing, and she was no novice at organising events. Perhaps she could make someone's dream come true and give them a wedding day to remember for the rest of their lives? Perhaps then she would feel she had done something worthwhile with her life.

★

Sara followed the crowds making for the beach – families, old and young – in the direction of the smoky tinge of olive wood and pine. The bonfire was well alight, flames leaping into the darkening sky as people stood around. She found Mel and her boys and joined them as Mel threw a dried wreath of flowers onto the flames. It seemed as if the whole of St Nick's town was gathering, watching, and to her horror, she saw boys were leaping into the fire, not into the middle but among the smouldering cinders.

'Why the hell are they doing that?' she whispered.

'It's an age-old ritual, all very pagan, I suspect. A rite of passage for good fortune and fertility and to rid the island of bad spirits.'

'Just imagine health and safety allowing this in Britain! What's with the wreaths?'

'Out with the old and in with the new; these flowers have done their duty protecting the house. I think that's why we do it. You have wreaths on the door at Christmas, I suspect for the same reason.'

'It's weird,' Sara said. 'I guess superstition is universal. My mum won't have lilac in the house or new shoes on the table.'

'No one wants bad luck,' Mel added.

Perhaps I should have had a wreath on my door but my bad luck was inside the door not outside it. I don't want to go back, Sara thought but said nothing. 'I'd like to stay on longer.'

'But what about your business?'

'Karen can cover for me... at least for a while.' Sara's head was spinning with ideas, smoke stung her eyes, blinding her. There was lyra music coming from a bar on the beach, everyone laughing and chattering, enjoying the spectacle. How could she leave all this? How could she leave Santaniki for damp old Sheffield, much as she loved her home city? That dream vision had lingered at the back of her mind all day and now this.

'It wouldn't work.' She was unaware of speaking out loud.

'What wouldn't work?' Mel shoved a drink in her hand.

'Nothing, just mulling over that idea.'

'Spit it out then...'

'Not yet. You're right, I have to think everything through before I take a leap in the dark.'

'Don't go leaping into the dark here, you'll end up in the fire and that won't solve anything.' Mel took her arm. 'I think you've had enough dreaming for one day.'

Sara knew her new-found friend was right.

July

9

In the villa set high on a rock overlooking the bay, Jack Bailey and Sandra Taylor took their G and Ts to the infinity pool. Renting this huge house was an extravagance but the young couple who owned it, lottery winners, she was told, had returned to London to await the birth of their first baby, but there were complications so they insisted on being close to their London family and they weren't planning to return for a while.

'Isn't this perfect, love? Just right. Are you okay?' Jack brought the drinks down to where Sandra was sitting in the shade with a magazine.

'Just tired as usual, the pills knock me out, that's all. I'm fine,' she replied, knowing Jack could be very protective and not wanting to worry him. They had been partners for over ten years now, meeting on a singles walking holiday on the big island, exploring deep gorges and river beds and white sand beaches on the south coast of Crete.

Now this lengthy holiday was to help her recuperate after

her operation. The diagnosis wasn't brilliant but there was life in the old girl yet. Jack was so kind and understanding and everybody agreed that a six-month break would build Sandra up before another round of chemo might knock her back.

This was a dream rental, a family house full of huge cool rooms, a film screening room and airy kitchen with all the mod cons, quiet, away from the bustle of Santaniki town where hordes of summer tourists spilled out of the ferry boats on day trips.

Sandra didn't want to be standoffish but too much canned music coming from harbour cafés made her head ache. Swimming in their pool was so relaxing, she could pretend she was in the turquoise sea down below. It really did feel like living with the gods. Yesterday they had made one trip up to Agios Nikolaos chapel but the steep climb caught Sandra's breath and she had to take a rest before reaching the ancient chapel, set almost into the rock. Outside there were benches to share their picnic of spinach pies, apples and a bowl of cherries with a flask of iced mountain water. In the chapel were golden frescoes so beautiful they seemed to merge into the walls, and silvery *tamata* – plaques donated to the saints as offerings for healing.

Sandra felt tears rising looking at the pleas; legs, heads, hearts. How many had been successful? she wondered. It was cool and musty so she sat drinking in the scene. I wish I were more religious, she sighed, but she felt the peace in this sacred place. She lit a candle and watched the flame flickering, a candle of hope for herself and others.

She sensed there were her own affairs to set in order,

just in case... but one day at a time. Enjoy the moment, she prayed.

Jack brought his binoculars to scour the rocks in search of local birdlife. They had returned many times to Crete and now to Santaniki. It was their paradise island but this year it was special. Both of them had been married before. They had five grandchildren between them but although Jack's family were close and welcoming, it was a great sadness to Sandra that her own daughter would not speak to Jack unless spoken to.

Julie was a law unto herself and she had taken against Jack from the start, goodness knows why. He was warm, friendly and eager to please. Julie was cold and distanced herself from them both. Even when Sandra broached the seriousness of her illness, Julie showed little interest in helping them both through the fear. What had she done wrong to make her own daughter so angry and dismissive? She felt the tears dripping again. This worry gave her sleepless nights trying to work out how this came about.

Julie was always a daddy's girl and Paul had spoiled her. They used to gang up on Sandra and go off, leaving Sandra to stay home to see to things alone which was fine by her.

One day Paul came home from work with a pain in his side. They operated for an appendix but there was peritonitis and a serious infection that would not heal. He died within three days and Julie, who was then fifteen, would not be comforted.

Sandra got used to the silences, the slamming of doors, the absence of any affection. It was as if Julie switched off from her. She suggested bereavement counselling that had so helped her come to terms with the shock and loss of her husband but Julie refused to even consider this. The spark suddenly went out of her daughter. Julie later trained as a social worker and married Colin after a brief courtship: one weekend they went off in secret to Gretna Green, told no one until they returned.

Sandra was denied the fun of planning a wedding, watching her daughter try on dresses, inviting friends to share the big day. It felt as if she was being punished for Paul's death and for not being enough and for not being him. It was as if there was a steel wall between mother and daughter and Sandra didn't know how to fix things between them.

Her dearest wish was for Julie to come closer and talk things through with her. She sent postcards, texts, photos, never forgetting the family's birthdays and giving lavish gifts to her grandchildren, Gemma and Scott, but never receiving a thank you reply. It was as if, being with Jack, she didn't exist anymore as a gran or part of their family and it was breaking her heart.

She'd also invited them to come to enjoy this big villa, offering to pay for flights, but Julie emailed a curt reply, *Booked for Tenerife this year. Crete is too far and not for Gemma, perhaps another time.* Sandra clung onto that 'another time' but she knew deep down it was not going to happen.

'Don't you go upsetting yourself,' said Jack. 'She'll come around in her own time.' He was ever the optimist. Time was running out though. The future was uncertain and she wanted to make things right between them.

'Do I have to be in my coffin before she turns up?'

'No more of that talk, you're getting stronger by the day,' he replied. No, she wasn't, and she feared that pining for Julie sucked her strength and resolve but she still smiled and nodded, playing along with his confidence.

As she was sitting in the silence of the chapel, she suddenly found herself relaxed. Perhaps there was another way to reach out to her daughter. If not a funeral, why not a wedding? She and Jack had been happy to live together without a thought of tying the knot but their affairs would be better if they were a couple. Sandra looked up at the icon of the blessed Maria holding her child. Where had that idea come from? Thank you, Sandra thought, for an answer to my heartfelt prayer of desperation.

Sara had returned with reluctance to Sheffield, to her office where Karen her assistant was keeping the kettle on the boil, arranging appointments, following up enquiries. It was hard to go back but she knew she would not be staying long. She stared up at the grey skies, the sameness of familiar streets. The thought of returning to the island stalked her every move but she needed time to get her head round the idea of this new business venture, owing her parents an explanation as to why she would not be staying long.

Sara took herself up to Hope Valley to walk the hill trails and think through her new future, trying to imagine what was needed to bring this idea into being. She could see everything unfolding in her mind's eye but it needed grounding in reality. Her evenings with her parents were spent online eyeing up the competition, what packages they offered and how they advertised themselves to couples. It was hard to imagine herself being able to nudge in and make it a success but what she needed was a unique selling point, something different, but what?

One evening over supper with her parents she explained how being on Santaniki had made her rethink future plans. 'There's nothing to keep me here now... I need a challenge, to take a risk. I wish you could see it out there. It's unique and I feel at home... Don't laugh, but I feel it's calling me back. I dreamt this wedding idea, bringing couples over to tie the knot in the sunshine.'

Her mum looked at her dad. 'You must be psychic... you remember Dad's best man, Jim? He's just got wed to Phyllis, both widowed and second time around. They went somewhere in Greece and did just that. Just a small do. We were invited but didn't feel it was right with you being so down and all that.'

'Oh, Mum, you should have gone,' Sara said. 'I spoilt your plans.'

'None of that, we had a golf break in Scotland while you were away.'

It was the phrase spoken off the cuff that brought a grin to Sara's face. That's it, she thought. There it was, her unique selling point. 'Second time around' covered all ages, not just pensioners. They could be family gatherings or private ceremonies, where couples could holiday and doubled it up as their honeymoon.

'Judging by the look of their photos, it went champion,' said her father.

Later, Sara couldn't sleep. A second time around gave couples a chance to have a different experience, putting the tin lid on their first wedding day. She felt a buzz of excitement, punching out ideas onto her iPad. Each package had to be tailor-made, bespoke to their needs to include children, grandchildren, a family affair or a private affair suitable to mature clients. They could find a villa and bring over friends and family, choose their own food, music and each wedding would be unique. Second time around had to be special.

First, though, she would visit Phyllis and Jim to see what they felt about their wedding. Did it come up to expectation? What touches made it special for them? Then she must search out local wedding fairs to look at current trends and size up opposition. She was glad she had returned home.

Sara needed to do her homework, looking at the cost of relocating, advertising, funding. She must find a good web designer, source a loan from the bank to set up the business. Were the gods on her side in this venture? So much to do but *siga, siga*, as Mel advised; slowly, slowly, she must test out the dream.

The thought of returning to Santaniki to live was exciting as well as daunting but she recalled Maslow's pyramid: the more you plan, the better the outcome. It was up to her to make this venture work.

August

10

Local resident Pippa Delamere was relaxing with her partner Duke, Griff and Mel in the taverna when she suddenly felt queasy. 'Give me a second,' she told the band, shooting off to the loo in the taverna.

'You okay?' Mel said. It had been quite a night. Simon, Griff and the guests from the retreat house had filled the taverna for their last night party. The band gave them a set or three to remember. Mel, who loved singing with the group, was belting out some eighties numbers, Griff was on keyboard with Pippa on guitar and Duke on the sax.

Pippa returned. 'Sorry, I had a funny turn but I'm fine now. I can help you clear up...'

'No, off you go, thanks for a great evening but you do look peaky,' said Mel.

'I'm just a bit whacked,' Pippa replied.

'Have a drink before you leave then?' Spiro offered.

Pippa shook her head. 'Better not or I won't sleep. Come on, Duke, time to hit the sack.' They strolled hand in hand up the hill to the little cube stone house they called home, a rather decrepit old building that had lain empty for years. It was just three rooms, a vegetable plot with plenty of space for a hen run and a goat. Pippa felt so tired she just crawled into bed half-dressed and went out like a light. In the morning she woke bog-eyed and feeling sick. Duke was worried. 'You've got to go and see the doctor.'

'It's just a bug and the heat. I'm fine, don't fuss.' Pippa got up feeling wobbly. This had been going on for days and it worried her but she didn't want Duke to see her fear. They had been partners for years. Duke was a roadie with a band that promised much until drugs got the better of the group. Pippa was his girlfriend who bailed out, seeing there was no future in the Serpent's Tail. Duke followed her. She could not go home because her patrician father had shown her the door when she refused to be shackled with a chinless wonder who owned acres in the shires but who bored her rigid.

Boarding school and cookery courses in Switzerland had destined her for her photo in *Country Life*, one of those girls in pearls, but she was too much of a free spirit to be reined in by his bullying. Pippa loved the Glastonbury festivals where she ran a veggie stall cooking fast food for hungry musicians. Duke was a regular customer, handsome with soulful black eyes and a mane of dreadlocks. Together they toured Europe in a van, ending up on Santaniki.

Aged hippies they might be but they could sing and play, and Duke mucked in at the olive and grape harvests, cleaning pools, labouring for builders and keeping their veg plot in good order. Pippa had helped out at the dog rescue pound until it was closed down by the council, and wanted for nothing. They lived off the land, loving the freedom, tending their stock. Almost forty, Pippa felt that life was perfect... until now.

Deep down she feared the worst: the sickness and the dizziness, the bloat, hot flushes and irregular periods. Perhaps it was an early menopause but in the back of her mind she remembered her mother dying of cancer when Pippa was a teenager. No one had spoken about her illness to her. She was away at school when the head called her to her study and told her the worst news possible. Was history going to repeat itself? She could not sleep, feeling her bloated stomach. Better to know the worst. There were new treatments now. She would be brave and make an appointment at the health centre.

Next morning, she sat in the waiting room trying not to tremble, dashing to the loo until it was her turn. Shaking and anxious, she sat with the doctor explaining her symptoms. 'My mother had ovarian cancer...'

'Let me examine you,' Dr Makaris said as she lay on the couch while he pummelled her stomach. 'You feel sick, your periods are scant?' Then he smiled. 'Don't worry, I think this is not cancer, Philippa... There's a baby in here, about four months at least.'

Pippa sat up. 'How come?' The doctor shrugged his shoulders and laughed.

'The usual way, of course. We could do a test now and see.'

Pippa produced her sample and watched as the blue lines appeared then burst into tears. 'I thought it was...'

'No, look, new life, congratulations. My wife will want to see you and check you over regularly.'

'Thank you.' Pippa jumped off the chair. 'I can't believe it... I'm too old.'

'So what? Life begins at forty, you English say,' he replied, writing out a prescription for vitamins.

Pippa staggered out to the sunshine, stunned by the news. She was going to have a baby, a child of her own. They had been careful for years and now this news. How would Duke take it? A great worry was lifted off her shoulders but... a baby in their humble shack? Things would have to change now there was a new life to support.

Back in Sheffield Sara was busy putting plans together. She visited her parents' friends to hear their experience.

'We had a lovely holiday, love, just the two of us,' Phyllis said, pouring tea into china cups in their cosy front room. 'We were so sorry to hear about your...' She broke off.

Sara smiled, shaking her head. 'It's okay. I'm fine now. Tell me more about your wedding.'

'It was just the ticket for us, a quiet ceremony. We did all the legal stuff here, it made it easier, and then we flew to Santorini to a posh hotel who found someone to hear our vows. It was very romantic.' Phyllis flashed pictures in front of her. 'I loved my dress, it was a cool floaty kaftan. They did my hair and nails and Jim wore chinos and a shirt.'

'Did you mind no one being there to share it with you?' Sara asked, thinking of her own parents who were lifelong friends.

'No, a bit too expensive for them to travel and it was our private day. They all came to the register office and we had a gathering of friends afterwards in a hotel. We just wanted to do something different for us, no one else. It's been a long time overdue. Two pensioners acting like lovebirds and we had a holiday of a lifetime into the bargain, didn't we, Jim?'

'Was there anything that you would have changed?'

'No, but I saw one bride arriving with a dress that looked that heavy she could hardly carry it. Poor lass would be very hot and sweaty in the gown, and imagine it trailing in damp sand! Our ceremony was perfect for us and they gave us a quiet room away from the bridal party that followed us... talk about rough... Shouldn't say that, should I? Some Brits give us a bad name with their shouting, fighting and drinking. Why are you so interested?'

Sara revealed a little of her ideas. 'Just thinking it through at the moment but it's not as if I don't know how to organise parties.'

'Can't you do it here, love?' Phyllis asked.

'Santaniki is the perfect venue. I will have no competition. I even met someone from Sheffield out there who has a taverna. She's being helpful. Besides, I need a change away from here.'

'I don't blame you,' said Jim. 'Go for it, girl. You're young. It's so easy to stay put and rot without a challenge.'

'How do you like the name "Dream Island Weddings, second time around"? I thought I'd cater for more mature couples.'

Phyllis shook her head. 'No, you do right. "Dream Island Weddings" is a bit vague. And second time around can come at any age, don't you think? Next-door's daughter was divorced at only twenty-six. Things have changed since our day.'

Sara nodded. 'I do think there's a market for the second time around but I need to think it through. Thanks for listening.'

'I hope I haven't trodden on your dreams,' Phyllis said. 'You have a good idea. We went to a wedding fair where we got our ideas. That might be useful for you.'

'I'm glad of your advice and I don't want to narrow the market. It's a bit of a risk.'

'You're a doer, Sara Loveday, allus was, allus were. We wish you all the luck in the world, you deserve it.'

They shook hands and Phyllis kissed her. Sara smiled all the way back to her office. She couldn't wait to get back to Santaniki and share everything with Mel. She must discuss the idea with her own business assistant as well before she took this leap in the dark. Was this just a fanciful notion or a genuine plan? But first, she needed to find a local wedding fair.

There were crowds queueing outside the hotel to enter the wedding fair, all those hopeful brides with their besties and mothers, poring over dresses and brochures, sampling dishes and tipping back the free wine. She found a stand for Paradise Tours where a girl she recognised from college was waiting for customers. She had not changed with her cheesy smile, whitened teeth, bleach-blonde hair. Her nails were like talons. 'Oh, it's you, Sara Loveday. Like the tan... What are you doing here? How can I help?'

The stall was covered with romantic shots of locations and brides posing under blue skies.

'I thought Paradise Guide to the Greek Islands was a travel agent?'

'They are but now expanding into the wedding business. It's very profitable.'

'I'm thinking of branching out into weddings myself,' Sara said, her heart sinking at this news.

'Really? I'd have thought it was the last thing you'd want to do after...' The rep paused. 'Sorry.'

'That's okay.' Sara swallowed her feelings but the rep had more to say.

'You know it's a crowded market out there. I hope you speak Greek, we have translators, guides and our own experienced wedding planners, accommodation agencies, the lot.' She was boasting that her company had resources Sara could only dream of.

'I have my own sources too and yes, my Greek is coming on well,' she lied.

'Do you know all about the red tape? I would advise you not to pitch in there. You won't stand a chance as we could beat you at every quote. You wouldn't want to live out there anyway. You're a city girl... Where are you thinking of?' She was probing but Sara shook her head. 'Not sure yet but thanks for the warning. It's good to size up the opposition.' Sara couldn't resist the jibe.

'My advice, for what it's worth, is to stick to what you know: home weddings in the Peaks would suit you fine. Crete, Santorini and Corfu, forget them. Stick to parties and anniversaries, christenings and Christmas parties. That's your ballpark.'

Sara smiled through her teeth and picked up a brochure. Here was a grade one cow, the sort who looked you up and down to find your flaws. 'Thanks, you've been very illuminating.' The rep stared after her, not understanding the sarcasm of her comment.

Sara moved on and picked up glossy brochures for Wedding Bliss, a very expensive, bespoke outfit, guiding brides into their pricey menus and entertainment. The Bliss package was a sausage machine, pay upfront with few refunds and not very inviting. She trundled from stall to stall looking at the expense of the wedding dresses, feeling depressed, but there were some good ideas for weddings on a budget.

Sara did not think thirty thousand pounds plus for one wedding day was justified but couples made their own choices. It was obvious by the look of some punters that they had oodles to spend. It was a useful if disheartening exercise but was bringing her fanciful ideas down to earth. There was so much to mull over but she sensed she'd know whether developing this business was realistic when she landed back on Santaniki.

11

Pippa sat drinking Mel's lemonade. 'I can't believe it. I'm nearly five months gone and never knew. Duke is still in shock. We thought all that passed us by because it never happened and we forgot about ever having a family.'

Mel held her hand. 'It couldn't happen to a better couple,' she said.

'I'm not so sure. We're not exactly very civilised. The house is cramped and damp in the winter. There'll have to be changes and a baby will shake both of us up but it's a gift out of the blue and I do want the best for it.'

'Did you have a big family?' Mel asked – Pippa never talked about her past.

'I had a nanny and a pony, a mother who died when I was at school and a father who was never there. You can sometimes have everything but love and attention,' she replied. 'Duke was brought up by grandparents, he doesn't even remember his parents, so not exactly the best background for us to bring up a child, is it?'

'Rubbish, it's you who'll do the best for the little one. You're making me broody.'

'It's all the clothes and equipment, and I don't want it stuck in a drawer for a cradle. We've never had to think of anyone but ourselves and we do live from hand to mouth.' Pippa was in tears. 'How will we manage? I do want to do things right.'

'What's that supposed to mean?' Mel could see Pippa was struggling to take in her new condition.

'Maybe it's my upbringing but I don't want my baby to be a bastard like Duke was. I want us to get married before it comes... Am I going mad? I can't believe I said that!'

'Lots of children are born to couples who are cohabiting, there's no shame in that any more, Pippa. You are happy as you are, why change things?' Mel was puzzled.

Pippa shook her head. 'No, if this is a gift, I want us to be a respectable couple, and have a christening. I know it sounds silly coming from me, the hippy, dippy Pippa, but I think this is Philippa Columbine Marianne Delamere coming out in me.'

'Have you spoken to Duke?' Mel could not believe what Pippa was saying. Pippa was always laid back and Duke could be horizontal at times. She hadn't even known her full name until now.

Pippa shrugged her shoulders at Mel's question. 'I don't know how he'll react... we've never bothered to discuss marriage. It's always sounded so uncool, bourgeois, but perhaps I am my father's daughter after all. What do you think?'

Mel couldn't reply straight off because in Italian and Greek culture marriage was the normal way to raise children. She sensed for the first time that Pippa was feeling the burden of her upper-class upbringing. Such things went deeper than she had ever acknowledged. 'You must talk it out with Duke. The civil ceremonies here can take some organisation but you've got time enough to talk to him. Explain what's bugging you. I know he'll be sympathetic. You've been together so long.'

'True,' Pippa said. 'From now on it won't be just two of us but three of us. How will we cope?'

'We'll all help you out in any way we can. Go home and talk it through with him.'

Pippa left her lemonade and it was then that Mel could see the bump under her T-shirt. How strange she had never noticed her guitarist putting on weight. Duke was a free spirit and a law unto himself. She wondered how he'd react to being a married man.

Sara sat once more on the veranda of Ariadne's villa. It was a relief to be back in its warmth but she was feeling guilty that she had forgotten all the garden chores she promised to do before she left, and there was no sign of Griff returning to water plants. Gardens didn't rate high on her agenda now that she was here to start her business in earnest, but this was now her own rental home so she must make an effort to tidy up the parched plants that had died. It was beginning to look like a desert, dusty and forlorn.

The past weeks in Sheffield had been a blur of preparations so that she could come back fully in control of all the information needed for permissions to marry abroad.

She had a domain name and a website being organised for her. Competition on the web was fearsome, with so many packages that alarmed her until she realised that no one was offering Santaniki as a destination. She was going to advise most of her clients to have a civil ceremony in the UK first and a symbolic ceremony here on the island but she needed to find perfect locations for photography shots before she lifted off. There was no time to allow mistakes. Pouring her heart out to Mel over supper in the taverna, she was still dithering about her decision. 'Have I thought of everything?'

Mel was looking across to Spiro. 'What if a resident here wants to marry? How would you deal with that? They can't go over to the UK to a registrar's office. With residence permits, couples are entitled to a civil ceremony here. You need to offer to give them your services too. We happen to know a couple who might just want this but on a very tight budget… Could you help them?'

That sent Sara into a panic. 'I'm not sure I've got those details under my belt yet.' At least she was being honest. 'The event party would be no problem. I could customise to their ideas and budget but you will have to guide me through all the regulations and the translation work I need.'

'We can find you a translator but a try-out might be a start for you.'

'Is it anybody I know?'

'It's all a bit hush-hush yet but we'll let you know if it's a goer… We can't speak out of turn but it will be an interesting challenge for you to cut your teeth on.'

Sara shook her head. 'Here's me thinking it would be easy-peasy to start up here but there's more to this wedding business than I ever thought. Perhaps I should stick to just parties and catering.' She felt nervous and disheartened, her confidence rocking. Had she made a big mistake in coming back here?

'I don't think you could make a living just from parties here. One thing at a time: get your facts in order, talk to the mayor, find suppliers, check them out. Have your hair and nails done in the town and pass around your business cards in Greek and English.' Trust Mel to give her an honest opinion.

'I'll have to find a Greek teacher, and soon. I can't go relying on you two to translate for me. There's so much to do and I have no business cards.' How could she forget promotional material as simple as a business card? There was location work to do and photography shots.

'And you still have your business back home to run,' Mel added.

'Not exactly, Karen is taking over from me, I hope, in the long term. For the moment though, I will still organise some business from here.' What have I done? she screamed to herself, her heart thumping with anxiety.

'Then you'll have to make it happen, won't you?' Spiro wasn't listening, distracted by a smell of burning coming from the kitchen.

'Mama!' He rushed out, hearing the smoke alarm. His mother emerged, waving a burnt towel. '*Po... po... po.*' Mel rushed in with him to see the damage. It was just a burnt pan this time – her eyes were rolling with exasperation but she said nothing for once.

Sara knew it was time to leave. There were endless lists to

make of all the things she had forgotten to explore. Time to
find beach shots, venues for romantic angles, but who could
she ask to guide her? There was one guy who came to mind.
She was not even certain he would oblige but needs must
when the devil drives.

September

12

After the open mic night at the taverna, as they were clearing their kit away, Duke sidled up to Griff. 'Fancy a pint?'

Griff nodded, knowing there was no course to supervise and it was one of those starlit skies with a warm breeze, a night for lingering. Pippa had gone back uphill and the two of them had hardly spoken all night. Something was wrong. He did hope they weren't going to split. 'Everything okay?' he asked, plonking himself down again. 'I thought Pippa looked tired and very quiet for once.'

Duke poured his Mythos into a glass. 'She sprung one on me the other day,' he said. 'She's pregnant, more than halfway, they reckon, and now she tells me she wants to get hitched... At our age...'

'Congratulations, but it sounds as if you're not too keen.' Griff shook his hand.

'Don't get me wrong about the baby, never thought we'd ever have a sprog, but it changes things.' Duke sat back. 'I can't take it all in and it's not like her to go all legit on me. Marriage is a big step I'm not sure about.'

Griff didn't feel like a Relate counsellor – who was he to advise anyone? – but he felt honoured that Duke had confided his misgivings to him. 'I suppose being parents feels like a new adventure and perhaps Pippa wants to feel secure,' he offered.

'She's reverted to type. You can take some of the past out of your life but once a posh girl... She wants to do things proper.' Duke was trying to explain his confusion.

'And you?'

'I'm just a mixed race working-class lad, born out of wedlock. Never knew my parents, brought up by my gran. Marriage was never anything I reckoned to bother about and neither did she until this. She wants the baby brought up like she was. I understand that but I don't want to go down some aisle in a tuxedo, all doodied up.' Duke shook his head.

'It doesn't have to be like that. Folk have all sorts of weddings these days and you can make it your style. Do the legal stuff at the town hall and then have the biggest bash you can think of to celebrate this unexpected arrival.' Griff was thinking off the top of his head, not sure if it was going to be any help at all.

'You got a point, man. I was afraid of all that formal stuff. Pippa must have been to posh dos in fancy hats and frocks but she left all that behind when we got together.'

'Exactly, so talk it over with her, suggest some ideas and I bet she'll be relieved and come up with ideas of her own.'

'Thanks, mate, you've given me another way of thinking about it. Nothing needs to change much, just a party with music, dancing, friends, and no need to stand on ceremony is there… Although knowing Pippa, she'll want some sort of blessing, a few words to match the occasion, not that I'm much good at that,' Duke said, leaning forward, looking relieved.

'I could help you if you like.' Griff was glad that Duke was buying into the idea and taking some responsibility.

'I'd better get back and sort this out between us. The atmosphere's been a bit frosty of late.' Duke leapt up. 'You've taken a load off my mind. I owe you.'

Griff stayed staring up at the stars and listening to the bell owl hooting in the distance. At least someone was happier for his suggestions, not that he had any experience of weddings except for his brother's big bash. They'd made a good fist of it, with church bells and a marquee on the lawn, everyone in morning suits and huge hats. Flissa had been his girl then and enjoyed every second.

Yet he felt a strange tinge of envy thinking of the joys ahead for them. Not two beans to rub together in the world's eyes but he sensed this would be a family where love provided all the wealth necessary.

Next morning, he was surprised to see Sara Loveday stroll up the drive. Spartacus, now fully recovered, bounded down to greet her. 'Don't worry, he's very friendly, just curious.'

'Sorry to bother you but Mel said you might be able to help me.'

Griff paused in his pruning. Sara was wearing cut-off jeans, a skinny top and sun hat.

'If I can – want a coffee?' She nodded and followed him into the main house.

'Wow, this is quite a place!' she said, staring at the portrait of Elodie Durrante in the hallway. 'Ah, this is the famous novelist? She reminds me of Agatha Christie in her latter days.'

'Don't be fooled by her grandeur, the old girl was a game old broad in her day. She had more lovers than days in the week, I'm told, and judging by her memoir, she kept them all in line. This foundation owes everything to her generosity.'

'The house is very quiet today. Mel told me you were booked up.' Sara was peering into rooms, curious about the building.

'Next week will have full occupancy with some romantic novelists coming; Lacey Sweetlove is running a workshop. Have you heard of her?'

'She's in every supermarket and bookshop but I've only read one once. They're good if you like lots of hot sex,' she laughed. 'It should be an interesting course.'

'Oh yes, Don will have a field day. He's staying on to work, or so he says. I think he's hoping for some practical lessons from her, the old rogue.' Griff grinned, pointing to a man toes-up under a sunshade.

They took their coffee into the shade of the olive grove. Sara looked round. 'It's just that I'm looking for photogenic venues for my new brochure. This is a fabulous situation, set on a hill with a sea view and a vine-covered terrace.'

'For your brochure, are you a holiday rep?' Griff was curious.

'No, I'm just doing a recce as I have an idea for a business out here. It's early doors yet but Mel suggested you might have noticed some good spots on your travels.'

Griff paused to admire her enthusiasm. 'What's it all for?'

Sara hesitated, looking at him with large, amber-green eyes and a freckled nose. 'I was an events manager in Sheffield but I think that weddings on this island would be good for tourism and local traders. Every other island has bespoke packages; they give the couples an idyllic experience, the whole works: photographs to remember for a lifetime in beautiful vistas... that sort of thing.' She sipped her coffee and fell silent, waiting for him to make a comment, but what was there to say?

'What's your USP, your unique angle to all this?' he asked. Hoping it wasn't some half-baked scheme that had no foundations.

'I'll specialise in second time around weddings; families wanting to have a symbolic ceremony surrounded by their children and friends, gay marriages and anyone wanting a very romantic setting with a private ceremony.'

'I see.' Griff could only imagine crowds of rowdy tourists invading beaches. It all sounded a bit naff but he said nothing.

'I mean, just look at this garden in the olive grove,' she continued. 'Imagine what it could look like trimmed up with lights and garlands. Is it available for renting out?'

'Not sure, the trustees would have to decide that.' Griff didn't want folk trampling over his garden leaving beer cans and litter, disturbing the ecosystem.

'Where else do you think would make a beach wedding setting?'

'Depends on the time of year. The beach gets crowded in the season and I'm not sure I can help you over that, Miss Loveday.'

'Sara, please.' She sensed his disapproval and rose quickly. 'Thank you for your time, it was just an idea. I could imagine a lovely woodland wedding here, very private with fairy lights at dusk, a midsummer night's dream setting.'

Griff saw the dreamy look of hope in her eye. He couldn't bear to stamp on her romantic schemes but then he had an idea. 'Strictly between ourselves, I know a local couple who might use your services but it wouldn't be the usual frilly frock affair but something suited to them.'

'Really? That's the second time that's been mentioned to me. It would be exactly what I'm looking for to make a client's day special.'

'I could speak to them, not promising anything, mind, it would have to be very modest. I hear some wedding packages can be extortionately expensive.'

'Tell me about it… I went to a wedding fair in Sheffield and was shocked at the prices some agencies charged. I want to get my business off the ground and for that my rates would be at least half price, even less for a special deal.'

'How long are you on the island?' Griff asked, seeing her face beaming with interest at his suggestion.

'As long as it takes… Nothing to keep me in Sheffield any more,' she said with a sigh. For a second Griff wondered what Sara was running away from to pitch up here, leaving her business back there.

'It's just that this event might be sooner rather than later and I know residents need permits and certifications just as those coming from abroad do. That might take some time,' Griff advised.

'Thanks for this, Griff. Bear me in mind if they might be interested. I could be very reasonable as it will be a chance to start up in a quiet way.'

'It would be no hole-in-the-wall sort of nuptial as they have loads of friends, but I'll speak to them, if you like. It's up to them to take it from there.'

'Of course,' she replied.

He watched her almost skipping down the drive, waving a farewell and feeling a twinge of both pleasure and lust. Who could ignore those long legs in denim shorts? He was getting as bad as Don. Griff hoped he had been discreet. It was up to Sara Loveday to prove her talent in organising something memorable for his friends. Word of mouth was the best advertisement for any business. He hoped Sara knew how to deal with free spirits like Pippa and Duke. They might prove to be a challenge with some very whacky ideas.

13

Sara was making inroads to the weeding in the olive garden when the doorbell rang and there was Mel's friend, Pippa, on the doorstep. 'Can I have a word?'

'Come through, I'll find us a drink. It's nearly wine o'clock.'

'Oh no, I can't.' Pippa patted her stomach. 'Her ladyship can't have it.'

'Lemonade it is then… Congratulations, I wouldn't have guessed,' Sara said. Pippa's tanned face looked radiant.

'Everyone's being very discreet but I gather Griff hinted that there might be a wedding in the offing.'

It was no use being coy, thought Sara. 'Actually, he never said who were the lucky couple. He told you I was starting up a wedding planning business then?'

'It's not as if we couldn't do it all ourselves.' Sara could see Pippa was relieved to sit down. 'But I'm no spring chicken these days and get tired so easily and I want us to celebrate before her ladyship's arrival…'

'And Duke, what does he think?'

'Formal stuff isn't his bag. We just want a simple ceremony but I told him if we were going to do it at all, it must be totally legit, no jumping over the brush. I want all our friends to join in. I know we have to present documentation to the mayor but we are residents and we pay our dues. That bit Mel and Spiro are helping us with but time is of the essence. We want it done as soon as possible. What do you think?'

Sara was taken aback. How soon did they need this? Time to be honest. 'You have to understand this will be my first wedding and I need to know your ideas.'

'We have no money to speak of but out here we can keep it simple: after the morning civil wedding stuff I'd like a ceremony at dusk followed by a party – I'd like Sally the vicar from St Paul's to give us a blessing, but not in church. Duke isn't keen on four walls.'

'You're thinking of a gathering under the stars?' Sara asked.

'Yes, how did you guess? Griff has offered the olive grove if the trustees agree. It would be so romantic. You only do this once and I just want it to be special.'

'Then we have a reception – at the taverna?' Sara was trying to glean Pippa's dream.

'Of course, with music and dancing, a right old bash. We could run to that but about your fee?' Pippa hesitated.

Sara smiled. 'I have an idea about that. As it's my first event here and I need photos for my brochure and settings, if you give me permission to use some of your pictures, I will waive my fee... After all, it'll be a first for all of us.' They both laughed.

'That's very generous. We need to think about catering and I will need a dress, or a tent by then, nothing white or lacy, just a simple dress.'

'I'm sure Mel will help you there. Do you have family to invite to join you?'

Pippa shook her head. 'Only Lygeia, my cousin, and she's the biggest snob in the world. She had six bridesmaids, a wedding in Claridge's, a dress with a cathedral train and a family tiara. No, I don't think this would interest her at all. I'm afraid my family are a washout.'

'I'm sorry to hear that but I'm sure you both have many friends here who will make up for them. And Duke?'

'His gran has passed away so we're both orphans of the storm who washed up here. Couldn't live anywhere else now though.'

They sat down on the veranda while Sara made notes. 'I will need a date and your full names.'

'Do we have to? For my sins, I am Philippa Columbine Marianne Delamere, as in the forest, but I want Pippa for the ceremony, and, wait for it, Marmaduke Albert Millar. Poor kid with that handle but Duke to everyone here.'

'You need birth certificates, passports, probably an affidavit to prove there is no impediment to you marrying... that's about it for the Greek bit but it all has to be stamped and translated into Greek. The sooner we get this set up, the sooner we can fix a date and book the garden. It's all very exciting.'

'I shall look like a beached whale by then.' Pippa patted her swollen stomach. 'This was a complete surprise to us but I'm not grumbling. Now I can get on with preparations. We might be looking for somewhere bigger to rent in one of the villages at some point. The houses will be cheaper if some expats haven't snatched them for holiday homes.'

'Don't overdo things in your condition, easy does it,' Sara warned. 'Let us know if you need help. I'll check up on what's needed with Mel and let me know what you decide about catering. We'll make it a night to remember but it's your ceremony so every detail of yours counts.'

'You're a star, Sara. I hope when your turn comes it will be just as exciting.'

If only, Sara thought, but said nothing. Her past was not for sharing.

The meeting of the Foundation Trust sat down around the dining room in the retreat house. Apologies, minutes of the last meeting, news of the reprinting of the Durrante memoir were read, followed by Any Other Business.

'What's this I see here about a request to use our garden as a wedding venue? I hope we all agree, it is most unsuitable to allow such a pagan ceremony to take place on these premises.' Norris Thorner waved his minutes. 'I mean, what next, pop concerts?'

Sally Pearson, the new vicar in residence at St Paul's, quickly butted in. 'It's hardly pagan, Norris, a young village couple want a blessing and an exchange of vows in the open air after a legal civil ceremony in the town. Pippa and Duke want their union legitimised before their baby arrives.'

'Young people these days do it all the wrong way around. In my day couples waited until marriage before...' Norris was riding his high horse. 'I'm glad my Daniel and

Soraya are going to do things by the book. Her father, Yuri Shevchenko, is coming over in his yacht to oversee proceedings and Dorrie is busy preparing for their visit.'

'Well, it's all different now, the world has moved on,' argued Simon Bartlett. 'Couples have their own ideas on cohabiting, to marry or not.'

Griff waited until everyone had had their say before adding his own pennyworth.

'The olive grove is hardly used and the courses will be coming to a close soon so why not open the garden for events and celebrations?'

'But all the noise… all that music until dawn. Poor Dorinda has to take a sleeping pill on such nights. It encourages strangers into the olive garden. Who knows where it will end? And I don't suppose you contacted Ariadne Blunt? I gather she still is on our committee?'

'Yes, as a matter of fact I have contacted our founder member,' said Griff. 'She emailed me a letter which I will read out.'

Dear Trustees,

Thank you for inviting my opinion on this new venture. I heartily agree with opening up the retreat garden for open-air celebrations. I think Miss Durrante, whose presence I always feel within the grounds, would rejoice at such a use. She was the most romantic of authors and a wedding under the stars would please her, I'm sure. I expect security would be an issue and any feasting best supplied by supporting our local tavernas. Then everyone gets a slice of the cake.

My thoughts are with Pippa and Duke who were stalwart members of my Christmas choir and their music-making always a pleasure to hear. Pass on my good wishes, our good wishes, in fact. It's good to know there will be new life amongst us.

I do miss our island but the chances of returning soon are slim. My partner continues to make progress after her big operation but it will be a long convalescence and I can't leave her alone to take a trip back, much as I would like. I gather Miss Loveday is keeping our little villa in good order and I'm glad to know it's in safe hands.

If you wish me to stand down, do not hesitate to contact me but my dearest wish is to see the trust prosper and income from any source must be welcome.

Best wishes

Ariadne

'I think that says it all,' said Griff, putting down the letter and taking off his glasses. 'If you would like to vote on the decision, I suggest we do it now. All those in favour...' Hands went up. 'All those against...'

Only Norris raised his hand. 'I think it's better if I resign my post then.' He stood up to leave.

Griff raised both his hands in protest. 'Do stay, we need your expertise to keep the funds in good order. You are the most trusted member of our team and we would hate to lose you.' Griff had past experience in the boardroom of smoothing ruffled feathers. Norris sat down and everyone breathed a sigh of relief. Finding a competent treasurer was not easy. The only other contestant was still in London for the duration until his baby was born. The couple renting their house, that some wag had nicknamed 'The Bunker' because of its resemblance to a guard post on the Atlantic Wall, were letting it for six months.

Griff decided to give Pippa and Duke the decision in person, only to find Sara Loveday sitting at their table discussing plans with them. 'Great news, you can have your fairy lights and the olive grove. All we need is a date fixed.'

'What's the weather like in November?' Sara asked him.

'October would be more reliable,' Pippa said. 'Santaniki can have a mind of its own here. Perhaps we could put up a gazebo or something,' she suggested. 'Guests will get soaked if it rains.'

'I'll fix something up,' said Duke. He looked at Griff. 'With a little help from my friends.'

'What about a yurt?' Griff suggested. 'We can hire one large enough for the wedding party. The rest of the evening the guests will be in the taverna. If the night is warm and clear then we can hold everything outside and there's no problem.'

Pippa looked at Sara. 'Too expensive, I'm afraid.'

Sara nodded, then looked at Griff, shaking her head.

'Transport is next on our list. I don't think Pippa should walk, in her condition,' she said.

'I want a donkey cart, decorated with what we can find, to escort us down together. I know Katya's father has one sitting in his yard and I'm sure if we gave them an invite to the party…' Pippa suggested.

'By the way, we've submitted everything, just waiting for approval and we declared neither of us have been married before,' she continued, touching Duke's hand.

Griff looked around their little stone bothy. It really was primitive, just three rooms with a fireplace in the corner, a raised bench, table, stone sink and a well outside, but Pippa had put down kelims, rugs and sheepskin fleeces, making it very cosy and comfortable. In the next room was an iron bedstead and washstand. There was not much room for a baby and he must ask Sally and her husband if they knew of any small cottages coming up for rent, especially at the end of the tourist season.

How strange that after only a year he felt so protective of his friends here and at the retreat house. Joining their little band in the taverna helped him socialise and he loved exploring the wide-open spaces where he could wander with his dog. He was so glad for the couple that their wedding plans were going well.

Yet there was something else on his mind as he walked back from their cottage, something no one could ignore and it was the stink from unemptied bins in the heat. The vermin, cats and dogs roamed over them. At times the stink made him gag. There was no landfill so rubbish was ferried over to the big island. Only yesterday on his bike he saw a gully where fly tipping covered the greenery with mattresses and broken chairs. Why didn't they just burn stuff? Then he realised there was the fear of setting the hills on fire in the hot summers.

Did no one care for their own beautiful landscape? He hated to see guard dogs sweltering under plastic shades, chained, thirsty and flea-bitten. These thoughtless actions riled him, especially since he had rescued little Spartacus. Griff paused, knowing he was merely a guest here. This was not his culture but he felt he must question these matters at the next open meeting of the local council.

14

'No time like the present, Pippa. We have to find you a dress,' Mel said as she was bashing down some pizza dough while Sara was chopping vegetables. 'And have you thought of a menu yet?'

Pippa was folding napkins. 'What do you recommend? There'll be a crowd…'

'Let's go traditional, for starters and main. Mother-in-law will approve of that, but for desserts I suggest some good old English puddings: apple pie, meringue pavlovas and a chocolate recipe I brought over from home. We have to have something to mark your origins. Are you making notes, Sara?'

'In my head… as for the dress, I can't see anything here but beach clothes and kaftans,' she added.

Mel paused, wiping flour off her face. 'I have an idea. How about a trip to Chania on the ferry, a girls' day out, a bit like a hen party. What do you think?'

Pippa laughed. 'You think of everything and I'd love that.'

'Hair and nails we can get over here. Tula's daughter has a little salon.' Sara had been doing her homework.

'I can't afford anything very fancy,' Pippa added.

'Don't worry, we'll have plenty of choice. Chania is full of little boutiques and baby shops. You'll come too, Sara?'

Mel wanted Sara to have the full experience of her favourite city with its backstreets full of leather goods, shoes, jewellery shops and restaurants. 'We can stay the night and enjoy an evening out. Is there anyone else who might like to join us?'

'Why not ask Della Fitzpatrick?' Pippa said. 'She works in the NATO base, Sara. Della was our Pilates instructor and sang with us in the choir and she's fun.'

Mel was feeling protective of Pippa. They had bonded together in the band and she wanted her to have a great wedding. Sara was doing a brilliant job extricating all those little alternative details that would be truly Pippa and Duke, and Mel wanted to help where she could.

Sara was savvy, cutting costs where she could, haggling over prices. Thrown in at the deep end and being so busy, she was settling into island life much better than Mel expected. Sara had a driven sort of energy, as if she must succeed at all costs. Mel wondered what had made her up sticks from the UK so eagerly. She knew very little about her private life, sensing something had gone wrong, but her past was a closed book.

The day dawned and it was sunny as usual when they gathered on the harbour waiting for the ferry. Della

Fitzpatrick was going to meet them after work so there was a whole day ahead to shop until they dropped. At nearly six months Pippa's pregnancy was beginning to show and they mustn't tire her. First, they must find the dress and accessories. Mel knew just the places at the back of the harbour of this old Venetian town, where you could peep through gaps and look to the sea like the Lagoon in Venice. September was still full of tourists. The ceremony was in late October so the sooner the bride was satisfied with her outfit, the sooner they could enjoy the rest of their day. There were so many windows to peer in. Pricey boutiques were out but there were still little outfitters in the backstreets to explore.

All Pippa kept doing was cooing over the baby emporiums with frilly cotton dresses, miniature boys' trousers and jackets for the christening day; another big fat Greek affair.

'Time for all that when Baby comes, it's you we want to sort out now.' Sara urged them onwards. This was a mission.

Pippa stopped suddenly. 'We've not got any rings yet,' she said, peering into a jeweller's window full of gold necklaces and pendants.

'You don't have to wear one...' Mel was pulling her away.

'But I do... I don't want people thinking things.' It was funny how her friend was reverting to type, wanting to be seen as a proper married woman.

'Pippa, dress! You can sort that out when the time comes.' They linked arms and found the nearest café to refresh themselves as Pippa's bladder had a will of its own.

'I'm not doing very well, am I?' the bride-to-be said.

'We've hardly looked at anything yet,' Mel replied. 'You

rest your legs and I'll go out on a recce with Sara and we can perhaps point you in the right direction.'

Leaving Pippa with her iced frappé, the two of them set off. Shop after shop they scoured until they found a tiny place where a young woman with plaits around her head was sewing in the street. 'Can we look round?' Mel asked.

'*Endaxi*... of course.' Her accident was clipped. 'I make them to order.'

Inside was a rail full of soft linen dresses decorated on the shoulders or around the neck with appliquéd flowers and leaves. Simple but beautiful. Mel looked at Sara without saying a word. They both smiled. Eureka! Pippa was ushered into the little store and they stood back to let her browse. It must be her choice, not theirs, for the big day. The dressmaker did not hover either.

'It's for her wedding,' Mel whispered and the girl nodded.

'Just one moment, I have some more in the back,' she said, disappearing, bringing out a mid-length linen dress in a rich turquoise blue; the sleeves were short, appliquéd with stars in gold and silver embroidery and the neckline was scalloped, edged with tiny pearls. 'This is just finished,' she said.

Pippa fingered it, shaking her head with delight. 'It's beautiful, simple and loose. Can I try it on?'

Mel watched, tears filling her eyes. Her friend had found her bridal gown. Pippa slipped into the little curtained-off corner and came out shining. She looked in the mirror. 'Is this really me?' Letting down her sun-bleached hair, suddenly she looked eighteen not thirty-nine.

'You look amazing,' Sara said. 'The colour suits you so well; it's the colour of the sea and the detail is perfect.'

'But can I afford it?' she whispered. The dressmaker smiled. 'For you it will be...' she whispered the price. Mel didn't want to haggle. The price was perfect. It would be a dress to last a lifetime and unique, made with skill and love. She knew all the bridal stores with their voluminous gowns costing thousands. They were not for the likes of Pippa, but this little backstreet was perfection. Mel high-fived Sara, mission accomplished.

Sara asked for her card. 'I think we can bring people here again for the coolest of dresses.'

Everyone was happy. Pippa kept peering into the bag. 'Thank you, how clever to find such a gem in the undergrowth. Wait until Duke sees it.'

'Not yet, not until your wedding day. If we're going to be traditional, he can wait to see you in all your glory,' Sara ordered. 'I will keep it safe until then... now for pretty sandals.'

What was it about seeing Pippa's bare feet and purple toenails that made Mel suddenly think about treading grapes? 'Don't forget it's the grape harvest, soon... all hands to the deck but not you, Pippa,' Mel ordered. 'We do it the traditional way, so shorts on and bare feet – we're going to dance on the grapes. This you must see, Sara.' Mel laughed, seeing the look on her face. 'It's good exercise.'

Spiro came back from his dance rehearsal and joined Griff, Simon and Duke round the taverna table. Irini was busy clearing away and the boys were asleep in the spare room. 'What's new?' he said.

'We're having a meeting, sit down and help us out.'

Spiro kicked off his boots. 'My feet are on fire.'

'Spiro,' Irini called, seeing him peeling off his boots, about to sit down. 'There's a hole in your shirt, does she not mend them for you? Off on the town leaving you with no meat on the table. I don't know what she will do next.'

'Mama, when has Melodia got time to sew anything? You keep her feet in the air all day and our boys run her around but still she smiles and sings like a lark.'

Griff laughed as the two shouted at each other. How different from the muttered sarcastic mumblings of the English when quarrelling politely. He fetched Spiro a beer.

'Get that down you. We have a problem and we don't know how to explore it with the demos.'

'I'm listening.'

'It's about the bins,' said Griff.

'And the stray dogs,' said Simon.

'And don't forget about the fly-tipping,' said Duke.

'Who is dipping flies?' Spiro looked puzzled. They explained about the smell of the dead cats and rats, the flies, dogs abandoned in the hills, dumped from cars and left to fend for themselves.

'Now the dog refuge has closed and it's illegal to have strays, there are complaints that too many poor creatures are stuck out in full sun. Jules from the dog pound did her best and the vets came over to neuter as many as they could but funds ran out and now the strays are everywhere. I know a couple who are rehoming six at their own expense.'

'But what is this to do with me?' Spiro replied.

'You are local born and bred. How do we approach the council, the mayor and the authorities to take more control of this?'

'I don't know,' said Spiro, scratching his head. 'The cats are useful to kill the rats.'

'But there would be fewer rats around if the bins were emptied more. It's a health issue. Don't people care?' said Griff.

'It's always been like this,' Spiro replied.

'But if Santaniki wants the tourist business to grow, stinking streets don't encourage visitors… We have so many comments in the retreat house I feel embarrassed.'

'What can I do?'

'If we write to the authorities here, will you translate and arrange a meeting for us?'

'Okay, I will try but we do not like foreigners interfering.'

'It is the responsibility of the demos to deal with strays, to catch, inject, spay or castrate and then to rehome,' Simon said. 'Some of the councillors are responsible, some are not and I know funding is limited. They need a reminder of their duty here. I have been here over twenty years, foreigner I may be, but I care about this place and the poor animals too.' He was incensed.

'Then perhaps you try for election then you can have your say.' Spiro was on the defensive.

Time to lay off him. 'Point taken,' said Griff. 'No offence… but we have to flag it up. If we put up posters would that help?'

'Don't ask me, just do it... Sorry, I must go help Mama.'
Spiro stood up, carrying his boots into the kitchen.

'Have we offended him?' Duke asked.

'Don't know, it's at times like this I feel a great gulf
between our opinions and the local culture,' said Simon.
'They are the hardest working people I know with the
closest of family ties, the most hospitable and generous folk
but when it comes to this they turn a blind eye. What can
we do to stir up some action?'

Griff was not to be disheartened. 'I could shame them
with pictures of Spartacus when I found him in the hills and
how he looks now. We could ask if they will fund another
vet to come over and do a health check, if necessary out of
our own pockets?' he suggested.

'But maybe it's not the culture to have man bits cut off,'
Duke added.

'Spartacus could tell them the benefits of it though. For
many here, a working dog is a tool, expendable, and when
old they are shot; and as for the puppies and kittens, they
are just a nuisance and fed by tourists in the cafés. Perhaps
we could start a campaign, better than doing nothing.'
Griff concluded, 'Guys, I think we have gone off piste re
the bins issues but we've now got some good ideas to meet
again with something concrete. I have photographs of
Spartacus when I picked him up. Simon can do the text for
a poster. Duke, perhaps you can distribute some in Greek
and English?'

Griff walked home, glad to get these concerns off his
chest, hoping he was not alone in this campaign. Maybe
other expats could make locals see the benefits all round

of clean bins and less strays because more tourists meant more money in the bank for everyone in the town. Short hands and deep pockets wouldn't do but a little bit of fundraising, information and compassion might win the day. Spartacus's adventures would make a good shaggy dog story.

15

Sara strolled up to the *plateia* in her denim shorts and flip-flops. The square was packed with vans and men chucking grapes into what looked like a cement mixer. There was a large communal tank into which the mash was being tipped. This was the modern way of harvesting the juice but Mel said they were going to do it the traditional way.

'Come around the back into the garden.' Here there was a large open space with a stone threshing wheel circle used as a sitting area, and to the side a stone pit where Katya and the two student waitresses were bouncing up and down in a sort of well that was full of grapes. They were holding hands and dancing, having fun, while Irini and Spiro and the boys were emptying more baskets of russet fruit. Raw juice was pouring from a channel into plastic containers. It looked a brown muddy mess.

'It's your turn now,' Irini said, pointing to the grapes. 'Don't look like that, you'll enjoy it and it's better than ten thousand steps to fitness. You will do well. You have big feet...'

Sara was trying to stifle a giggle, big feet indeed, as she climbed into the *patitiri*. She'd show them. Mel and her boys were now squishing around, pounding the fruit with bare feet.

She felt the strange sensation of mush between her toes and she began to march up and down. It was fun. 'What happens to the mash – does it go like manure onto the field?' she asked.

'Good lord, no,' Mel shouted. 'Nothing is wasted. When the juice runs out, the skins are left to ferment into *tsikoudia*, raki... moonshine to you and me. The vine leaves, you know we use them to wrap *dolmades*. It's the same with the olive trees – when the branches are pruned, the wood goes to heat the fire or for wood sculpture.'

'It makes better village wine doing it the old way.' Irini pointed to the plastic barrels. 'We let the juice stand and some goes into oak barrels...special,' she smiled, touching her lips. Sara had tasted the end product – some was like thin sherry, the rest she could take or leave – but said nothing. She looked around at the boys still pounding away.

'You wouldn't do this in Sheffield,' Mel yelled and Sara laughed.

'If they could see me now in Sheffield, Health and Safety would have a fit,' she replied, knowing her own sweating feet were part of the harvest. This year's harvest she would have to taste and as for the raki, the white spirit that burnt her throat when it was offered in tiny glasses as a digestive treat at the end of every supper, she was getting a taste for that. Heaven only knew what its alcohol level was. Griff told her it was used on insect bites and wounds. She hoped she wouldn't have to try that remedy.

'Hose down your legs and then we eat.' Irini pointed to a trestle table with a white cloth and plates. 'It is thirsty work, come... all is prepared.' There was a huge *pilafi* dish, salads and a plate of courgettes in thin batter that Sara demolished with gusto. How did they do all this, serve tables in the taverna, crush grapes and now this feast for the eyes as well as the taste buds? The colours of the island were in their dishes: reds, greens, colours of the rainbow. No wonder the old folk here lived to a ripe old age, with no chips and booze.

When she stood up, her muscles were aching, but she wouldn't have missed this tradition. Going to Chania with the girls, meeting Mel's friend Della for an evening on the lash by Chania harbour was magic. Now the wedding to prepare for made her feel she was part of the community. The only thing lacking was her Greek. If she was to stay here, she must make an effort, hard as it was, and not keep relying on Mel and Spiro to translate. Perhaps in the winter she would join a class to bolster the little language she had. Sara didn't want to be one of those foreign residents who never bothered to learn a word. Why should the locals have to speak English all the time? No, she must take herself in hand. She owed St Nick's so much, it was the least she could do.

Jack and Sandra from 'the Bunker' sat in the taverna looking at the poster of a scruffy, skinny dog sunk in a rubbish bin with the title: *It's a dog's life... No home, no food, feeling sick. Surely there is another way?*

'It's enough to put one off one's dinner,' said a scruffy old Greek man in the corner.

'But it's true,' Jack replied. 'There are strays everywhere.'

'Then let them get put down,' came the reply.

'They can't help being chucked out or dumped or breeding like rabbits.' Sandra felt sorry for the poor mutt in the picture. 'Whose doing was this?' she asked Mel who shrugged her shoulders.

'Not sure, but it's long overdue... Stavros, it's time you went home. I need your chair and your smoke is stinking out the tables.'

The man shuffled off muttering to himself, gesturing defiance in Mel's direction.

Irini had other ideas. 'It's the English interfering again. They should look in their own corner. Here we care for our family when they get old... we do not shove them into homes and visit them once a month. Do they care for animals more than their own flesh and blood?'

'Mama... shush, not all families are like that. My own nonna lived with us for years.'

'You are half Italian,' came the reply.

'I thought there was a band tonight.' Sandra changed the subject, knowing it was none of their business to express an opinion.

'Not tonight, our sax player and the guitarist are getting married soon so we're giving everyone the night off but there's a big party on Saturday night and you're more than welcome to join us.'

Sandra smiled. 'We'd love to if you're sure.' She liked Mel who helped them choose from the menu. They ought to mix more in the English crowd but she got so tired and breathless lately with the chemo pills and that sicky feeling made choosing dishes difficult.

'I thought there was a dog sanctuary somewhere,' said Jack.

'It had to close due to the authorities not approving and lack of funds. There was not much support. But I hear there's a new campaign to raise awareness of animal welfare and rehoming them.'

'Oh, good.' Sandra looked around the taverna. 'It's all looking very decorative. I like the stripy bunting.'

'We're doing it up for the wedding,' Mel said as she cleared away their plates. 'It's going to be a grand do. Pippa and Duke are having a quiet ceremony in the retreat house garden and she's coming by donkey and cart, if the cantankerous old beast will oblige. Honestly, when we went to look at poor Ajax, it was a scene straight out of *Steptoe and Son*,' she whispered with a chuckle. 'Let's hope a lick of paint and some flowers will disguise the cart and Katya's family will give poor Ajax a makeover.'

'We saw the doctor's wedding procession but this sounds very different.'

'Oh yes, it will definitely be different. Sara Loveday is organising it. She's setting up wedding packages for visitors from England. It's a new venture, though she is very experienced in event management in Sheffield.'

'I thought you sounded like us – from up north,' Sandra said.

Mel laughed. 'I'll never lose my accent.'

'Is this Sara planning parties as well?' Sandra asked.

'Not really, wedding planning takes up her time. She is busy preparing her new brochure.'

'Really?' Sandra replied, squirrelling this information away. What a coincidence as she was still thinking of the future. If her treatment went pear-shaped, she wanted some memories to look back on when times were hard; a family gathering if possible. Jack must be provided for. Cohabiting was fine for the young and fit with years ahead of them.

In her heart she feared her future might not be the full three score years and ten but how to approach Jack to propose to him? He was convinced that everything would be fine but stage four cancer was incurable; treatable yes... Don't dwell on that, she thought, fixing her smile.

Mel looked the same age as Julie but with an energy and cheery persona that her daughter had never had. Julie sulked, living in washed-out leggings and faded tops as if she didn't care for her appearance. Colin didn't seem to mind what she wore.

As a child Julie was skinny, full of mischief with a mop of golden curls. 'Bubbles', they called her, but bubbly she no longer was. How Sandra longed for that little poppet, piggyback-riding on her dad. Those golden days were long gone and she ached to hold her, to soothe away all the grief that lay like a heavy stone inside her child. Why does she still punish me? she cried into her pillow that night. Why did her daughter shut them out of her life? It had to be sorted once and for all... Would a wedding here help or make it worse?

*

Sara was making a long to-do list, check, check, check. Only the weather was now beyond her control but every other detail was, or at least she thought it was until she cornered Duke in the street. 'I was wondering if you'd organised a ring?'

He looked nonplussed. 'Hasn't Pippa bought one?' he replied.

Sara held her hands up in horror, typical man leaving everything to the wife. 'She shouldn't have to buy her own ring,' she said. 'It's a bit late now but have you got anything that might do? Do you know her size, even?' Duke was so laid back, almost horizontal at times, but he needed to make some effort.

'Hang on,' he said. 'I've got a gold signet ring. I think it was my grandad's but it's a bit battered. Don't know why I kept it.'

'It could be altered to her size, refashioned later, but you'll have to find her size, and soon,' Sara ordered.

'I'll root in her trinket box. She has a few bits from her family that she wouldn't miss if I took one for size.'

'There's a Danish jeweller up in Sternes village. Mel told me that Chloë Bartlett buys her necklaces from there. She might alter it. Get yourself to Anna's workshop pronto and see what she can do. Have you got your own outfit sorted?' She didn't want Duke turning up in his old tie-dye shirt and cut-off jeans.

Duke laughed. 'I'm sorted, something I picked up in my roadie days so don't worry, I won't show up in shorts... Bit nervous though. I've asked Mel to sing for us. I've suggested something as a surprise for Pippa. Griff's helped me write some words.'

The civic ceremony was organised for the morning. Their papers were all in order and just Mel, Spiro and Griff had been invited.

Sara wanted them in the retreat garden checking the decor. There was no yurt available and the gazebo they'd found had seen better days.

'Haven't we all,' Griff quipped as they began to disguise the wear and tear with bunting and flowers; the last of the plumbago and the bougainvillea. Sara was up and down to the retreat house so much that Spartacus wagged his tail to greet her as an old friend.

He was now the star of the 'Spot the Dog' campaign, a little competition for schoolchildren to take photos of stray dogs without collars, puppies and cats that had no homes, and give them names. The younger children could draw them and there would be a prize for the best entry.

'Not going to be easy to change minds,' Griff explained. 'It's already caused some controversy among locals.'

Sara hoped none of this would spoil the party atmosphere. This was to be Pippa and Duke's big day. The professional photographer from the big island was coming to do some specialised shots she hoped would give a romantic atmosphere. The hair and beauty was all organised. They planned fizz and nibbles on the veranda with more shots after the wedding. It was now up to her to set the table with flowers and greenery. They were expecting Pippa's friends from the book club, the regulars to the band nights and local residents. Sally the vicar was a fount of information and Sara knew the ceremony was in safe hands.

This was a good learning curve in this new setting but in its own way nerve-wracking. What if it poured down? What if the locals stayed away because of Griff's campaign, or the donkey cart fell to bits and Yannis's boys drove them to the wedding in smelly farmyard shirts?

Mr and Mrs Thorner declined an invitation on the grounds that they were otherwise engaged. Dorrie was off to London to check her outfit for their own 'wedding of the year', but not before sending Sara a note hoping that she wouldn't make a precedent of using the trust's garden for alternative nuptials. How they would deal with any same-sex celebrations, heaven alone knew.

Last, but not least, was the pretty dress she bought almost as an afterthought; a raspberry pink shift with matching shoes and a Thai silk wrap if it turned chilly. Sara did not want to waste the opportunity to give it an outing.

With Simon and Griff's help they found a trailer for all the empty water bottles, glass and recyclable waste. As the sun went down Sara stood admiring the olive garden, praying tomorrow would prove to be special for Pippa and Duke's big day.

16

Mel woke Pippa from her deep sleep. She had spent the night in their spare room oblivious to the boys who were out playing football in their back garden. 'Wakey, wakey, it's your wedding day,' she yelled. Duke and Pippa were following tradition by spending the night apart.

Pippa staggered up from the pillow. 'Let me lie in…'

'No, we've got hair appointments and the civil ceremony will not wait.' Mel was being bossy but as a sort of matron of honour she felt duty bound to get this show on the road before Sara arrived.

'I feel like a beached whale, the little sod's kicked me all night. Duke is convinced it will be the next Lionel Messi. I'm happy not to know either way.'

The morning flew by. Sara had gone to help Griff and his staff to set up the little bower while Mel's student waitresses prepared everything for the wedding table on the veranda. Spartacus got under everyone's feet and was banished inside, much to his disgust, where he whined for attention. Don was charged with tidying up but his idea was to flick a duster in the air. The flowers arrived and the weather was set perfect for the day. The wedding party took Spiro's taxi to the town hall. It was all very low key. Pippa had wanted to save her outfit for the blessing in the olive garden. Mel and Spiro together witnessed the brief formalities before speeding back for the main event. Mel hoped her mother-in-law had kept Markos and Stefan in check in their new clothes.

Ajax and his cart arrived, now looking more like a wedding cart with white sheets and cushions on the bench. Katya had sweetened the floor with rosemary and thyme. Duke strolled down in a blue silk shirt and chinos with his dreadlocks tied back neatly. Then Pippa came down the stairs in her dress with a circlet of flowers round her hair – she looked radiant. 'Will I do?' she whispered to Mel.

'You look like an earth mother,' came the reply. There was a glow around Pippa that came not only from pregnancy but from happiness.

The donkey clomped down the street and neighbours came out to wish them well – *chronia polla*: many years – but the young driver still looked as if he'd come straight out of the farmyard. They paused while passers-by took videos. At one halt Pippa got off to stand in front of Ajax, smiling.

'Look out,' yelled the driver as Ajax took a chunk out of her bouquet. Everyone roared but Pippa was not amused. Griff, who was following behind with the other guests, caught the action. It was then that Mel noticed there was no other photographer in sight.

'Where's your photographer?' she asked Sara.

Sara looked flushed. 'He didn't show. I got a garbled email to say he was not feeling well and had missed the ferry. What the hell am I going to do?'

'Ask Griff. Look, he's got his camera in his hand.' Sara hurried off to catch up with him, not easy in a tight skirt. She was rushed off her feet. This was her first wedding and she was doing it almost for free so she could have genuine shots for her brochure. There would be plenty of mobile phone snapshots but they needed proper ones for the bride and groom.

Mel was hugging her own special gift. All those years ago she was afraid to sing in public. Setting up this band changed all that and she had found the perfect song and lyrics. They had roped in a local jazz band ready to play them into the garden on arrival and Sally would be waiting.

Mel was not prepared for how much detail had gone into the decorating of the old tent into this leafy bower. It was almost mediaeval. Their closest friends were gathering, sitting on chairs. The vicar stood in her robes. Mel noticed Chloë Bartlett, Simon's wife, wearing a beautiful silk polka-dot dress, Simon himself looking smart in a pinstriped shirt. Della Fitzpatrick arrived on the ferry with her American boyfriend, Joe. The book group filled a row even without Dorrie Thorner eyeing up the proceedings for any mishaps.

She took her place beside Spiro and the boys as the little ceremony began. It was just a few words and a blessing. Duke's adjusted ring was placed on Pippa's finger without any problem. Pippa was tearful. Then it was time for Mel to stand up to the mic to sing Etta James's great classic: 'At last, my love has come along…'

Pippa and Duke kissed and everyone clapped as they turned to their friends to lead them down the path back to the veranda of the house.

'Is that it? Not much of a ceremony,' Irini complained, sitting in her best crimplene black and grey striped dress. 'All that fuss for a few minutes.'

Mel ignored her as the drinks and nibbles, sugared almonds, nuts, little cheese pies and slivers of pâté on toast were passed around and everybody mingled. It was just as Pippa and Sara had planned but there was the delicate problem that no proper photographs were being taken.

At last Sara found Griff with Spartacus, clearing chairs away. 'Griff, the photographer is not showing up and I desperately need to have some good portraits for my brochure. This is such a perfect setting... please can you help?' she pleaded. Spartacus jumped up to greet her.

'What, me take his place?' he replied.

'Mel said you would and I'm desperate. I tried to catch you up before.' How could she explain her tight skirt and high heels had hampered her chasing him earlier.

'Just a sec, hold the dog, I'll fetch my camera. You'll have to choose the angles. I take landscapes not portraits. I'm a purist and don't trust just digitals but I'll take from both.' He disappeared, returning with his Pentax, not the latest range but it looked reliable.

'You're lucky, I've got space on the card still. You'll need to gather the congregation again with the vicar to make sure we get a shot of everybody.'

'Thanks.' Sara tried to stay calm but felt foolish as she ushered bride and groom, guests and the vicar back into the garden amidst the flowers for a group shot. Then Griff ordered the guests to look as if it was the start of the ceremony, not the end.

Sara picked a spot on the veranda for the couple to sit in a relaxed pose, sipping fizz, but somehow Spartacus wheeled his way between them and it made a good shot. Then they posed the couple holding hands looking out over the sea, very cheesy but romantic. Griff photographed the table carefully recreated by their helpers to look informal, relaxed, taking in the colour, the texture, the scenic beauty. Sara knew it was a tall ask but Griff manfully took his orders from her.

'I owe you,' Sara said, grateful for his help.

'Wait until you see them first,' he replied. He did have a nice smile, Sara thought; good teeth – but that made her laugh, thinking of how judges eyed up horses in the Great Yorkshire Show. She bit it back and hoped that out of his pictures there would be some decent ones.

The afternoon drifted into a hazy evening. Mel, Spiro and Irini left to prepare for the evening feast and Sara felt the heat and tiredness because she'd forgotten to eat.

'Here's a cup of tea for you, it's going to be a long night,' Griff said. He pointed to the house. 'It's time for a siesta.'

'I'd better go and check up with things at the taverna. I hope the wedding cake has arrived and nothing else goes wrong,' she said, anxious to be on her way.

'You worry too much, it's been a splendid occasion, everybody smiling...'

'It's my job to do the worrying if I am to make a success

of this business. I will have to sharpen up my act, be on call just in case... This event is just a rehearsal.'

'Sit down,' he ordered. 'Three minutes won't change anything. I hope you've hired a jeep to get you there,' Griff checked, and she nodded.

'I can't thank you enough for stepping into the breach and I will pay for all the prints.'

'Forget it, it was a pleasure to take them. Pippa and Duke looked so happy. I wish all weddings were like that,' he said.

'Sounds like you've seen your share of mishaps,' Sara replied.

'My cousin had the biggest nuptials in the county but six weeks later the bride eloped with one of her bridesmaids... how about you?'

Sara smiled, knowing she was not going to reveal her own sad experience. 'They happen,' she replied. 'Too much planning, too much money, wanting to please parents, too much time on Pinterest, I suppose. I'd better get used to dramas and be prepared with tissues, counsellors and unpaid bills. I really must go.' Her jeep was parked by the road. It was time to check at the taverna and escape Griff's probing gaze and questions. He was the last person with whom she wanted to share her tale of woe.

Sandra and Jack were sitting at the tables that were spread out into the town square, watching the Cretan dancers leaping and turning. It felt special to be invited to this wedding party and the taverna was adorned with flowers and banners. Everyone was dressed to the nines in costumes of all shapes and colours. How different Greek women were to the British in their subdued linens and silks. Sandra was wearing her favourite sundress covered in red poppies. The bride wore her turquoise dress, floating like a galleon in full sail. They sat next to Mr and Mrs Bartlett who were very friendly and pointed out all the local expats.

'Do you enjoy reading?' Mrs Bartlett said.

'All the time,' Sandra replied. Resting up with a good book helped her fatigue fade away.

'We have a book group once a month. Would you be interested in joining us?' she added.

'That sounds lovely, yes, but we are only here for a few more months.'

'That's what we all said but look at us now. I'm Chloë and my husband's Simon,' she said. 'The man on the end of the dancers is Spiro, Mel's husband. He's looking very fit.'

'And very handsome,' Sandra replied. They both giggled. 'You're not too old to notice, are you?'

It was the turn for the audience to get up and dance in circles. Sandra wasn't sure she could manage but Jack pulled her up. 'Let's have a go and if you get out of breath…'

'I think I'd better go to the ladies first,' she said.

Sandra pushed her way to the toilet. Her bladder was unreliable but she was game for a few twirls as the music was the magnetic 'Zorba's Dance'.

There was only one woman in the loo, standing by the sink. It was the bride and she was staring down at a pool of water at her feet, looking shaken. 'Where did that come from?' she cried. 'I'm soaking, my poor dress... I can't go back in there. They'll think I've wet myself.'

'You have, love,' Sandra replied. 'Your waters have broken... it's your time.'

'But it can't be, it's too soon. I've got more weeks to go yet.'

'Your baby thinks otherwise so you'd better sit down, but not in here.' Sandra was taking control.

'Can you fetch Mel? She'll know what to do,' Pippa said.

Sandra shot out of the toilet, searching for Mel in her lilac dress. She was about to go up to the mic to sing. 'Mrs Papadaki,' she tapped her on the arm, 'I think you'd better come. It's the bride, she's going into labour,' Sandra whispered

'But she can't! She's still got weeks to go.'

'This baby wants to come but I take your point... I was a nurse and the waters have broken so she needs to be seen to now in case of infection.' Sandra spoke with urgency as they all made their way back to the loo. 'Is there a doctor in here?'

Mel pointed to a man in spectacles and a lady in a silvery dress. 'His wife is the midwife, slip over there and tell them.' Sandra sidled over, recognising the two of them from the wedding procession. 'Excuse me,' she whispered. 'Pippa Millar has gone into labour.'

All eyes were following the procession as the doctor, the midwife, Mel and Sandra headed in the direction of the ladies' toilet, curious as to what was happening. Jack stood up. 'You okay?'

'I'm fine but there's a bit of a drama in the ladies, that's all.' Sandra made her way towards the toilet then turned back. She did not want to interfere as the doctor and his wife were now in charge.

'Someone better fetch Duke,' Spiro said. Everyone knew Duke, the groom.

'I'll fetch him,' Sandra offered, making a discreet exit, squeezing between guests to where the groom was busy congratulating the dancers.

'Excuse me, but I think you are needed in the ladies, it's your wife. The baby is coming.'

'She okay?' His dark eyes were filled with concern.

'Don't worry, the doctor and his wife are there. It's all under control and I think it'll be ages yet. Babies take their time even when they're very early.' Sandra was trying to reassure him. The guests sensed the drama unfolding. It was like a wave of news rippling from table to table... the baby is coming.

Then Mel appeared. 'Please, no fuss, the party will go on but we must get Pippa down to the clinic,' she announced as the medics, bride and groom processed past, trying to smile as if this was all part of the celebration.

'Done a good job there, lass,' said Jack as Sandra slumped down, her heart beating fast with all the excitement. 'She is in good hands. Poor girl on her wedding day... I hope it all goes right, being premature. Still, it's the right way around now, not born in the vestry, as they used to say.' Sandra laughed.

The disco band struck up again and the guests danced on but Sandra felt tired. The slightest excitement got her out of breath but she had her inhaler.

Somewhere down in the town another party would

be going on and it wouldn't be over until well after dawn broke.

Griff, Don and Sara sat speechless at first, sipping their iced beers watching Spiro and Irini and the waiters filling glasses and handing round plates of wedding pastries and sweets. No one was going anywhere. 'You couldn't make this up, could you?' Griff said, shaking his head in disbelief. 'Now, Don, here's the plot of your new novel.'

'A wedding and a birth in the same day, not bad...' he replied, smiling at Sara.

'But it's been a great day. My first wedding and it will be one to remember. I hope everything goes well for Pippa, with no complications. Do you have nephews and nieces?' she asked them both.

'Six of them,' Griff replied. 'My brother and his wife can't seem to help themselves. He's the one who runs things back in Shropshire. Have you any?'

Sara shook her head. 'I'm an only child.'

'Lucky thing,' Don said. 'You wouldn't want a family like mine thrust upon you...'

'It couldn't happen to a better couple,' Griff added. 'Don't think they're prepared, though, and it'll be a squash in the little shack. I wondered if they would accept the guesthouse for a while? I gather it's not the first time it's harboured newborns. It wouldn't interfere with the other residents and you said you were going back home.' Griff turned to Don.

'I'm being shoved out to make way for a baby? I was

thinking of staying on. Still, I know when I'm not wanted.' Don pouted but then laughed.

'I'm going back home so you'll have to keep the place in order.'

'Not quite my style, old boy. Perhaps I will inflict myself on one of my brothers. I shall return as a deadline is looming.'

'You're leaving too?' Sara was surprised.

'Only for Christmas, things to do back home.'

'It must be lovely having a big family celebration. Our Christmases are quiet, lots of walking in the Peaks.'

'How simply ghastly.' Don grimaced. 'Griff has been putting me through my paces to no avail. Now he takes Sparky in my place.'

'I shall be working on my brochure with your shots,' Sara said.

'Sure. Perhaps we should meet up somewhere when I get them sorted. You could choose them and we could Photoshop them together. I do have some IT design experience if that would help.'

Sara felt embarrassed. Did he think she couldn't handle it herself? Her business was none of his concern but he was trying to be helpful. Why did she feel reluctant to get him involved? 'Thanks, but I've plenty of contacts in Sheffield.'

Don was eyeing them both. 'That's you told, son.'

'I just thought they can be expensive and you won't have made much from this wedding.' Griff was oblivious to Don's remark.

'I never expected to make a profit. It was a try-out, but I shall check out photographers in future. It could have been a disaster.'

Griff lifted his glasses. 'I just thought it might help. I didn't mean to patronise.'

'Thanks all the same but I have to deal with this my way,' Sara replied.

'Fancy a dance?' Don said, dragging Sara onto the floor. 'Can't miss the chance for a smooch with a pretty girl.' Sara laughed as he stumbled over his feet. 'Sorry.'

Griff was watching them both. Sara felt her cheeks flushing. She would prefer to be dancing with him but she wanted no distractions. Don was a harmless flirt, and it suited her to let him amuse her with his antics, but she had the perfect escape.

'Sorry, do you mind, I'm a bit concerned about Irini and the girls in the kitchen. Irini is much better but I don't want her to overdo things. I must take Mel's place,' she said, not looking at either of them as she made her way out.

'What did I say?' Don shouted. Sara paused.

'My thanks to you both for today. You really did help me out of a hole.'

Griff looked up. 'Think nothing of it.'

Sara felt mean but she did have to leave. Griff was a nice guy, too nice, in fact. How could she miss his interest in her? But she didn't want any more complications. A man like Griff would want more than she could give. He was not on her to-do list.

Mel held the tiny baby in her arms and felt her breast tightening with yearning. It was a little girl and how she longed to have a daughter of her own. She was beautiful, her skin a little bit wrinkled but she was breathing well, tiny but perfect, her hair was dark and she was a good size for such an early bird.

Pippa lay back, exhausted. It had been a long birth, hours of pacing the floor, but the midwife and her husband, who had brought most of the babies in town into the world, knew what they were doing. Duke had held her hand until the delivery was over. He wept at the sight of his child. 'No one tells you it will feel like this,' he said as he held the baby as if she was fragile glass.

'Have you chosen the name?' Mel asked.

'I was so sure it would be a boy called Theo, but Pippa must choose,' Duke said.

'Not Theodora,' Pippa chipped in. 'Something different. I have my own idea but let's wait to see if the baby likes her name. I'll not thrust Columbine on her, and there's no rush.'

Mel left them sitting, adoring this beautiful gift of life. How envious she felt, but she knew she had two healthy boys and what mama did not love her sons?

Next morning, Sara was waiting at the taverna collecting up the decorations and helping Katya and Irini collect the rubbish in a sack for recycling. There were so many bottles and napkins and cigarette packets. Spiro would take them to the makeshift bins. Mel hadn't slept all night, worrying about Pippa in labour. Sara took the bride's dress to wash and then they went to the shack to collect clean clothes.

'Griff said they could use the guesthouse if things got too squashed but I think it's homely in here and babies don't take up much room, do they?'

Mel laughed. It was clear Sara had no idea about bathing tubs, changing mats, buggies, cots, sterilising equipment, nappies, mattresses and liners but she said nothing. Perhaps Sara's turn would come one day. They found a drawer full of baby clothes, knitted cardigans, pretty feeding scarves, baby-gros that would be far too large for this little tot.

Mel knew there were still little cotton nightdresses somewhere in a case that Irini's neighbours had made for her own babies. They were cool and just right for Pippa to use. At least her friend had quietly squirrelled away nappies and vests and a beautiful lacy shawl as fine as gossamer that looked locally knitted.

'Have they got a name for her?' Sara asked.

'Not yet; they plan to wait a while and see what fits.'

'Perhaps they'll choose something Greek like Zoë or Phoebe, Xanthe or Daphne,' Sara continued.

'Knowing Pippa, it'll be something alternative, a little hippy. Anyway, let's give their place a once-over and put in some flowers and bring in the cards from the doorstep. Everyone will want to shower them with gifts and have a peek at the new one,' said Mel. 'The mother must rest before the visitors come.'

'When I go back home, I'll try and find something. I have a friend who designs children's clothing, all organic cotton and ethically sourced and I'll buy something for when she is bigger, to grow into. I'm so glad it all went well.' Sara was ferreting about to find cleaning products.

The house must be sparkling clean when they came home later in the week. Prem babies needed checking and Caliope would want to keep a close eye on her progress.

'You're not staying for Christmas then?' Mel was disappointed.

'No, I'll leave early in December to get all the business side of things sorted. I do need some bookings for next summer but I may have left it too late already. Griff is sending photos and I hope there is something worth printing but I've seen a preview, not bad for an amateur.'

Why was Sara so dismissive of Griff? He was one of the good guys in Mel's book. She had hoped there was a spark between the two of them but evidently not. 'Are you still going with the "Second Time Around" idea?'

Sara was busy sweeping the floor. 'Not sure now. The website is crucial and I'm not convinced I've got it right but I'll have time to work on it back in Sheffield.'

'How do you feel about going back?' Mel hesitated to say that Sara could have months here to escape away from the realities of a British winter. Christmas was always an emotional time but it was up to her friend to decide. 'I bet you're dying to get back to see your friends… anyone special?' She was fishing for information but none was forthcoming.

'That song you sang in the garden ceremony had me in bits,' Sara said. 'I realise real love is about sharing, being there for each other like you and Spiro. "Our life is like a song…" I don't think that will ever happen for me.'

'One day your love will come along…' Mel whispered.

'But not yet, stop it! This won't get the job done. Where's

the duster? You pack and I'll clean, a bit of teamwork not
sob stuff,' Sara ordered.

'Slave driver!' Mel laughed.

Going back home would be a test of Sara's resolve. Was
this island wedding planning business just a dream or a
real goer? Only time would tell. Back in a Yorkshire winter,
working on the project without sunshine, taverna life and
Ariadne's garden to hide in, should reveal how realistic her
chances were of making this business a success.

December

December

17

Sandra brought Jack his G and T by the pool. It was late afternoon but still warm and sunny as she sat down beside him. The appointment in Chania had gone well, things were still under control with stable tumour markers. The cancer wouldn't go away but they were treating it like any other chronic disease. Her scan results were hopeful. There was still more time ahead to plan a future and there was only one thing on Sandra's mind.

'Wasn't it grand to see the baby? It was kind of them to invite us after I sent that present. They want us to wet the baby's head after the christening but it got me thinking, love – isn't it time that me and thee got wed to make an honest woman of me before I pop my clogs?'

'None of that talk,' Jack snapped. 'You'll see me out.'

'No, I won't, and you know it. I just want our affairs to be in order, and besides, it will be lovely to tie the knot right here on the island.'

'I thought it was the man who did the proposing, you brazen hussy,' he laughed. 'Are you sure you want a fuss?'

'If cancer has taught me anything, it's that time is a gift and to spend it wisely by having something to look forward to. That's what living in each moment is about. We could make it as special a day as we want it to be: just you, me and a few old friends.'

'And Julie?' he said.

'I was coming to that. I want us to go home for Christmas and I'll visit her and talk things through. She could be my matron of honour.' It was her dearest wish to set things straight.

'Steady on, lass, I don't want you getting upset. We both know what a wet blanket she can be.'

'But I've made my mind up, Jack, it's what I want.'

'I see,' said Jack, smiling. 'Then you'd better get down on your knee and ask me proper. My knees aren't up to it. If I get down I'll not get up again. I suppose I'll have to fork out for a wedding ring then,' he laughed.

'After all these years together only the best... No brass curtain rings from Woolworths for me,' she said.

'You'll be lucky.' He leaned over and kissed her. 'We'll make a right party of it but it'll take some organising and I don't want you getting exhausted.'

'That's where young Sara will come in. She can sort all the official stuff. I'd like to help her set up a business here and she's from Yorkshire so she'll do us proud.'

'You've thought it all out, haven't you?'

'It just feels the right time. I'm feeling good and I want a celebration. You and me, we've been good together and I feel lucky to have found such fun second time around. So, why not make the most of it while we can?' Sandra held his hands tightly.

'There you go again, doom-mongering...'

'I'm not, I'm being realistic. Here we are on our dream island, looking out at the horizon... Let's share our good fortune with our friends and have a ball, Jack.'

'Aye, happen you're right; make hay while the sun shines.'

Griff arrived in London in time to visit his old friend Felix MacLeod and his partner Alexa and her daughter Olympia, who was nearly two. He brought them olive oil, fresh halva and a good bottle of Cretan rosé.

'Good to see you, old chap. How is your island idyll going? Bored already?' Felix shook his hand.

'Interesting... Much better than I thought. Our courses are booking up for next season and I'm going to stay on.' He turned to Alexa. 'Your father is a great asset on the trust committee.'

'They're coming over next week,' she said. 'Will you be around too?'

'For a while, until duty calls. My brother and his family expect me to stay and play Father Christmas for their children's party.'

'We've got a few friends coming at the weekend before everybody departs for the season, can you join us then? It'll be the usual crowd but I'm afraid Flissa will be coming with her latest beau. Would you mind?'

Griff did mind. She was the last person he wanted to see

again but he smiled. 'Not at all, she is all in the past now, but I won't stay long.' He made an excuse to get back to his old flat. It smelt damp and fusty. He ought to let it out but it was a useful bolthole. The tiny mews apartment was down a cobbled alley off Wigmore Street that once belonged to his mother's family, passed on to Griff from the trust while his brother inherited the estate. When his business failed and he had to sell his own place, it was a relief to have this pad in town to call home. It was furnished, central enough, but it was hardly cosy or warm. Leaving St Nick's was a wrench as he felt the keen wind and damp air in the London streets.

It was a culture shock to return to crowds, the noise of police sirens in the night. There were neon lights, street decorations flashing, all very festive, but behind the jolly Santas it was all sell, sell, sell. In the backstreets were rough sleepers with pathetic little dogs for company which he couldn't ignore. Christmas was a sad time for so many. He would spend some time as a volunteer in the night shelter of St Martin-in-the-Fields. There was no rush to get to Rufus and family.

In the flat, his mind's eye recalled sunsets over the Aegean, racing with Spartacus up the hill to the olive groves and the pinewoods. His dog was staying with the Papadakises as the boys wanted to take him out for walks. He had visited Pippa and Duke before he left, offering them the guesthouse again, but they said they were happy in the shack.

He was introduced to the new baby who they had named Harmony, a hippy sort of name that suited her because she was a dark-haired beauty. Pippa carried her wrapped in a shawl where the baby sucked at her breasts, not a bit like his sister-in-law's brood who were wheeled around the park in an ancient Silver Cross pram and fed by the clock. He was going to find a present for Harmony in Hamleys.

Griff began to wonder if coming back for Christmas was a good idea. He had promised to meet up with Sara in Manchester to discuss her brochure and his photos. They were online and easy to access but he sensed she was happier to share her views with him in person.

On Saturday night he donned his leather jacket and his best jeans and headed along to Felix's house off Kensington High Street close to Olympia. He would not stay long, wishing to avoid Flissa where possible. How could he forget how she deserted him when the chips were down? Once his business partner had vanished to the Cayman Islands leaving Griff to face furious investors, she made feeble excuses and a sharp exit from his life. Flissa was ever the gold-digger and he hoped her latest find would see through her scheming.

There was such a crush of gathered friends, he could barely squeeze through the door but then a familiar voice yelled, 'Griff, how lovely to see you... Darling, this is Rufus's brother, Jolyon de Grifford, but he only answers to Griff. And aren't you tanned?' She greeted him as if nothing had happened between them. 'Meet Jace, he's from Yorkshire but don't hold that against him.'

Griff had forgotten what a ridiculous hyena laugh Flissa had. Admittedly she was still glamorous, slim, dressed in her usual black, flashing scarlet nails that looked like talons. He nodded to the tall man politely. 'You're down for Christmas then?'

'No, thank God, we're off to St Lucia for the hols. Jace's business takes him all over,' Flissa butted in, flaunting her new beau's success in front of him.

Griff wanted to move on but Flissa grabbed his arm. 'You okay? I hear you escaped to a Greek island, what fun…'

Griff flashed his charm in her face. 'Never better and you look as if you found a good asset in Jace.' He couldn't resist the sarcasm.

'We met at a conference, not my usual type but these gruff Yorkshire men have a certain charm. A bit rough round the edges but you can't have everything, can you?'

'Good luck. Now I must see Felix.' He extricated himself and found Felix handing round the bubbly.

Once they all had a drink, Felix tapped a glass for attention until the room fell silent. 'Everyone, I've something to announce.' Alexa was standing next to Felix in a glorious fuchsia pink concoction that must have cost the earth. 'Alexa has done me the great honour of agreeing to become my wife.' Everyone cheered.

'About time!' someone yelled as Alexa held up the sparkling diamond on her engagement finger. Griff felt pleased for them both.

'When, when?' someone else shouted.

'Next summer on her Greek island and you're all invited.' There was a cheer and Griff's immediate thought was that this wedding would put Sara on the map. It was funny how protective he felt of her venture. 'Congratulations to you… Can I kiss the bride? Do Chloë and Simon know?'

'They were the first people we told, of course. Mummy is in ecstasy planning my nuptials but it's months away. I just wanted a quiet affair but Felix wants to make it, well, we'll see...' Alexa confided to Griff.

Griff swallowed his champagne and sidled out of the door. He had made an appearance and was genuinely thrilled for his oldest friend but it made his own isolation out of step with his contemporaries. One by one they were all pairing up again. Still, tonight he was helping down in the city shelter. He had offered a week's volunteering in the kitchen, and then it would be time to make for Shropshire and the family. As Uncle Jolly, he had a role and a welcome awaiting there.

He was glad that some street sleepers would have a nourishing meal: these were the strays of London. The retreat must, however, be his first priority. There was redecorating, finding guest speakers, keeping the house dry and the little museum updated. There would be lively nights at the taverna, a busy New Year ahead.

After a hectic night at the shelter he walked back in the small hours through the shadowy streets, feeling grateful there was a part of him yearning for the quiet beauty of Santaniki, the retreat and the doggy antics of Spartacus. He couldn't wait to return.

18

Sara's Christmas flew past with a relaxing visit home due to her parents' thoughtfulness. There were just the three of them enjoying TV and going for walks to pubs in the Peak District. She had time to put the final touches to her online brochure, its layout and text. She took presents from Mel to her family and was feted by her sister, Rosita, with wonderful home-made panettone. They in turn gave her things Mel requested that Sara was happy to take back.

Griff emailed to suggest meeting up at Salford Quays and she invited her mother to come too, to enjoy a night together to go to the theatre and the museums in Media City. It was easy to feel guilty in deserting them to live on a Greek island but they were in good health and happy that she was finding her feet again.

'Who is this chap you're meeting?' her dad asked.

'Only Griff, he runs the artists' place… you know, the novelist's house.'

'I loved her books,' her mum replied.

'Then you must come over and visit in the summer and that's an order,' Sara said. They would squeeze into Ariadne Villa's second bedroom and she would enjoy showing them around the island.

'So, you're staying on then?' She sensed her mother's disappointment.

'I can't run the business from here. I have to be on the spot just in case things go awry. Like when Pippa's photographer didn't turn up for the wedding. It would have been a disaster but Griff stepped in and his pictures are good.'

'He sounds an interesting young man,' said her father with a wink.

'Hardly young... just a friend so don't go getting any ideas. He's Mel and Spiro's mate, not really mine.' Sara felt mean for dismissing Griff so readily but she didn't want to raise any hopes of romance.

'We're so glad you've settled down, back to your old self. We were so worried for you. Troubled hearts go with us wherever we flee to... But I can see you are putting it all behind you.' Sara could see the concern on her mum's face.

'I'm fine now, honestly. It was right to get away. I still blush when I think of it all and I'm sorry I embarrassed you as well.'

'We're proud of you. You stood up for yourself when it mattered. What you did, you had to... You were let down big time.'

'Let's not talk about that any more,' Sara replied. 'I've better things to think about now.'

'That's my girl, I can see the spark back in your eyes.

Just you go back and make it all happen. We'll come to see you when the weather gets better. It's been lovely having you here and don't leave it so long next time.'

In the end her mum got a bad cold and stayed put. Sara headed for Media City on the train, wrapped in a faux fur coat and beret to meet up with Griff who was waiting by the Imperial War Museum. It was strange to see him in a leather jacket with a long scarf, jeans and boots, not shorts and sandals. He looked good, she had to admit.

It was a freezing morning so they headed into the museum's café for an early lunch. She showed him her layout and Griff made suggestions as they sat choosing the most romantic of his photographs. 'You are selling a dream, an idyllic celebration, and it's your brochure that will clinch it. I brought a few I picked up online,' he said, pulling up rival wedding planning sites to compare with hers. 'Still thinking about the second time around theme?'

'Yes, but I want to remain flexible too,' she replied. She was touched that he seemed genuinely concerned about her progress.

'Then the brochure must make sure that you aim in that direction without losing any other couples who might be interested in just an island destination. The text is important, more important than the pictures.'

Sara pulled up her online notes. 'I'm not sure I've got it right. The menu on the top needs sharpening up, and I need more details of legalities, costings, catering, location. All options must be clear in the overall package but I've decided not to offer guest accommodation – that they must sort out for themselves according to their budget. You're right, though, I need better text.'

'I can help you if you like,' Griff said. 'Send me a copy and I can look it over. You need to get this out straight away. After New Year is when couples make plans, so not much time.' He leaned in towards her, raising an eyebrow. She caught a whiff of expensive aftershave.

'No pressure then,' Sara answered, feeling her cheeks flushing at his gaze. He was being kind and perhaps thought her text amateurish but she was not going to give him the satisfaction of admitting this yet.

Time flew past as they chatted whilst walking across the bridges, pausing to take in the Quays' vistas. To passers-by, they must look like a regular couple out for a day in Media City. It was still decorated for the season with snowmen and there were hordes of visitors.

Sara felt strangely comforted by this thought. And then uncomfortable. They were friends, nothing more. She checked her watch; there was just time to view the Lowry gallery together. The wind whipped off the water. 'Hope it won't be so cold in St Nick's,' she whispered.

'Better bring your fur coat, it's not so idyllic in winter... rain, snow on the tops with unpredictable storms, violent at times and flooding. I don't think you should suggest weddings off-season unless they're locals. By the way, Felix and Alexa got engaged. There's going to be a Bartlett wedding on the island in the summer. You must make a bid for the contract as half of London will be coming. Chloë and Simon may need your help. Even Chloë will find it hard to do everything herself and Alexa has firm ideas that might have them clashing. Mediation might be the order of the day.'

'I'm not sure.' Sara hesitated, knowing this would be a challenge. What she had seen of Chloë Bartlett, Queen Bee of the book club and a churchwarden of St Paul's, she would make a formidable mother of the bride.

'Faint heart never won fair contract,' Griff quipped. 'Have faith in yourself and remember the mantra: think big, keep it simple and do it yourself.'

'Are you staying on next season or off to pastures new?' Sara changed the subject, uncomfortable at the focus on all her plans and the interest in his blue eyes.

'They want me to continue and I have no other plans except to add new courses and workshops. The Foundation has to pay its way and I am heading the Spartacus project. We want to set up a proper charity to help rehome dogs, foster out strays and educate the local children so it will need a good fundraising committee. Would you be interested in joining us?'

'I heard about that from Mel. Yes, it sounds a good cause. If I can help in any way, I will.'

'Talking of online PR, we want to sell a shedload of Elodie's memoirs online to link to the retreat house and the museum. I'm sure there must be many would-be novelists who would love to write where she did. Have you read any of hers?' Griff asked.

'Just *The Cretan Dancer*. I liked the subject; a very romantic bodice-ripper – I can see why she still sells.'

'Her agent hinted there's an option out for a film, all

hush-hush yet, and it may not come to anything, but these things take time and money.'

Sara looked at the time. 'Better be off to catch my connection. I can't thank you enough for taking the trouble to come over. But, oh, I never asked how your Christmas went.'

'As usual with my brother and his mob, chaos. One little darling got a bead stuck up her nose and a trip to A&E. Another kid ate so many chocolates he was sick. The toddler was having tantrums about sharing his present with his sisters while the baby just played with wrapping paper. I did my Father Christmas but they pulled my beard off and shouted, "It's Uncle Jolly!"'

Sara chortled. 'Uncle Jolly?' picturing the scene as his disguise was blown.

'That's why I prefer Griff to Jolyon. We all went to church for the Christmas Eve pageant, *The Donkey's First Christmas*, and it pooed all over the chancel, such an awful stink. All the kids were delighted though. I must admit I'm a sucker for an old-fashioned country Christmas. You never know what will happen next...' Griff paused, shaking his head. 'I saw my ex, Flissa, at Felix's engagement party. She brought along her latest, a gruff Yorkshire chap from your neck of the woods. What about your Christmas? Anyone special waiting for a kiss under the mistletoe?'

Sara bristled at his throwaway remark. 'I really must go,' she said, making her excuse to leave the conversation right there. 'Bye and thanks for lunch.' She fled, leaving Griff staring at her abrupt departure.

*

Was it something I said? Griff wondered, watching Sara scurrying away towards the station.

The woman was such a puzzle, like a door that opened and then shut in his face. What was it that drove her to abandon her family and business to set up in St Nick's? There had to be a man behind this. She said so little about her life in Sheffield except that she was close to her parents and an only child. Why was she so guarded?

He had no right to talk. His own business disaster had left him broke and embarrassed. He, too, had taken the chance of a new life. Simon and Felix knew his story but few else, so who was he to criticise Sara for refusing to disclose her reasons?

Over the past months Griff had grown to enjoy her company but her reluctance to open up made him feel she didn't trust him with whatever her secret was. The only man who got under her guard with his flirtatious teasing was Don Ford. They had danced and laughed at Duke's wedding. To his surprise he found himself jealous of their closeness. There was so much more to Sara Loveday than just a pretty face and a steely determination to succeed. What was she really like behind all that reserve? Griff smiled, knowing he would make it one of his New Year resolutions to find out.

19

Sandra and Jack couldn't believe how cold they felt in the chill winds coming off the moor. They'd gone for a drive to look over their town but the driving rain did nothing to cheer them. Coming home to an empty house felt strange. Jack brought out the Christmas decorations, more out of habit than desire. 'It's going to be a bit of a let-down after St Nick's and I'm nithered,' he said. 'Have you rung Julie yet?'

'She was out but I'll take round a card and some honey and oil, then we can make arrangements for a proper visit. Val next door has asked us round for Boxing Day and I feel we ought to do something ourselves to announce our engagement. What do you think?'

Sandra was admiring the antique ring she had chosen from Fattorini's in Harrogate. It was a hoop of amethysts and diamonds set in gold to replace her original wedding band. It was now time to let Paul's ring go into her drawer. She wanted to tell Julie the good news before anyone else but feared Julie might not be so enthusiastic. She rang up again to say they were home for Christmas and she'd got some bits to give them. But it was the answerphone again and Julie had never given her her mobile number.

Sandra bought a Christmas holly wreath for the door, wrote some cards and letters but she felt uneasy. Better to go now and get it over with and teatime was a good time to catch Julie after work. The cul-de-sac at Meadow Croft looked festive with Christmas trees in the windows, fairy lights in the gardens and wreaths on the doors. She saw lights in Julie's house but Sandra hesitated, feeling nervous as she rang the bell.

The door opened and Julie stared at her mother. 'Oh, it's you. I wondered when you were back.'

'I did leave two messages on your phone. I brought you some Cretan honey and olive oil. Can I come in?'

'I suppose so.' Julie did not offer a kiss or a hug, leaving Sandra feeling the chill of this welcome. 'How long are you staying for?'

'Time's our own these days but we couldn't miss Christmas here. How's things… Colin all right?'

'We're fine, your granddaughter's got a new boyfriend and they've gone to Tenerife for Christmas. You want a drink?'

'That would be nice.' Sandra's heart was crying out for some warmth in the offer. Taking off her coat and gloves, she sat upright at the kitchen table. Everything was in its usual place, not a spoon or a cloth on the granite surfaces. 'So, what's new?' She was trying to relax but Julie was making the tea with her back turned.

'We're going to friends for Christmas. We didn't know if you were coming back, Mum,' came the reply.

'That's okay, we'll have it on our own. My next-door neighbour has invited us for Boxing Day. I was hoping to see you all together…' They sat across from each other, the table like a barrier between them.

'Sorry, I've nothing in the tins to go with the tea. Colin doesn't like mince pies,' Julie said. 'I'm not doing much for Christmas as we're dining out this year.'

Sandra nodded, recalling those happy days when Julie used to help fill the mincemeat in the patty tins and put a wish list up the chimney for Father Christmas. Her daughter looked tense, her brow furrowed and she had put on weight that didn't suit her.

'I've got some good news…' Sandra took a deep breath. 'Jack and I have decided to get married. I'm not getting any younger and what with my health, I want to make the most of things.'

'I see.' Julie looked out of the window. 'What's brought this on all of a sudden?'

'It just feels the right time, love. Look, he's bought me this ring,' she said, stretching out her left hand. Julie barely glanced at it.

'Where's your wedding ring… Dad's ring?'

'I thought you'd like to have it one day. Oh, please say you're happy for me and Jack.'

'What do you expect me to say, congratulations?' Julie stood up and went to the sink.

'Oh Julie, why are you so angry? What have I done

wrong? It's been twenty years since Paul passed away. Am I expected to live in purdah for the rest of my life? I can't change what happened and I know you were gutted but it wasn't my fault, or yours, he got sick.'

'I don't want to talk about it. You do what you want, it's no skin off my nose,' came the guarded reply.

'But I want you to be there for me. Come to Santaniki and be my best man – or my best woman.' Sandra tried to smile.

'Don't be daft, where do we get the money to go gallivanting when we've got college fees to pay?'

'You know money is the least of my problems. We would pay your fares and the house we rented is huge. There's room for all of you. Please say you'll be there for me?'

Julie turned to her, arms folded across her chest. 'Why? You've never bothered before and Jack isn't my cup of tea.'

'He's kind and helpful and it's not been easy living with the big C. Jack makes me happy and I just want my daughter to be happy for me too. You're my girl. I suppose I'm asking for your blessing.'

Julie looked surprised. 'It's not me you should be asking, is it?'

'You mean from Paul? He's gone, love. He was generous to a fault. He wouldn't mind me finding some happiness.'

'But I mind you jetting off into the sunset with your lover boy, living the life of Riley while we're stuck here working our socks off to pay fees.'

'It was your choice to send them to private school and if it's the money, let me help you out. But it's not that, is it? You resent me starting over with a new man. Love isn't a piece of cake that gets cut in pieces until there's none left; love has an endless supply and keeps on giving. I don't know how long I can keep cancer at bay. It'll get me in the end but I want to enjoy the future I have left and I want you to be there for me... for us to have good times together. None of us know what's around the corner.' Sandra felt her disappointment choking in her throat.

'Don't be morbid, Mother. You look fine to me.' Julie looked at her watch. 'Any road, I'm going out in ten minutes to pick up Colin from work.'

'Will we see you over Christmas or New Year?'

'I'm not sure... we've made plans.'

Sandra knew this was hopeless so put her gloves back on. 'Oh, well, don't let me stop you. Think about my offer. You're still my little girl. We had such good times, didn't we? I'll just have to live off those memories. I'll be off now. Have a nice Christmas.' She stood up to get her coat. 'I can see myself out.' She couldn't wait to leave or let Julie see her tears. Her heart ached with sadness that she had tried and failed once more to make a bridge of understanding between herself and her daughter – she wouldn't ask again. 'Bye!'

'Mum...' Julie shouted but the door was shut and Sandra didn't hear her calling.

February

20

When Griff returned to Santaniki, Spartacus gave him a rapturous welcome. Mel's boys, Markos and Stefan, loved walking the dog but Irini was relieved to see the back of him. Mel and Spiro went off to Athens on a short out-of-season break. He saw the lights flickering in Ariadne's villa. Sara had returned without contacting him but he wasn't going to interfere with her plans,

There was so much mail to see to and repairs to check over. The retreat house smelt damp and chilly. Rufus's house was buzzing with visitors and parties but it all left him empty inside. As for his time in London, he was all too aware of being a failure, reminded of the duplicity of his business partner's greed and cunning. Griff had paid his dues quietly and left the only business he had known to escape into this new life. He must make a success of this post. No point in going over all that again.

Listening in to one of the writers' courses in the autumn, he was intrigued by the idea of keeping a log of thoughts and feelings every day, something that no one else would ever read. It all sounded very New Age but he would give it a go, sitting down each morning to put his heart on paper. It was oddly liberating letting off steam as his words sped along the page. There was so much confusion inside him waiting to be released. It was time to clear his head, moan and groan, and then see what evolved as he aired his innermost wishes.

He filled pages of an exercise book with anger over his past, anger over Flissa letting him down and feeling life was passing him by. Then there was his concern for the fate of the stray dogs and cats that sparked his Spartacus project. It was about time to make sure it got off the ground.

First things first, a meeting of the community must be a priority to gauge interest and commitment. No use it being just a foreigner's idea, it had to win the hearts and minds of the local residents. Perhaps he could invite a vet from the big island to give a talk with illustrations about animal healthcare, raising funds to pay for a spaying week. It was better to get things going before spring came and the bitches got into season. Griff sat down to make a list of emails and dates.

Spartacus was a photogenic little mongrel with appealing eyes and a ruffle of grey and white coat. He was a joy to behold, lively, faithful and good company on dark nights. He was disobedient at times, sparky, no man's slave, with a will of his own but he did know who was the boss. On dark nights when Griff lit the olive wood fire, Spartacus would sneak up and rest his chin on his legs, happy to just sleep and snore. He would make a good poster boy now his life of hunger and dirt was ended. Not every dog or cat could have that luxury but if they were spayed and checked over, it was a start, a fresh start, just as he had found hope and purpose here on St Nick's.

Griff mustn't trespass on the legal duties of the demos who were obliged to see to strays, but a private charity could work alongside them to help foster and rehome suitable dogs abroad. But a charity was going to cost. Perhaps they could perform a jazz night fundraiser to start the project off.

First, he would speak to the mayor and the demos to get them onside. Perhaps some of the tavernas would adopt a stray, keep an eye on them, point out those injured or sick. His mind was bursting with ideas which he noted in his log. Now, though, he must see to this house and check the artists, authors and musicians who were booked in for the season, tidy up the garden, prune back bushes and practise on his keyboard. He wondered how Sara Loveday was making out with her wedding planning. He'd like to help her but sensed she saw his interest as an intrusion; better to stick to his own plans and keep out of her way.

Sara had three tentative enquiries from her island wedding brochure. She suggested that they might like to come out to view the setting and discuss their ideas with her. One couple immediately dropped out, not wanting the expense of an out-of-season trip, but two others decided to visit before Easter for a long weekend. Sara booked them into the best hotel and organised their flights but only one couple turned up.

They were the perfect clients who explored the island, chose the exact spot, discussed the wedding breakfast, put down their deposit and confirmed their far-off date. Everything else was done online. But you would not get rich on one booking. It was lucky that Sandra and Jack turned up at her door one evening to discuss their own marriage plans.

'We want it to be in our home by the pool in our villa. There'll only be a few of us. We want a little blessing in the Anglican church first, then a party.'

Sara was delighted to be asked, hoping Mel would organise catering from the taverna when she called in to tell her this news.

'Have you spoken to Chloë about Alexa's wedding yet?' Mel asked. 'Get in there quick. I know Griff gave you the heads up.'

'Yes... yes, but...' Sara was hesitating.

'What's bothering you?'

'It's Chloë. I think she'll want to do it all herself and she is such an organiser. I don't want to be pushy.'

'Come on, Sara, that's not going to get you noticed. Chloë may be Queen Bee but she's only got two hands like everybody else. Simon is a sweetie. Talk to her at the book group tonight.'

'I'm not sure...' Sara was dithering.

'If you don't, I will and that's an end to it.'

It was Dorrie Thorner who set the ball rolling that night after the wine and tapas break in Chloë's magnificent stone house. Sandra, like Sara, had joined as a temporary guest, being an avid reader of romantic sagas and crime. They were discussing *A Gentleman in Moscow* by Amor Towles that enchanted everyone except Dorrie. 'It was too long for me and the print too small and I got confused jumping back and forward in time,' she announced.

'I thought it was magical, and such a warm character to follow,' Sara replied.

Dorrie ignored her, turning to Chloë. 'How are your wedding plans going? We're so glad Alexa has chosen to celebrate here like my Dan and Soraya.' Turning to Sandra and Sara she explained in great detail how wealthy Soraya's Russian father was. 'Now we'll have two splendid events to look forward to.'

How presumptive of Dorrie to think her invitation was automatic, Sara thought, glancing at Mel who rolled her eyes. 'We are all well ahead with our plans. Soraya and Dan are coming over in her father's yacht for the final details. They are bringing their wedding planner to check out suitable venues. Yuri is such a generous man, wanting only the best for his princess.' Dorrie was boasting to anyone who would listen.

'I'm not sure what's happening,' Chloë said. 'Alexa has got her own ideas and everything is still very vague. They've decided to do the legalities in London first, with perhaps a blessing here at St Paul's afterwards.'

'Norris can play the organ then,' Dorrie continued.

'You should get Sara on the case,' Mel announced, winking at her friend. Sara sat back into her chair, embarrassed. 'She did a great job for Pippa and Duke.'

'The least said the better,' Dorrie commented. 'I mean, the baby born on the very same day, and christened Harmony. What sort of Christian name is that?'

'A lovely one for a gorgeous baby,' Mel snapped, seeing

the sneer on Dorrie's face. 'We could do with a lot more harmony in this sad world, the world she'll inherit.'

Dorrie took no hint from the feeling in the room that she'd overstepped the mark. 'Alexa will make a beautiful bride, even if it is the second time around.' There was a deafening silence at this remark. It was the perfect cue for Sara to speak up.

'Actually, that's my special focus. Second time around is just as special as the first. Couples are older, wiser, more aware of the reality of what it all means. They say a wedding is easy to arrange but a marriage takes longer, so I wish them all the joy in the world.'

'Hear, hear!' Chloë added. 'Second time around with Simon has been the happiest time of my life.'

'And me, with Jack,' Sandra chipped in.

Mel whispered, 'You hit the nail on the head there.'

Everyone was clearing up to leave when Chloë sidled up to Sara. 'Come for coffee tomorrow morning. I liked what you said there. Perhaps we can discuss your ideas further. I'm sure Alexa would be interested and it would be a weight off my mind. It's her day, not mine... You sometimes forget that, don't you?'

Sara smiled. 'I'd be delighted.'

'I'm sorry Dorrie said what she said. She's so caught up in her son's wedding. I gather the Russian papa has grand schemes and I fear poor Dorrie won't get much of a look-in. Daniel's a good son, despite all her forthright opinions. Each to his own views,' Chloë said with a wry glint in her eye. 'Dorrie won't want to miss out on an invitation to our wedding. She'll be sweetness and light until the card is on the mantelpiece. See you tomorrow then?'

'There,' said Mel as they walked home. 'All sorted.'

'Not exactly. Alexa is the bride and she'll have to decide.'

'Of course, but if Griff puts in a good word to Felix... I gather you met him at Christmas back in the UK.' She tugged her on the arm.

Sara was ready for this one. 'It was just a business meeting to look at the photos in Manchester.'

'Oh yes... was it a long lunch?' Mel laughed. 'Don't be so uptight.'

'Forget it... I have a business to kickstart: three weddings so far but hardly a lift-off. I have to make them work with no distractions.' Sara paused.

'Griff's gone out of his way to help you, putting in a word here and there, I gather. Are you not the tiniest bit grateful?'

'I am, it's just...' Sara couldn't think of a smart reply. 'I don't want to get involved with anyone. Don't push me, and anyway, he's not interested in me that way.'

'How do you know that? Come off it, don't be coy. He's interested and you know it,' Mel replied, looking her straight in the eye.

'I'll be seeing you.' Sara turned in the direction of Ariadne Villa and sped down the hill hoping she hadn't offended Mel. What's up with me? Soon it would be a year since... None of her clients would want to know what a disaster she had made of things. All that mattered now was to make sure that their weddings here would be memorable and epic.

March

21

Griff invited the deputy mayor, Dimitris, the doctor, the priest, local residents and Simon for lunch at the retreat. He wanted cross-party approval for his plans. Sparky was clambering over feet under the table and Griff brought out before and after pictures of his rescue dog.

'Lucky Don and I were up in the hills when I found him collapsed in a dreadful state. I don't understand the mentality of folk who do this to a dumb animal. Perhaps it's time to educate people to show that animals have feelings too and in better health they will perform their duties with more vigour.'

Dimitris looked at Sparky. 'You've done a good job, Kyrie Griff, but strays are part of life here. With the recession some have to abandon them. Better to shoot them, I suppose.'

'There was a decent rescue shelter but it was closed. Why?' Griff asked, knowing it caused controversy amongst the expat community.

It was Father Mikhalis who spoke. 'It was little more

than a dog pound, barking day and night. Kyria Julia was overwhelmed and sick herself.'

'That's right.' Spiro nodded. 'Before your time.' Griff sensed he was trying to stay neutral.

'I heard there's been more poisonings lately? All I ask is the chance to form a charity to raise funds for regular vet visits to neuter the strays or find new homes for them so no unwanted puppies are destroyed. This would be, of course, expanding the good work the demos does. There are charities who will rehome them abroad.'

'But they are OUR strays. Taking away their bits is not the Santaniki way,' Dimitris said, looking for support.

Thank goodness, Dr Makaris came to Griff's rescue. 'Vaccination and spaying costs but it is better than leaving them to starve. Griff is right, those left to guard orange groves need good shelter, water and winter protection; owners need to take advice.'

Everyone nodded as they sipped their ouzos and munched on a selection of nuts and snacks.

'What do you have in mind?' Spiro asked.

'I thought a poster of Spartacus before and after to shock. Visits to the school to get our children involved. We could ask the vet to come and give a lesson in animal care.'

'That will be expensive.'

'Not if we find the right vet. Perhaps a *glendi* with dancing and feasting in honour of St Rocco or St Frances, patrons of animals, on their name day. We must educate the next generation. Working dogs are not just tools, useful equipment. Animals are living, breathing beings, worthy of respect, and should not be just beaten or left to starve or shot for no longer being of use. Owners could bring their pets for a special blessing.' Griff was thinking off the top of his head. 'A parade of pets, health checks. Just a few thoughts,' he offered.

He brought out chicken souvlaki and the cake Spiro had brought from the taverna to sweeten them all up. He wanted to encourage responsibility in a gentle way, not thrust his opinions down their throats, but he sensed the reaction was mixed. He hoped his enthusiasm was catching. Once they had left, he wondered if he had gone too far.

Griff wanted a breath of fresh air to clear his head. The first guests were due in tomorrow for a yoga workshop for writers. The patio needed clearing and yoga mats airing and disinfecting. The local ladies were in, changing sheets and housekeeping, laughing and chatting like starlings, and the kitchen crew were preparing for the season's buffet lunches. It was all busy, busy, as Irini often said while delivering instructions from her armchair. Mel, Katya and Sara dashed around like scalded hens. Easter was coming and everyone was washed out even before the onslaught of tourists arrived.

Griff jogged slowly up the hill towards the higher olive groves and orange trees. Sparky was in his basket with a sore foot, sulking about being left behind, but Griff wanted to clear his mind. He was trying to think of a name for his new charity. Santaniki Protection and Animal Rescue Centre was a mouthful but perhaps SPARKS wasn't a bad acronym. It was his rescue of Spartacus that started the whole idea off.

Running was a lifesaver when his business collapsed; focusing on each forward step allowed him to rethink his options. Griff found himself close to the very spot where they had found the exhausted starving little dog with no collar or chain but with welts on his back where he been beaten.

No one in St Nick's recognised him or was bothered when he adopted the mutt. Now the posters were going up around the town. He hoped that there might be some interest but it was Metrakis, the drunken menace, who was spotted tearing them down wherever he saw them. 'You foreigners butting in... Our dogs are our dogs, not yours,' he yelled when Spiro turfed the man out onto the square with a roar of Greek expletives too fast for Griff to follow.

Climbing higher onto the rocky outcrop where once a homeless family had sheltered in caves, he stopped to catch his breath and stare down at the turquoise bay. He never tired of the view or this wild landscape. It lifted his spirits in the early days when he had retreated to Santaniki to lick his wounds, feeling a failure on every level. The island magic touched him, renewing his energy and resolve to give something back into the community here.

Was it the light and warmth, the lush green fruit groves, the white limestone rocks tinged with ochre and the last of the wildflowers? Was it the friendly warmth of the people in the quiet grandeur of the retreat house? He wished he could have met Elodie Durrante, the famous novelist. It was strange how he felt her presence in certain rooms, especially in her study that became a little museum in the tourist season. It was here Ariadne Blunt found her private journals that Simon had edited and brought out as an e-book and in print. They had a shelf of her books to sell during the courses.

Griff thought he wasn't psychic in any way and yet he sensed a tinge of Balkan Sobranies and a feeling of encouragement and optimism whenever he entered that room. He decided to broaden the scope of their courses, to use all the large garden for craft work, night camping, stargazing in the hills. There were endless ideas flowing through his mind as he lay back, entranced by the vista, until he felt a dark shadow behind him, turning around to face Metrakis and one of his sons.

'Off my land!' the old man bellowed in broken English.

Griff replied in Greek, 'This is an open trail, a shepherd's track,' determined not to give in to their menace.

'You steal our dogs.'

'What dogs?' But neither man replied as Stavros Metrakis lifted his gun as if to shoot him but Griff stood his ground, towering over the squat farmer. 'That's not going to help anyone.' He saw Metrakis hesitating.

'Bugger off!' Metrakis swore. 'You stop your interfering or else...'

There was no point in staying to argue his corner. While the men were laughing at his retreat, Griff knew he had made an enemy for some unknown reason. What was it with Greeks and their guns? For hunting, yes, but for some, was a gun in their hand a symbol of their manhood, their heritage and much more?

Those two were bullies and you didn't cross them lightly. He knew enough about feuding families to realise this family saw themselves as rulers in these hills. Step out of line or speak loosely and accidents might happen that could not be proved to have been deliberate. There was a dark side to every rural community. Silence was the safest bet amongst frightened folk. That's how men like Metrakis kept their power.

Griff was shaken by the encounter, knowing they could have shot him and claimed it was accidental, but why such threat for looking after dogs? How pathetic in comparison to all those Cretan island resistance groups who fought for their country in the war, brave, foolhardy at times, who went to their executions like warriors. Heroism at its finest. These two were just thugs with their pot bellies and swarthy beards. He pitied their wives, if they managed to attract any.

The pleasure of his run was gone, their threat unsettling. It was all too easy to see this magical island as a benign paradise but it was like all other close-knit communities. There was a shadowy side and in isolated pockets only a thin crust of civilised behaviour. Griff felt his indignation rising up like bile in his throat. If Metrakis thought he could scupper their charitable scheme for a rescue centre, let battle commence.

In the taverna that evening, he joined Simon, Mel and Sara. 'Has Spiro spread the word?'

Mel laughed. 'A festival for dogs. I'm not sure St Nick's is ready for this,' she cautioned as she stroked Sparky. 'We'll do our bit as long as I don't have a wedding booked.'

'October the fourth is St Frances's name day. The weather will be warm, tourists still about. It gives us time to organise the event; a garden party in the retreat?'

'Your courses will still be in residence,' Sara said.

'The more the merrier. It will be something to add to their stay. I will talk to the school teacher and staff to see what they think.'

'I hope you know what you've started. It won't go down well in some quarters, yet another stranger interfering in local culture,' Mel warned. 'Dogs and cats keep vermin down.'

'There'd be fewer of them if the bins were sealed and tourists picked up their litter,' Griff snapped back. 'But that's another matter.'

'Be careful,' Mel whispered. 'Walls have ears and not all my customers will see things as you do.' She nodded in the direction of Stavros Metrakis, who was listening in, twirling his amber beads with a sullen look on his face. 'He's not one to cross. Ask Irini about his family. His sons are bully boys.'

Griff eyed the bulk of the overweight man huddled in the corner with contempt. 'I had the pleasure of his company earlier today.' He raised his baseball cap in mock greeting.

Metrakis, the man with three chins, turned to smirk and drink with his cronies who looked up at the group with suspicion. Griff sensed cruelty and menace in the face with the hooded eyes of a raptor. Why did the man suddenly remind him of his former business partner: jovial in his cups, hale fellow well met, but underneath a sinister cunning that knew no bounds?

Chloë laid the table out on the veranda. 'I love spring, don't you? All those wonderful wildflowers. Have you been up to Agios Nikolaos chapel high on the rocks? There's a carpet of wild chamomile, daisies and poppies. You must see the wild orchids and tulips. It's just beautiful.'

Sara shook her head; between being busy online and trying to tidy Ariadne's rampant garden, she had hardly left the villa. 'I must try and get up there,' she replied.

Chloë's house looked down towards the glittering silver bay, an ancient stone house built on a series of neatly planted terraced slopes, and above the house was an olive grove and bushes full of oranges, pomegranates and lemons. It was a dream setting.

'Alexa wants a garden ceremony here but it is such a steep slope, I can't see it myself,' Chloë confided.

Sara had discreetly surveyed the terrain after the book club one night. 'There is a flat area just before the olive grove and perhaps that would make a platform.'

'Oh no, that's far too small. With all her London crowd and local friends, we're expecting at least a hundred guests, and then there's the wedding breakfast to consider.'

'Griff said Alexa wanted a small affair.' Sara was hoping she hadn't spoken out of turn.

Chloë poured the coffee. 'That won't do. I mean, what will our friends think if they are not invited?'

'Perhaps there's a compromise,' Sara suggested. 'A ceremony here and a party later.'

'But where? I thought they might have had a blessing in our little church but Alexa says no. I suggested photos taken outside the chapel on the rocks up the steps but she said that was too narrow a path and Olympia might fall off. I'm hoping to fly over to help her choose her dress so it would be useful to have ideas.'

Sara brought out her iPad with Pinterest images. 'I thought you might like to look out over these settings, just ideas to share with her. Alexa emailed me with some decorative suggestions.'

'Oh, I didn't realise that.' Chloë looked a little put out. 'I suppose it is her choice, after all.'

Sara could see Chloë was feeling left out. 'There is one solution, though, if you want more guests, family and friends. The retreat garden is large and open if the committee would rent it out,' Sara offered.

'No, I wouldn't want it decked out like Pippa and Duke's hippy nuptials.'

'I don't think Alexa is thinking on those lines either.'

'You've discussed it with her already then?' Chloë said.

'It is just a possibility. The backdrop of the house, its views are rather spectacular in their own way.' Sara could see it all in her mind's eye.

'But I wanted our daughter to celebrate in our garden.'

'Don't worry, she's thought of that too,' Sara added, sensing Chloë's disappointment. She was finding it hard to let go of her own dreams for her daughter's wedding. Tact was needed here.

'Have you thought of the American custom of having an eve of wedding dinner, quite formal, a pre-party for close friends and family with a dinner laid out upon the flat area, drinks around the house on the veranda? It would extend the whole event,' she offered with her fingers crossed as Chloë sat down to sip her coffee, staring out over the bay. Lost in her own thoughts.

'Candles, silver, formal dress, yes, I can see that working. Their London friends can float around the gardens, admire the view sipping champagne... Yes, I think Alexa would like that. Shall I FaceTime her?'

'I'm sure she'll agree. After a long flight guests will need time to find their billets, perhaps have a siesta and come to. The party can be on the next night. Do you think you could plan something and I'll help with any details?'

'We'll need caterers. Do you think Mel would be up to it or should I book Fratelli's?'

'It's up to you both but I think Mel would want to bid for the chance.'

Chloë looked relieved. Sara smiled to herself – there was a semblance of a role for Chloë to play hostess so that the wedding itself in the olive garden of the retreat could be Alexa's choice not Chloë's. It was going to be a very English wedding among the expats, a compromise, and she trusted they would both go along with the idea

'I do hope I don't put Dorrie's nose out of joint,' Chloë added. 'These weddings will be quite close but very different in tone, I hope. I gather Shelley Dorney, the London society party planner, has it all in hand. The Russian father insists on only the best and I think poor Dorinda is a bit overwhelmed.

The Dorney woman is coming over to inspect the island soon. You may glean some tips from her.'

'I think I shall keep out of her way,' Sara replied, knowing she must see Griff before Chloë pounced on him with a fait accompli. There was the peace and quiet of the artists in residence to consider. It would be during their season of courses. Would they be willing to leave a long weekend free for this special event? It would do no harm to invite him to supper one night to discuss everything over a pot of lamb tagine. The olive grove was such a good venue.

There was more to wedding planning than just a date and a venue. Sara was learning how to tread gently over dreams, to make sure they were realistic, yet romantic and memorable. Alexa's wedding was important to her own business so everything about it must be perfectly planned to showcase that Santaniki Dream Weddings was here to stay.

'I hope the tagine is not too spicy.' Sara hovered over Griff as he sat by the table on the veranda. 'I never thanked you for giving my name to Alexa and Chloë. It seems we now have a plan. At this rate it could be a Christmas wedding. They keep changing the date, according to Chloë.'

Sara had spent half the afternoon making sure her favourite go-to recipe was up to scratch. If she was going to entertain then it must be right. It was a long time since she had had supper alone with a man.

'This is delicious. Sit down, you make me nervous in case I spill anything on this fabulous tablecloth,' Griff said.

He looked smart in his linen shorts and paisley silk shirt. 'You've gone to a lot of trouble and I can see all your hard work in the garden... Sparky, under the table... I don't feed him when he begs but the guests do, behind my back. Ariadne's cat isn't here, is he?'

'Orpheus, no, there was a note left to tell residents not to let him in the house. He is fed and pampered up the road but he will sneak into the garden and look all pathetic when I turf him out. I like cats and he's as soft as butter.'

Sara was indeed nervous. There was something about Griff's handsome profile, the tang of his aftershave, the way he slicked back his sun-bleached hair... In times past, she would not have hesitated to give him the full green light. Here was the romantic setting any woman could wish for; balmy heat, candlelight, the scent of jasmine wafting in their nostrils, luscious red wine and the privacy of a walled garden where anything could happen. She shook herself. But it won't, Sara Loveday. Stay sober, stay alert. If he makes a move be on guard and deflect before things turn steamy.

'Coffee? I have chocolates from the *zaxaroplasteio*,' she offered, jumping up.

'I'm fine... like your perfume.' He sat back and smiled.

'Nothing special... thank you. Are you sure you won't have a raki?' This was getting awkward but she must stand firm. 'How is the dog scheme getting along?'

'A bit of local opposition but nothing we can't handle. But tell me about yourself. Why did you decide to stay here? You have a business in Sheffield.'

'Not any more, my manager is buying me out. I want to

focus all my energy on my wedding business now. I see a great future here.' She yawned. 'Gosh, it's getting late.'

Griff sat up. 'What really made you up sticks and run?'

'What do you mean?'

'I sense something happened to you.'

'That's my business,' she blurted out with a sharpness she didn't expect.

'I see, sorry for prying. I guess that was a bit too direct a shot. Now I've offended you.'

'Not at all, I'm not ready to share my private business with anybody. I know there's speculation but we all have reasons to be silent on such matters, don't you think?'

'All work and no play.' He paused. 'We all need to relax. I find cycling and running so invigorating when the retreat business gets too hectic. By the way, there will be no problem hiring the olive garden in December, it could be tricky with the weather though. I gather this is a business meeting, after all.'

Sara felt her cheeks flushing. 'Of course, there's so much to discuss so I thought over supper would be best,' she stammered.

'Lighten up, Sara, keep yourself to yourself if you prefer but I've found sharing stuff with others keeps the demons at bay. Take it from one who knows. I'll not keep you any longer but thanks for an excellent supper... Sparky, time for your walk.' He left the table and made for the gate. The dog raced after him. Griff waved and disappeared leaving Sara staring up at the night sky with tears in her eyes. His challenge had unnerved her. That went well, she chided herself. *What do you expect when you pour icy water on any chance of friendship or understanding? He'll think you a stand-offish prig, and well he might.* Why did his good opinion of her matter? So much for a relaxed getting-to-know-you sort of evening; congratulations on a good piece of self-sabotage.

22

Nobody could miss the arrival of Yuri Shevchenko as his yacht sailed into St Nick's harbour in a cloud of red dust. The winds of the south were whipping up a sand storm, whirling around the streets sending everyone for shelter; suddenly his gleaming white leviathan, overshadowing every other boat in the port, was covered in red powder. Too large to come close, a motor launch carried his entourage, arriving to inspect Santaniki's prospects for the wedding of the year.

Yuri was a stocky man with broad shoulders, strutting with purpose; his smile was wide but his eyes were cold, his mouth set in a firm line at this unexpected gritty welcome.

Mel had pulled down the plastic screens to protect the tables from the storm but already a film of scarlet dust covered everything. She saw his entourage scuttling uphill towards the big taverna that would provide them with lunch.

Sara peered from behind the screen. 'I wouldn't like to get on the wrong side of him, would you?'

A tall elegant woman with streaked blonde hair pushed herself through the screens in a panic to shelter from the deluge. '*Kalimera*.' She grimaced. 'What the hell is going on? My suit is ruined,' she moaned, trying to brush the sand from her shoulders and hair.

'Don't worry, it will soon pass, just a desert wind storm from Africa,' Mel reassured her but the woman was not impressed. 'Are you visiting?' she asked.

'Thank God you're English... No, we are here to finalise the Shevchenko wedding. Soraya, Mr Yuri's daughter, has a list of questions. Does this happen often? We were not warned. Mr Yuri will not be pleased. Soraya wants a wedding on the beach by sunset so we've come to check out conditions. There must be no litter, no doggy doo-da and we want to find the best angles for their portraits. This is not my usual assignment; I leave the minor events to local planners but this is going to be some wedding. There will be no limit to the budget.'

'How exciting,' Sara offered, deciding now to glean some tips. 'You must be Miss Dorney. We've heard from Dorrie Thorner that you will be the wedding planner.'

Shelley Dorney took out a cigarette. 'I can smoke here?' she said and Mel nodded. 'This is such a quaint taverna, very rustic,' she said, surveying it with an eagle eye.

Mel brought out coffee and water. 'It has been in my family, my husband's family, for generations and is very popular with tourists.'

'Yes, well, this will be like no other wedding the island has ever seen. Soraya wants the full *Mamma Mia* experience. I gather there's even a church upon a hill that we could decorate?'

'Agios Nikolaos is a chapel but it's tiny and not available for photographs except by the priest's permission.'

'No problem,' said Shelley. 'Mr Shevchenko is Russian Orthodox and there would be a good donation to settle any difficulties. We had a drone to check over the whole island for a location but it is much smaller than I hoped and not a decent hotel to speak of. We did suggest Santorini, Mykonos, even Corfu, but Daniel wanted to marry here as his parents – you might know them – live here.'

'We know them well and they are looking forward to welcoming Soraya,' Mel said. Who was this patronising bitch dissing her beloved island?

'Soraya will stay on the yacht, of course, with her mother. There will be a flotilla of ships with guests so accommodation is not a problem but we do need a perfect setting. I want a private beach so there are no interlopers.'

'The best private coves are accessible only by boat and too shallow for the big yachts but we can provide everything, large sandy beaches, a good florist…' Mel suggested. 'They make floral arches, beautifully decorated with local flowers on little decks out into the sea.'

'I'm sure you can but this event is for society pages, *Hello!* magazine and the like. We will set up a scene, fly in thousands of fresh blooms and lighting experts for the day. Sergei Markovich will be designing the set and we are hoping to secure Kylie for the entertainment.' She was boasting, seeing the look of amazement on their faces.

'Kylie Minogue?'

'Who else? Yuri loves her but it will be guests only, of course. Security must be tight as Mr Yuri is an international figure.'

'I hope it will not be too hot. September is reliable but still very steamy and it will affect make-up, hair and body sweat.'

'Of course, we've got all that covered. Our make-up artists are used to filming model shoots in desert settings.' Shelley looked at her Rolex. 'When will this bloody thing stop? It's messing up my schedule. I hope this is not an omen. Mr Yuri is very superstitious.'

'Look, already it's going, it just leaves a trail of powder to wash off. You are safe to go now.' Mel raised the screens to let her out.

'Thanks for the coffee.' Shelley dashed off towards the entourage, her high heels clattering on the pavement.

Mel looked at Sara and burst out laughing. 'Patronising or what? The snooty cow, looking down at us as if we were chavvy peasants. Poor Dan Thorner, how did he come to be mixed up with this shower?'

'Talk about sinister, those men in black suits and sunglasses looked straight out of *The Sopranos*. Soraya must be someone special, her father's princess, but where is Mrs Shevchenko in all this?' Sara asked.

'Dorrie implied they were divorced and he has a new lady friend, twenty years younger, all tits and teeth according to rumour. I think even Dorrie is worrying how this will go. I bet Shelley Dorney doesn't give her a look-in,' Mel replied. 'I got the impression that St Nick's isn't quite what she was expecting. Still, it will be fun watching a parade of extravagant wealth but I bet it won't be half as fun as Pippa and Duke's wedding done on a shoestring with the wonky donkey cart. I don't think that they'll produce a newborn at the end of the night either.

'I even feel sorry for our rivals, the Fratelli Brothers,' she added. 'I expect they'll demand the use of their kitchen, bringing their own Michelin chef to provide lunch. That is one catering event I am happy not to be doing. But where on earth will Kylie Minogue sing?'

As the plans for Sandra and Jack's wedding were finalised, Sara made sure that they were clear as to their own ideas. At least Sandra wasn't a bride who wanted an exact replica of something she'd seen on Pinterest, all candles, fancy china and table linen; she had her own firm ideas about the cake, the table decorations and the layout. They were going to be married with a traditional church ceremony at St Paul's, just the two of them and witnesses from Yorkshire with no fuss.

Sandra's latest blood test was worrying and the stress of making sure everyone was invited and catered for took a toll on her energy. There was still no word from Julie despite her phone calls, and Sandra felt that all her plans were in vain.

Jack looked on anxiously. 'We can cancel this,' he said. 'You don't have to marry me if it's going to upset your family, love, or we can go back to Yorkshire and get it done there.'

'I'm marrying you, not them. If they don't want to come, they don't deserve my invitation. I have my own friends coming over and an old work colleague. I shall ask all the book club ladies too and we'll have a party even if it kills me.'

'Don't say that, you're upset. Julie doesn't know what she's missing. She needs a good talking to.'

'Please don't make it worse, Jack. Let her stew in her own juice.'

'You've got to rest and let Sara do it all. That's what we're paying her for. You could have your hair done.'

'What's left of it,' Sandra sighed.

'Get your nails done and all that women stuff. I hope you found a nice frock.'

'That's all sorted. Thank goodness for the internet. Sara found me some wonderful sites to look at and I was spoilt for choice.'

'Good, now go and rest as I've got a few jobs to finish.' Unknown to Sandra, Jack was taking matters into his own hands. He opened his Mac and sent an email that was long overdue.

Dear Julie,

I feel I must write to you as I am so anxious about your mother. Since Christmas she's been going downhill. I don't know what was said between you but she came back in low spirits.

I know I'm not your favourite person but I love your mum every which way so I just feel I must let you know that without you at our wedding, Sandra will be so disappointed. I hear her crying in the night. She puts on a brave face with her illness but the rift between you is making her worse.

I realise you never got over losing your dad and I'm no replacement for him or ever could be but after all these years, your mum has made me so happy and for some reason that has made you sad. I am no psychologist but I understand when my Denise left me for another man, I felt the ground under my feet collapse. It was a dark time and I felt such shame and despair I nearly ended it all.

You were lucky to have loving parents but Paul's untimely death left you devastated. Now you have a nice husband in Colin and children and a good family life together.

The greatest gift in my book is time… time shared with those we love, especially as we get older. Family time is precious for your mother now. Once it's lost, it can't be replaced.

She gets tired and sleeps badly and is no longer as energetic. Her tears flow with sadness, fearful for the future, but she is still independent but yearns for your attention. I know we are a generation apart as we grow older, you grow stronger. It's the way of things. Sandra so longs to spend time with you choosing an outfit, all that girly stuff, having a day out together, chatting on the phone, sharing gossip that mothers and daughters like to do.

In living here for the last six months, I know we have deprived you of her company but it is only for a year and half of it has gone already. Coming over for even a short holiday would give her such a fillip. I hope you don't take this wrong but you are loved and cherished by her.

Please reconsider your decision. The offer stands for us to gift you the expense of the fare for all of you.

By the way, Sandra doesn't know I have contacted you so let's keep this between ourselves. Kindest regards

Jack

Easter

23

How strange it was to Sara that suddenly the whole of the island was gripped by preparations for Easter. There were no Easter eggs in cardboard boxes or Easter bunnies and all the commercial trappings on the minimarket shelves. It was as if everyone suddenly began the slow rituals associated with a tradition centuries-old, full of meaning to families.

The carnival before Lent had been a riotous affair; hundreds of men, women and children in fancy dress dancing on floats, on trailers, crawling through the crowded streets. There were men in drag, children dressed as anything from cupcakes to animals, gaudy banners and balloons.

Clean Monday was the first day of Lent. Now there was a solemn atmosphere as the weeks up to Easter were when the faithful fasted. No meat was eaten and there was a rush in the harbour to buy fresh fish from the sea.

Mel and Irini began preparing their house for the season, making sure everything was shipshape, while on the beach the children went with Spiro to fly their kites. Sara went down to Sunset Beach to watch the hundreds of kites soaring into the blue, a symbol of man sending a prayer on high. As Easter week began, preparations began in earnest for the ceremonies. Mel asked her over to help with baking. 'We're making plaited breads and Easter biscuits. Would you like to try some? I'll show you how to do them.'

Sara was nervous, baking was not her forte, but she made a batch under supervision flavoured with orange oil that turned out uneven but not burnt.

Mel was wearing black jeans and top, as did many of the women in St Nick's. Sara decided to do the same to blend in with the locals. She noticed how many men were wearing black shirts too. This was her first Easter and she wanted to be part of it. On the Thursday she had fun with Markos and Stefan dying boiled eggs bright red. She was not sure why but Markos informed her that they played a game with them but not yet.

'Like conkers?' Sara said.

'What are conkers?' Stefan asked her. Her Greek was not up to a decent explanation or to telling them the rules. She had her iPad with her to show the boys how conkers on strings was played. Each in turn bashing them together trying to crack them. This kept them amused.

On Holy Friday, Irini and her friend Maria went to join the women to decorate a funeral bier on which lay the statue of Christ. Then in the evening at dusk it was processed all over the town in solemn candlelight and music. The *epitaphi* procession was a re-enactment of the aftermath of the crucifixion.

Sara watched along with all her neighbours. How seriously the Greeks solemnised Good Friday in contrast with the British Easter. How different the same day would be in England. It was all about shopping, Easter eggs, holiday traffic queues and the real meaning of this season no longer held much meaning except among devout Christians.

The high point was when she joined Mel, Griff and Pippa as they packed into the church late on Saturday, holding unlit candles. As it grew dark and the chanting droned on, people came and went out for a cigarette but at midnight, the priest came from behind the altar holding a Paschal candle with which he passed the light on from candle to candle. The darkness began to lighten as each one lit another until the whole church shimmered in candlelight. It brought tears to her eyes.

'*Christos anesti*,' they whispered to each other. Christ is risen. '*Alithos anesti*,' came the reply. Risen indeed!

Outside the church women carried baskets of dyed eggs and biscuits to give out to the congregation and Mel said that the ash from their candle must be smeared on the door for good luck.

After weeks of fasting for the faithful, the welcome smell of grilled lamb was in the air, ready roasted on the spit as families gathered for a feast.

'It's your first Easter here – it's unique, isn't it?' Griff leaned across the table of the taverna. 'Like nowhere else.'

'I had no idea,' Sara replied. 'So symbolic and moving. I didn't understand a word being spoken but I'm so glad I'm here to see it.'

'Come, Kyria Sara, *ela*... the fire is lit.' Markos took

her hand and led her to a piece of spare ground where the boys had built a huge bonfire on which sat an effigy dressed up and sitting on an old bike.

'Look, Judas is burning!' They cheered as fireworks leapt into the air and guns went off as usual. By two o'clock in the morning Sara was weary, and brim full with delicious dishes. She had managed to take a few photos and emailed them home but how could she explain to Mum and Dad how wonderful Easter was here?

Tomorrow it was back to work, replying to emails, but so far she had only one definite online booking and her bank balance was not looking too healthy until Karen's money came through. Yet nothing could spoil what she had witnessed in the past few days. From darkness to light, from fasting to feast, from death to resurrection. Now it was springtime and the flowers were in full bloom in the hills; tulips, orchids and poppies. There was a richness to life here that made up for her present cash shortage. Here she could live simply with vegetables, fresh fruits and local produce. All she needed was the faith that things would improve if she kept believing in her business acumen. Time to spread the candle ash over the door. She was sure Ariadne wouldn't mind. Both of them were in need of good fortune in the coming year.

Sara was worried about Sandra and Jack's coming event. It was as if Sandra had lost interest in her big day. As Sara busied herself tidying Ariadne Villa, she wondered how to inject some enthusiasm into the coming ceremony, so much so she even enlisted Sally, the vicar's help.

'Do you think her treatment is affecting her listlessness? It's as if she is grieving and unable to enjoy any of it,' Sara said, knowing Sandra was making few suggestions about her party.

'I think it's a family matter, a fallout. Sandra told me there is one guest missing, her own daughter who means so much to her and that's something we can't remedy, I'm afraid. Sandra is a fighter but the stress does not help her stability. She is such a brave woman and I've been on my knees praying for the best outcome.'

'How could anyone not come to their own mother's wedding?' Sara was puzzled.

'I fear you still have a lot to learn about this business. Every family has its own dynamics, who is in, who is out. I see it most at funerals and weddings. Does the father give the bride away, or the stepfather? What role is there for the new wife when there's an acrimonious divorce? Why was the brother not the best man, or the sister's child not a bridesmaid? You get the picture... All these issues come to play every time, even before the banns are read out.'

'I take the point.' Sara shook her head in dismay. Sally was being very gentle with her comments.

'I'm afraid you have to be counsellor, adviser and comforter, as well as making sure all the guests are seated in the right place. That's another nightmare. You put the wrong relatives together and there can be ructions. Most people can be polite for so long but too much wine, raki, whatever and there'll be trouble. Believe me, bloody noses, tears, fights and structural damage are all par for the course.' Sally laughed.

'Hells bells, I didn't envisage all this,' Sara confessed.

'I'm curious as to why you decided to choose this business?' Sally asked, sipping lemonade and giving Sara a piercing look.

'I wanted to make a bride and groom have a wonderful experience, a day to last a lifetime.'

'You're quite the idealist. I'll be frank. I find many marriages last no longer than their toaster; at the first sign of trouble they ditch it and each other.'

'That's cynical coming from a vicar,' Sara replied, shocked at Sally's comments.

'I'm just being realistic. Some people marry not for keeps but only until something or someone better comes along. It's a different generation now than that of our own grandparents. Divorce carries no shame and cohabiting and pregnancy is all matter-of-fact these days. I try to hope that those who do decide to marry are in it for the long haul. There are often subtle pressures from parents, career promotions in work as well as legal status and security all playing their part. I gather you've not been there yourself then?' Sally was probing.

'Almost,' Sara sighed. It was time to share her own story and she found tears flowing as she recounted some of what had happened last year.

'I'm sorry.' Sally touched her hand. 'Sounds like a lucky escape.'

'Why do I feel such a failure?'

'It was once explained to me that we have two sides to ourselves: the sunny bright side we show others as they show their sunny bright side back to us, but as we live and know someone better, the darker shadowy bits feel safe to reveal themselves and this can suddenly destroy our trust and our loving relationship, leaving us confused.'

'Crikey, that sounds well complicated to me... I thought it was for real and then suddenly I saw him for what he was. It was too much to bear.' Sara found herself reliving that moment of revelation, the weakness in her legs, the pounding heart and exhaustion draining her confidence.

'The sad thing, Sara, is until someone recognises their own weakness and dark self, they can't do anything to change their behaviour. They go on making the same mistakes and making others suffer. Recognition has to come from within and it is not easy to admit. It helps to forgive them this weakness.'

'I couldn't do that,' Sara snapped. This was turning into a counselling session. 'Anyway, this doesn't sort out our problem with Sandra, does it?' she added, changing the subject.

'Wait and see. I have a feeling it may all work out. I'm praying it will for Sandra's sake. She deserves a break.'

Sara strolled down the hill from the vicarage. She couldn't help chewing over all Sally's experiences. How naive she was being. There was much more to this wedding business than just flowers, bridal arches, table décor, seating plans and canned music. There was a lot to learn about human frailties and the reality of family lives. With loving parents, she was protected from such divisions or feuding. It was time to tighten up her psychology if she wasn't going to land in a whole heap of trouble. How she admired Sally's grasp of the realities around marriage. First thing in the morning she would sit down with Sandra to plan the table seating. Perhaps a mixture of local expats with her home guests might be the best arrangement.

24

Mel and Spiro sat down to a well-earned dinner of leftovers. It was after midnight and there was still the taverna to tidy up and much to chew over. 'Your mother is getting worse, Spiro. She nags at us all day long and I can't stand much more of it.' Mel felt it was about time her husband knew just what a pain his mother was of late.

'Mama is tired and demanding. She's afraid of being old and dependent so she takes it out on everyone, even me,' he replied with a sigh.

'No, not you… You can do no wrong and she's not that old. She just dresses as old.' Mel was feeling bitter and washed out. 'We have the christening party on Sunday and I want Pippa's baby to have a lovely day.'

'The baby won't know anything about it but we can get in extra help if you need it.' Spiro was trying to be helpful.

Typical man, he had no idea of the work involved. Harmony may be asleep but her parents would want a celebration to remember. Baptisms were huge events among the locals. There were balloons and decorations to put up, special dishes and tables to look good.

'Thank goodness the book club will muck in, even Dorrie Thorner, wonders will never cease, but it's just…'

'Just?' Spiro was puzzled.

'You and I get so little family time together with the boys; a day on the beach, a picnic or a trip to the waterpark in Chania. It's all work, work, work.'

'That's how it is in the season. This is when we make our money and times are hard. You can't expect me to down tools and lose business because you want time off. I know it's hard for an English girl to be a Greek wife.'

Mel sniffed her disapproval, shaking her head. 'There has to be some balance. The children need to see us all together.'

'They see us at dinner.'

'That's not what I mean and you know it.' The gloves were off. 'I come to bed and my skin stinks of kitchen fat, my calves ache, my eyes are stinging with weariness but I can't sleep. You turn up after dancing in town and snore like a pig all night. It's not fair.'

'I thought you like me dancing with the troupe?'

'How do I know what you get up to behind my back? Some of those young boys attract the tourist girls like flies to honey.'

'Don't be stupid. I dance and that is all. You said that I was unfit and needed to lose some weight and I have,' Spiro shouted.

'Don't call me stupid… I know Greek men flirt, drink and the rest… if they can get away with it. I know you smoke. I wash your shirts,' she yelled back.

'So, what if I do? A man needs comfort from a nagging

wife.' Spiro stood, his arms crossed, his chest defiant. 'You're not my mother.'

'Thank God!' Mel snapped, aware her arguments were going nowhere. 'It's all about what your mother wants, your taverna, your jobs. None of you appreciate anything I do. I'm going to bed.' She fled in tears and slammed the door.

'Melodia! Don't be childish. We can talk about this again when you've calmed down,' Spiro whispered through the door.

'You can sleep in your mother's flat… I want to sleep alone.'

She heard the door close with a bang. Markos woke up and demanded to sleep in her bed. 'Where's Papa?'

I don't know and I don't care, she thought. Why am I being like this? Perhaps it was the time of the month again or just that she had had enough. Tomorrow she must pin on her smile and make sure Pippa and Duke had a wonderful day.

Next morning, they both made polite conversation over coffee as if nothing had happened.

'Is Griff still going ahead with that rescue centre?' Mel asked.

'Not sure, the deputy mayor and the demos think it is unnecessary but no one has told him yet.' Mel knew Spiro had mixed feelings about the venture. 'You think it's my job to inform him? Everyone sees me as a bridge between foreigners and the town because I'm English.'

'Griff is determined to form a private trust, a charity with or without the demos' approval. Simon Bartlett and Chloë are on board. You must support them.'

'I don't know, it will cause trouble.' Spiro was in no mood for compromise.

'You mean from Stavros Metrakis and his thugs?'

'Metrakis is from the past, he lives in the hills, his sons are uneducated and he hasn't much influence down here. The dog to him is just equipment. When it gets lame or sick it's disposed of with a gun. That is their way… you can't change that,' Spiro argued.

'Can't we? A working animal deserves a retirement, like the horses on Chania harbour. They are found homes. It is only humane. Metrakis is an ignorant peasant and he could do with a good wash.' Mel had no time for the man who still lingered in their taverna eyeing the tourist girls in their shorts and tops.

'Don't badmouth him in public, Mel, he can go crazy when drunk. If you rattle him, he may take matters into his own hands.'

'Like what?'

'Nothing, just warning you not to get too involved.'

'That's not like you to defend a bully. You must see Griff and explain things.'

'Enough, I'm off.'

Mel couldn't settle. What was it about Metrakis that troubled her husband? Why did he make him welcome in the taverna and why did *Yiayia*, grandmother Irini, refuse to serve him? Spiro was holding back on something and she was determined to find out just what it was.

Sara sat in the little church as Sally baptised Harmony Marianne Millar into the fellowship of the church. It was a traditional ceremony and Mel, Simon and Chloë stood as godparents. Little Harmony slept through it all. Pippa wore her turquoise wedding dress with a crocheted shawl over her shoulders and Duke, well, he dressed as Duke.

Griff sat opposite in chinos and cream shirt and Sparky crept under his feet. Many regulars were far away and Mel explained how she wished she could introduce Sara to Ariadne Blunt and her partner Hebe but they were in North Yorkshire on the coast trying to nurse Hebe back to health. There were other absentees too but Della Fitzpatrick came with her friend, Joe. All those friends scattered to the four winds, unknown as yet to Sara. She hoped in time she would get to greet them on their return.

Expats were a fluid community, coming and going with the seasons, houses rented out, dogs and cats rehomed with neighbours. Was she here only for a season or two? Her business was in its early infancy, hardly viable, and she was living off savings but the thought of returning to Sheffield held no joy. The sale to Karen was going ahead. It had to be done but it felt like burning a final bridge. She could not be in two places at the same time and here was where she was choosing to live.

It was at times like this, seeing families celebrating a birth, that she felt her singleness. To have a loving relationship, a child perhaps. Would these things now pass her by? Jack and Sandra's wedding was next on the agenda. She noticed Sandra was blooming with a new lease of energy, much to Mel and Sara's relief. Perhaps there had been some good news about her health.

Sara looked across to Griff. What was he thinking? After the supper date, she'd avoided him where possible but in their close-knit group it wasn't easy. They held an open meeting to discuss a fundraising campaign for the newly named SPARKS. No one had yet got any original ideas for a moneymaking event that might attract a crowd and the animal blessing service had died a death. There was no support coming from the demos as yet but they still had high hopes of cooperation.

Griff and the kind vet from the shelter near Chania were going into the school with Sparky to talk to the children. The vet would use Sparky to examine for fleas and ticks, check his teeth and coat, asking the children to look out for sick dogs and cats. This was a start but vet bills, medicines, cages and a sick bay would all cost so the sooner they could come up with a viable idea, the better.

Sara had to admit the more she saw of Griff, the more she couldn't help liking him but where that might lead frightened her. It was barely a year since her own sad event and far too soon to be involved with another man; once bitten twice shy and all that. She blushed at such wandering thoughts as they stood to sing an old favourite hymn: 'All Things Bright and Beautiful'. This was going to be a lovely day with a feast to look forward to, even if she must change her heels for flats and her dress for jeans. She looked at her watch and nodded to the book club contingent. Time to get moving. It was kitchen duties for them all, and soon, or they would face the wrath of Irini.

July

25

Sara was watering the plumbago in the front garden when her English neighbour came running down the path. 'Have you seen Orpheus lately?'

Sara looked up. 'No, why?' Orpheus was Miss Blunt's cat.

'We've been looking after him and he's getting on now. I know he sneaks back into his home garden if I leave the gate open but he's not come back for his food. Oh, hell!' she cried.

'Where does he usually end up?' Sara asked.

'Who knows, but he's always by the side door ready for his meal. When it's not your own... I'm usually so careful. My husband's already been out looking for him.'

'Let me just put this away and come and join you. We can ask around. His fur is distinctive and he's friendly. Have you checked any old buildings?' Sara could see how anxious she was. They spent the morning searching down by the harbour in case he was scrounging fish bits, then along the tavernas, shouting his name.

'He's a bit deaf now and has a one-track mind when he is hungry, from his days as a stray. Ariadne adopted him. What can I do?'

Sara walked up to see Mel and ask around. She had grown fond of the little moggy with its stripy fur. There were always cats milling around in the square scrounging for scraps. Irini was sitting holding court with her neighbours, crocheting and eyeing up the visitors passing by. Sara described Orpheus in detail.

Irini put down her needle. 'If you want to find him, pray to St Phanourios, patron of all lost things. He does a good line in finding lost animals.'

Sara had never heard of this saint or his special powers. Mel came to the rescue. 'We ask St Anthony to come to our aid if we lose anything but St Phanny works as well. What's this about?'

Sara recounted the cat's disappearance. 'They usually return when they are hungry, don't they, but what if he's trapped somewhere? He's quite old now, and deaf.'

'Don't worry, he'll turn up. Mama will put in a word to Phanourios, he's usually reliable given time.'

Sara didn't know what to make of all this saint business. All she knew was her neighbour was beside herself with the responsibility of keeping Orpheus safe until Miss Blunt returned.

She met Don Ford strolling down from the retreat and he invited her for a drink. It was hot and sticky and he would be able to pass the word round to Griff.

'It's a while since we saw you up at the retreat. I gather

things are a bit frosty between you and our host.' Don sat back eyeing her response.

'Not at all, who told you that?' Sara felt herself blushing at this personal comment.

'My dear, a writer sees all… observes the little nuances that might prove useful for his next character. We have shards of glass in our hearts, don't you know.'

Sara laughed. 'Honestly, you talk a load of codswallop! How's your writing going, or shouldn't I ask?'

Don gulped down his beer. 'Hard going and got a deadline to meet.'

'Shouldn't you be slaving away at your Mac, not idling in the taverna then?'

'Touché, my friend… so I should but it doesn't work like that for me. I need to stroll out and think on my feet or in the pool but there's a noisy crowd there splashing about. I can't concentrate.'

'You can use my olive garden if you like,' Sara offered. 'It's private and quiet. I promise not to disturb your musings.'

'You are a saint… what can I do in return?'

'Have you heard of a St Phanourios, patron of lost things?' She explained about the lost cat. 'Ask about for me and tell Griff too.'

'Ah, you want me to be a go-between, how romantic.'

'Stop it, Don. Griff and I are just friends so don't go getting any ideas of matchmaking.'

'I wouldn't dream of it, darling. I was hoping you might be looking in my direction, not his.'

Now she could see he was teasing her. 'You are a menace

to anything in a skirt. I pity those would-be writers hanging on your every word. What power you must wield as you drop pearls of wisdom and encouragement into their ears.'

'You are too cruel but I may avail myself of your kind offer sometime.'

'You do that, the side door is usually unlocked. Just make yourself at home.' With that Sara left him to his beer. She had to admit old Don was fun but too observant for comfort. Did he spot that magnetism she felt when in Griff's presence? There were more urgent things on her mind as she made for home, hoping Orpheus had made an appearance at last.

August

26

On 27 August, the streets of St Nick's began to fill up for the *panagyri*; the feast day of Phanourios, patron saint of lost and found; be it a mislaid tool or a lost dog or cat, a forgotten coat, whatever. At dawn, stallholders were busy setting their places in the shade. From the harbour uphill to the town square, vans were parked, women displayed baskets of cakes and bread, tables were set with all kinds of toys, icons of the saint, and craft stalls were ready for the annual invasion of families, tourists and priests.

Sara could hardly move in the heat for the crowds milling around, ready to buy, sell or feast. Chloë, Pippa and herself had set their stall at the top of the hill, not the best site but with space to spread out information leaflets about SPARKS charity. They were focusing on rehoming strays locally and abroad. To raise money they had, with Sandra's help, run up gay bandanas for dogs, and found some cuddly puppy toys to sell, and there was a big bowl of water for passing pooches and a jar of dog treats to encourage owners to stop and browse. Jack and Sandra had fallen for a young stray they had named Dusty and were seriously thinking of adopting. Harmony was sleeping in her buggy in the deep shade of a mulberry tree, while Chloë had her eye on the purple berries to make jam.

As the morning wore on, the competition was stiff. Stall upon stall were selling beer, lemonade and sticks of grilled souvlaki. Sara was watching Irini's friends who were dishing out feast bread and something called Lost and Found cake, in honour of the saint.

Mel and Spiro were hard at work grilling lamb burgers with yoghurt and mint toppings, and dishing out frappés and ice cream. There was a line of craft stalls full of handmade work in competition with stalls full of imported souvenirs.

Griff found them all sweating in the sun. He was in a foul mood because one of the clients was proving a pain, complaining about the plumbing, the air conditioning, his mosquito bite and the fact that Don, the tutor, had made suggestions to his novel that he felt were impertinent.

'Go down to the taverna and cool off. We can manage here,' Simon ordered, seeing the grim look on his face.

'How are you all doing?' he asked, looking at the pile of leaflets.

'Not as well as we hoped.' Chloë looked around. 'Not sure we've got the right goods. It's too hot for people to climb up the hill. St Nick's is packed. I've never seen so many tourists.'

'But people have been interested in the posters of Spartacus.' Sara tried to sound encouraging but had to admit it was hard going. One man had picked up a leaflet and thrown it down. 'You English and your dogs. Here we care for our family until they pass away. You shove them into homes and pet your dogs in their place.'

What could Sara reply? It was the same old criticism, a fair point of difference in culture and traditions. They must be careful not to offend but animals had feelings of pain, hunger, abandonment and confusion. She was feeling the stifling heat. Chloë told her to go down into the shade of the taverna. 'Take a break. We're hardly rushed off our feet and Jack is coming to do a stint.'

As she walked down the street, there was a stall selling statues of the saint. They were skilfully carved in olive wood by a local wood sculptor who she had admired for some time. She decided to buy one to leave in the villa for guests as a thank you.

She plonked herself down next to Griff who was gulping down a Mythos beer. 'What do you think of that? I thought Ariadne Villa might like it when I leave.' Sara showed him the statue with pride.

'You're not quitting, are you?' he replied, looking up in surprise and ignoring the statue.

'Of course not, but I can't stay there indefinitely. Are you all right? You look done in. This heat... and this wannabe writer on the course?'

'Why is it one pompous man can be so irritating? Don says he hasn't a hope of being published unless he does it himself or takes some positive criticism. His prose is dead on the page and his plot is all over the place. There's always some plonker who thinks they know it all. Why he bothered to come, beats me.'

'Cheer up, they'll be gone at the weekend. I expect the heat gets to your visitors and makes them cranky. I think we'll be packing up the stall soon.' She saw a strange look on Griff's face.

'It's not only that, Sara. I've heard some disturbing news, hot off the press. They've found a bunch of corpses round the litter bin on the road to Sternes village… cats and vermin mostly. They think it's another deliberate poisoning.'

Sara went cold and looked up, hoping against hope this was nothing to do with Orpheus's disappearance. It had been weeks and not a sign of him. 'You know Ariadne's cat went missing… surely not?'

'Yes, I've only just heard. The demos are investigating. Bait was put down somewhere and the animals were lured to it. That's all I know.'

'Who would do a thing like that?'

Griff shook his head. 'Sorry, there are always people… it's not the first time this has happened.'

'Surely something can be done to catch this person?'

'They say there's enough evidence from the remains to get the poison analysed. That might indicate what substance is being used. It could have been Spartacus.'

'And Orpheus… I know what you are thinking. I can see it in your eyes. He's likely to be one of the victims. He's a wanderer, he got hungry.' Sara felt tears. 'How are we going to tell Miss Blunt and her neighbour?'

'It's not certain, he may not be one of them, but if it is, then I'll write to her. I feel sick at the thought that someone's out there. I wish I could shove the stuff down his throat and see how he likes the agony.' Griff banged his hand on the table. 'People must be warned to rein in their pets and I shall watch Sparky. What is it with these people?'

'I know Mel and Spiro have been arguing over our dog and cat rescue project. She told me there's a clash of cultures here. We are guest residents, incomers. They think us sentimental over animals. Do you think they will trace the source?' Griff looked despondent and Sara wanted to reach out to him but drew back. Why was it so hard to be natural with him?

'Don't repeat what I've said until it's official. I don't want to raise false alarm but it's not looking good for Ariadne's cat. It's been too long since you flagged it up. I'd better go back. I'm not in the mood for all this feasting and crowds. Thanks for listening, Sara. I'm sorry to burden you.'

'Not at all, what are friends for but to share this sort of news?' She watched him slink away into the crowd, her heart sick at the thought of what would follow. She stared down at the statue in her hand. Was he listening somewhere, had he pointed the council to this sad scene? Had Orpheus been found but not in the way they had hoped?

It was time to return to help pack up the stall but Griff's news felt like a stone in her gut. The feast would go on into the night with music and dancing and then, first thing, the priest would be chanting over the Tannoy to wake them all up.

Dorrie arrived full of yet more news of the impending nuptials, inviting them to a special meet and greet evening where they would be introduced to the bride and her entourage. Everyone was too tired and jaded to take her excitement on board and she sensed this, flouncing off.

'Oh dear, that didn't go down well,' Chloë said. 'I hear the weather is a bit iffy in the next few weeks, from the north, which can be bad news. Poor Dorrie will not like that.'

'Who is going to tell Miss Dorney that there might be an almighty deluge?' Pippa laughed. 'Mr Shevchenko won't like any weather spoiling his princess's big day but even he can't hold back the skies. Don't look so glum, Sara. It might do you a good turn.'

Sara tried to smile and join in but it was hard knowing there was bad news coming to St Nick's community. All she wanted to do was retreat to the silence of the olive garden, and worrying that poor Orpheus might be lost forever.

September

27

Excitement was building for the wedding of the year on Santaniki. Crates of champagne were arriving by ferry. Shelley Dorney flew in, striding across the beach demanding a carpeted duckboard walkway for the bride so she could wear her Manolo Blahniks, and her couture dress would not get soiled. They were going to erect a platform out from the shore where the ceremony would take place. It was designed like a huge water lily with the couple-to-be encased within it surrounded by flowers. The beach was to be closed off to the public, all litter, stones and detritus to be removed and the sand raked clean. She imported gold chairs covered in satin cushions. A flower designer was coming from London to prepare the scene.

There would be a large meet and greet for the bride and groom, arranged by the Thorners in the community hall under Miss Dorney's instructions. The hall was to be altered into a palace of exotic flowers with garlands hanging in great wreaths from the ceiling; only the wooden structures were in place so far. The walls were to be dressed out in swags of silk, and boxes of fine china crockery and glasses, engraved with the date of the wedding, were waiting to be assembled on a long table display for the guest buffet. The steep steps to the little chapel of Agios Nikolaos were to be swept and garlanded with pots of scented lilies, a special stair carpet laid from the bottom to the chapel door for a photo shoot. Nothing was to be left to chance.

Mel and Sara watched Shelley's progress through the town, picking holes in everything that she felt Yuri would not want to see. His princess must have everything she wanted.

Poor Dorrie smiled wanly at all these specifications. She confessed to the book club it was getting out of hand. 'That woman marches in with her lists, inspecting Norris and me as if we were also-rans, not the groom's parents. Daniel is worried that Soraya will be disappointed in our island. Whatever for? It's our home, our base! Would you believe she even emailed my other son, who has a little daughter, suggesting that she's too young to be a bridesmaid. She has ten already. We shall be the laughing stock of St Nick's. Ten bridesmaids indeed! Oh, and my new outfit clashes with Yuri's new wife's, the tarty one, not his first one, she's been ignored completely. I sometimes wonder if Daniel...' She broke off, almost in tears. 'I am glad I'll have all of you on my side. At least the party in the hall will be full of our guests, not theirs.'

No one spoke at first, sensing nerves had got the better of Dorrie. She had lost weight but looked drained and anxious. 'Cheer up,' Chloë said. 'St Nick's will never have seen such a spectacle, a flotilla of yachts, a carriage and horses ferried over from Chania and a posse of gorgeous girls with a princess bride.'

'You don't think it's rather over the top, do you?' Dorrie asked, her trembling hand shaking her wine glass.

What could anyone say? Sara thought the whole event sounded horrendous, such a display of wealth on this simple island where families were struggling to pay its taxes. How much of this extravagance would go into the local economy? After Sally's quiet lecture, Sara knew she mustn't judge every bride who wanted her dream wedding and this was Soraya's idea, not hers. Making unrealistic dreams become a reality was part of a wedding planner's job, smoothing out ruffled feathers, finding compromises. She was learning on the job, having blithely jumped into this business thinking it was just another event to manage. There was so much more.

Shelley had free rein with untold thousands. Most brides were not so lucky. She thought of Pippa and Duke's wedding day done on a shoestring and it was such a happy occasion. Sara smiled recalling her gran's Yorkshire saying: 'There's many poor folk in this world. They have money.' She was beginning to understand her meaning. Money wasn't everything and she just hoped all this expense would bring happiness to the young couple.

She had to admire Shelley's confidence and professionalism but there was a steel edge to the service she offered. This event would add to her kudos and bank balance but she didn't seem to care about the rest of the families, especially Dan's mother or Soraya's own mother.

For some reason Sara felt protective of their welfare. Surely it was the involvement of everyone in a family wedding that made them part of this show? That seemed to be missing here. They had to obey like foot soldiers under strict orders.

If she was organising this event, Dorrie and Norris would play an important part in the day. This was their island home. Surely their other son and child had every right to be included? This wedding was in danger of becoming the Yuri Shevchenko show. Thank goodness she did not have to kowtow to their demands.

Little did she know that the Fates had got other ideas in mind for the wedding of the year.

On the eve of Daniel and Soraya's wedding, a storm hit the island in a fury of wind and crashing waves. St Nick's was battered with rain, thunder and lightning with every attendant dramatic effect. It closed down ports and local shipping as the seas rose and crashed into the harbours, tossing boats into each other. Tiled roofs were flapping, chairs and loungers and parasols flying into the air as Sara closed the shutters, battening down the hatches preparing for the worst. The power was off and her newly planted garden shrubs lurched against the window. Then she remembered it was the night of Dorrie Thorner's meet and greet evening. There would be no yachts in the harbour, none of the Russian guests would be able to land in small boats and she wondered if she should offer some help.

Wrapping herself against the rain she slithered through the streaming torrent up to the Thorners' villa, not far from her own, part of her wondering if she should turn back as

Dorrie was prickly and perhaps thought she was muscling in on their big day. Dorrie could blow hot and cold but somehow Sara knew all might not be well.

Daniel was on the veranda, smoking, his brother trying to calm his little daughter, as the thunder rattled above. Dan looked up to see Sara. 'Thank God you've come, it's bedlam in there, panic stations, and poor Soraya is in tears.'

Sara could hear the wailing from the porch as Soraya stormed out. 'This is not supposed to happen in September. How can it do this to me? And who are you?' She stared at Sara, her ice blue eyes puffy with tears.

'I thought you might need some help as Shelley isn't here yet.'

'What can anyone do in this?' The bride-to-be flung her arms out in despair. 'It's all your fault, Dan. I didn't want to come to this shitty little island. I wanted Mykonos or Skiathos… even Kylie can't make an appearance due to a clash of dates.'

'I'm afraid this storm is all over the Med,' Sara offered, seeing Daniel turning away in frustration. 'Let's go inside and see how to make the best of the day. It may be fine tomorrow.' She edged Soraya indoors where Dorrie was wringing her hands in despair.

'What'll we do? Everything is planned but the forecast is dire, what shall we do, Sara?'

'Sit down, have a cup of *malotira* to calm things and see what we can salvage. The hall is booked.'

'But not decorated, Shelley was going to supervise all that. The flowers were being kept in cool storage and the room could be flooded out.'

'Then I'll get some help to finish it off.' Sara brought out her leather-bound pocket notebook. 'How many guests have arrived already?'

'Just locals, everything is at a standstill and Soraya is refusing to budge. Her father is stranded somewhere out there... what a mess! Norris is lying down with one of his bad heads, feeling the strain. No one tells you the stress of all this... At least the groom and best man are here. Our house is full. Soraya had planned to stay in a hotel with her mother but everywhere is in darkness.'

Sara could feel Dorrie's panic as all their plans were crumbling before her eyes. 'There's no reason not to hold the reception meet and greet.'

'But with no power supply?'

'Plenty of lamps and candles will suffice, outages are common here, aren't they? It doesn't stop feasts and parties, not with wood ovens and Calor gas stoves. You told me it was going to be a cold buffet with lots of wine and cheese. Mel will give us a hand, I'm sure.'

'But tomorrow... They are due to meet the mayor to sign their documents and then the beach ceremony. The platform boards will be wrecked. Thank goodness the carpet up to the chapel wasn't due to be laid out. It's all too much. Shelley should be here. She has all the notes...' Dorrie was flapping her hands and pacing the floor.

'One day at a time, Mrs Thorner. We'll salvage what we can and make it happen, perhaps not as grand as planned but there is no reason for them not to marry. Their party celebrations can come later when everybody has arrived safely. We can still make tonight special. Fratelli's can still prepare the catering, and we can ring round the book club to help finish off the hall tables, glasses and flowers.'

'Thank you.' She paused. 'My other son has come along. His wife isn't here. It's all too much. That Shelley woman just bulldozed over us. This wasn't my idea at all, not even a blessing in church,' Dorrie moaned while Soraya was swallowing a large glass of wine.

'We can't do anything without Shelley and Papa, can we? Stranded on this island, what a farce. The wedding might as well be called off,' Soraya cried, waving her glass and spattering wine over Dorrie's cream sofa. 'Ooops… Sorry.'

Dorrie rushed out for a cloth. It was time for Sara to step in with firmness before it all descended into recriminations. 'I know you must be disappointed but there are more ways to skin a cat, as they say. The whole of St Nick's is looking forward to meeting you both. We can still have the party as planned. There'll be food and drink, candlelight, live music. It could be fun and very romantic. What a tale to tell your grandkids one day. So forget about what can't be helped and enjoy the moment. Videos and photos can be emailed, perhaps, to your papa. It will be a night to remember.' Soraya's sulky lips changed into a smile. 'That's better, you can still wear your pre-wedding outfit. Now relax. Tomorrow is another day.'

Soraya downed another glass. 'But if it continues, what then? The sun must shine on my wedding day, not some soggy wet downpour. What about my bridal dress and train? They'll be ruined. What if the water lily has collapsed? What a stupid idea and it's all Papa's fault for wanting all this fuss. We might as well have exchanged vows in a London park.'

Dorrie was busy wiping down her sofa shaking her head at Soraya's attitude. 'There's no pleasing that one,' she whispered. 'Dear Papa spoiled her rotten, poor Daniel…'

Sara was not going to take sides. Time to muster help from her expat friends so that Dorrie got a special night. The heavens may have opened but no reason not to have a great evening after all. Most of their meet and greet guests were British and a little drop of rain and wind was par for the course. Sara took her leave and headed up to the square to the community hall, texting everybody she could think of before she realised without power and no internet service, she would have to go and knock on doors as it poured down.

They were a motley crew of helpers who set to in the hall to make the best of things. At least they had the fancy china and tablecloths ready to be displayed, Fratelli's delivered the pastries and cold buffet, candlesticks and lanterns flickered on the ledges. The stage they lined with pot plants and shrubs. There was nothing they could do with the garlands but Spiro got a ladder and Griff brought a huge sack of greenery which they hung from the wooden circles instead, adorning them with balloons.

Chloë and Mel made the tables look presentable. Irini loaned her silk flowers to cheer things up. It was all very makeshift but candlelight could hide a multitude of sins. The musicians hired for the night turned up and there was plenty of background music to fill the room. When they were satisfied, everyone dashed back home to change. If this was to be a grand occasion then only party frocks would do under macs and umbrellas. They assembled like guests at a ball. Soraya made her entrance in a mid-length satin gown with a boat-shaped neck and very fifties in style. Daniel thanked everyone and admired what they had achieved in a few hours. Dorrie and Norris looked relieved and the evening proceeded without a hitch. The food was plentiful and delicious, toasts were made to the bridal couple but Soraya said little. Disappointment was etched on her face for all to see. They emptied every one of Papa Yuri's champagne bottles. Poor Norrie got plastered. They had never seen him so lively, shaking hands and hugging his neighbours.

'I hope to goodness the rain stops tomorrow or there will be all hell to pay,' whispered Chloë to Sara. 'Well done, you saved the evening.'

Sara was not so sure. There was nothing she could do if it rained tomorrow. All that mattered to her was that Dorrie and her family had a good evening. The rest was up to Miss Dorney to rescue and put a smile on Soraya's face at last.

28

The day of the wedding dawned bright as if nothing had happened the night before. It was the wind that did most of the damage along the shoreline and the waves rolled in like a surfer's dream. There was still no sign of the yacht. The appointment at the mayoral office had to be kept and Dorrie asked Sara to accompany them down in case anything went wrong.

Sara prayed Shelley had done all the paperwork correctly and Spiro taxied them into town where Soraya was waiting with Dan in her second wedding outfit: a two-piece, tight-fitting lacy trouser suit with wide lapels on which sat a diamond brooch the size of a small saucer. 'Her papa's gift,' whispered Dorrie. 'Not quite a kettle and table mats, is it?'

The legal wedding ceremony took about three minutes, they signed the documents in triplicate, smiled at the local photographer and that was that. Soraya searched the horizon in tears, waiting for the sea to settle and a sighting of her father's yacht. Then suddenly it was there in the distance and everyone cheered. Soraya was taxied back to Dorrie's house to change into wedding outfit number three: the Paris creation.

Sara was curious to see what happened next, waiting for the motor launches to disgorge the guests in their finery. Already a team of local chippies were hurriedly trying to fix the waterlily platform but the waves had smashed the faux leaves, leaving a sorry mess. There was only time for plan B, a simple duckboard and raised decking. The set designer would have a hissy fit but what else could be done?

At least the formal ceremony was not due until much later and would give time for tempers to calm down, for all the girls to be made-up and the flummery of flower arrangements erected to disguise any damaged structures.

The bridesmaids staggered off the boat looking green and dishevelled. No one was in the mood for laughter. Mr Yuri's expression was like a wet weekend in Hartlepool. The poor horse and open carriage from Chania was lifted off, ready for the procession. Locals and tourists stared in amazement as the boxes of roses and blooms and accessories were piled up on the harbour.

Back at the taverna, Sara relayed all she had seen to Mel. 'This, we must see. I'm not going to miss it for anything.'

As if reading her mind, Norris popped in with an invitation. 'After all you two did for us yesterday, it's the least we can do and if anyone queries your presence, send them to me. This is our island and we have to have some say in matters.'

Mel asked Irini and Katya to cover for her. The boys would stay and play with friends. Lunches were quiet with time for them both to shower and change so they could join Chloë and the book club ladies for the ceremony. The gold satin chairs sank into the damp sand, the duckboard was lined with white roses and ferns, the archway was covered in red roses and gold ribbon and they brought a trio of chamber musicians to play in the bride. It was a pity their instruments were out of tune.

After a short delay, Soraya arrived on her father's arm in her third wedding outfit, a froth of silk and lace cascading into an enormous bustle and train. She looked drained and anxious in the early evening heat. 'That dress will kill her… it's so hot,' Sara whispered, noting how the train was already soiled with sand. They watched as the vow-taking began, kisses exchanged and everyone clapping until one of her ten bridesmaids collapsed under the weight of her dress and huge bouquet.

Sara watched Yuri's new wife's hair extensions droop into rat's tails. The wedding arch was wilting in the sun, the duckboard carpet was sagging under all those spiky heels. At least those with large hats had some shade. Sadly, Sara thought it all rather tacky and shallow but again Sally's words echoed in her mind: *You must never judge someone else's dream.*

Then it was time for the bride and groom to kick off their shoes and wander onto the shore for those romantic shots by the photographer from their chosen magazine. The guests were left to head for the huge marquee erected for the wedding breakfast. Sergei, the designer, had done them proud, using up all the spare flowers that should have gone to the community hall the night before. You could hardly breathe for the scent of lilies and roses. The chefs were waiting for the bride and groom to arrive back and wine flowed and flowed. But they didn't return and guests grew restless. Yuri kept looking at his watch and the chefs in their whites looked on, impatient. The noise grew louder, the drinking harder, they attacked the raki bottles and when the couple finally arrived, a party was in full swing without them.

The chefs came with dishes but they were ignored. They were past eating and Dorrie watched in horror as a fight broke out and a table collapsed. This seemed to sober up the guests. Yuri rose to make his speech. Norris began to sneeze and drown out his words which did not go down well. Somehow the toasts were made. Then it was time for the bridal procession to make its way around the town by lamplight with guests following behind the open coach.

'Look at all that food gone to waste. It ought to be shared out along the harbour or in the square,' Mel suggested as they left the tent. 'What a shambles that was. There's a party on the yacht, I gather, but we won't be invited to that, thank goodness. I think the bride has another gown for that as well.' She laughed. 'Nice for some. I wore a dress from Monsoon… just the one. What will yours be like?'

'Never thought about it,' Sara lied. How could she explain away the oyster silk dress she had once worn and given to a charity shop? Funny how whenever she saw that colour, she felt sick. 'We could ask if they would mind us making up doggy bags for the dog pound. Griff has got a makeshift shelter at the bottom of the retreat garden.'

Later, looking back over the great wedding disaster,

Mel and Sara chewed the cud as they lay in the September sunshine. 'I think we did well in all the chaos of the storm. We made the best of the meet and greet, everyone mingled and the hall scrubbed up well. I thought the buffet was okay and they drank Papa Shevchenko dry. You were a star. You worked miracles,' said Mel, lying back with her arm above her head.

'I hope I did what was needed,' Sara said, pleased at all the compliments she received.

'Don't be so modest! You went the extra mile and bust a gut making sure to give them a good pre-wedding party despite the awful weather. It was a flood down the main street.'

They were sunbathing out on Sunset Beach, knowing how the storm had wrought havoc everywhere. 'I'm glad it's all over.' Sara smiled. 'Even Shelley Dorney said she couldn't have done better under the circumstances. Praise indeed!'

'Your local knowledge was key to your success, Sara. You showed you cared and roped in everyone. Shelley wouldn't have had any of your contacts. The girl done good. I hope you sent them a bill.'

'I couldn't,' Sara replied. 'It was only my time.'

Mel sat up and nudged her. 'Your time is as good as anyone else's. Honestly, I despair of you sometimes. However did you make a living in Sheffield?'

'That's different.'

'No, it's not. Your time is valuable. You came to the rescue and sacrificed time you could have spent on your own business. It's certainly worth a fee.'

'I can't bill Dorrie...'

'You can bill Shevchenko though… stepping in to prepare and supervise things.' Mel saw her friend hesitating.

'I'm not sure, he rather scared me like some gangster…'

'Perhaps he is,' Mel quipped. Sara was too trusting and reticent. She had impressed everyone with her calm efficiency. Dorrie would not be so snotty at the book club now that Sara had saved the day.

Two days later, the flotilla of Shevchenko's guests in their yachts glided far into the horizon with the newlyweds aboard, off to safari in Africa. Mel was glad that they were gone from the island; all those blonde, leggy glamour girls made her feel homespun and lardy. Spiro's eyes were on stalks watching them parade in their skimpy, figure-hugging outfits. They were like creatures from another world.

When Sara returned to Ariadne Villa, she found Griff hard at work strimming around the rockery and the stone walls.

'Hi,' she said shyly, aware her bikini was showing underneath her thin wrap. 'Sorry, I forgot you were coming.'

'I wanted to thank you for the dog leftovers. It was a kind thought. I snuck a few shots from the bridezilla wedding. I thought you would like to put them on your webpage.'

'It was Shelley's show, not mine,' Sara replied.

'You stepped into the breach and kept Norris and Dorrie from nervous breakdowns. Have a look.' He had left an envelope under the shade.

'I'll get some of Irini's lemonade and cinnamon biscuits.'

Sara went to change quickly into shorts and loose top. They sat on the little stone patio with its view down to the sea and looked at the photos. 'These are good. I like the barefoot couple walking in the sand with her dress trailing behind her. I could use these as there're no faces to the camera and it's very romantic.'

'You were amazing, considering that bunch of posers and hangers-on. They must've consumed the Greek national debt over three days and at least thanks to you, some of the traders got a look-in, fixing hair, bringing flowers to rescue the hall. I hope you get some punters after all this.' Griff smiled.

'It's back to the simple weddings for me. Jack and Sandra's will be next. That is just a quiet family affair and I'm looking forward to it.' Sara smiled at him, trying to ignore how good-looking he was, his hair sun-bleached and his long legs tanned to leather in his cut-off jeans.

'In December there's Alexa and Felix's,' Griff added. 'He's asked me to be the best man. Are you helping Chloë?'

'I think so, nothing firmed up yet as to the actual day but Alexa keeps in touch. The couple want a winter wedding, a bit risky after this last deluge but I'm ready for anything now. How about you – any more news on those poisonings?' The gossip about who might be poisoning the poor beasts had died down recently.

'Not yet, but the stuff has gone to a lab. Everyone's been warned to keep their dogs on leash when walking. Who knows what tempting morsel will lurk in the undergrowth and dogs love to sniff out bits of food.' Griff paused, sitting back in his chair. 'It's a setback to our fundraising campaign. Everything's gone quiet. The school visit was cancelled. The vet was called to check over the strays impounded by the council and not exactly encouraged to join our committee. I think they are being cautious until they see how our enterprise evolves. I've made before and after posters of Sparky to replace the ones torn down. I won't risk sticking them everywhere but discreetly on noticeboards with a number to call us. We'll be keeping things low-key for the moment but I'm determined to get our funds going. How else can we start?'

'I've had an idea for that, not sure it would work, but how about a party after Christmas or New Year, a fancy dress party. Everybody loves Abba so why not a tribute night with the full gear, a showing of the film, perhaps an open mic and find some memorabilia to auction, a competition with lots of food, the usual raffles? This came to me in the middle of the night when I couldn't sleep.'

Griff grabbed her hands across the table. 'You genius! Spot on... with plenty of time to plan and get the whole town involved. We could find a tribute band, run a best costume competition. You're not just a pretty face, Sara Loveday, genius!'

'Thank you.' Sara blushed. 'It could be fun and, who knows, warm enough to barbecue on the beach. We could do the whole *Mamma Mia* thing.' She felt the heat of his hand as it warmed right through her body, and withdrew hers gently but reluctantly. She could feel his breath and the faded tinge of expensive aftershave. The intimate moment passed. They looked again at the photos and tried to concentrate on choosing the best.

After Griff left, Sara sat down with her handy notebook and made lists.

What would she do without her lists? The pages were getting full as her ideas flowed.

How this last year had flown by. Sheffield was a world away now and soon her parents were coming for two weeks so she must clear the spare bedroom she used as an office. Sara couldn't wait to see them as now it looked as if she would be staying on this Christmas; what with the Bartlett wedding and the Abba party. She would have to let her parents down gently.

This was home now as long as this villa was free. She loved its cosy ambience, the bookshelves, the outlook and the quiet companionship of the ticking wall clock. The olive wood was stacked for when a fire was needed. There were rugs to roll out when the floors were chilly and the woolly wraps she knitted ages ago would warm her through. So far it was warm and sunny so her parents would be able to bathe in the heat and eat al fresco.

She could still feel the heat of Griff's hand, the look of admiration in his blue eyes as they laughed together. Could she trust this growing closeness? Only time would tell if there could be anything more between them.

October

29

Sandra stood in the bedroom facing the mirror trying on her outfit, her hands shaking as she fingered her oyster-pink dress with three-quarter sleeves. It was two days since Julie and Colin's unexpected arrival and she still couldn't believe the miracle sitting beside her or that her silent prayers had been answered. 'Am I mutton dressed as lamb?' she asked Julie, who was smiling.

'You look lovely, slim and neat… Jack will be very proud of you. I'm sorry for doubting him.'

'I still can't believe how you've changed your tune, love. What's brought this on? I thought you disliked him.' Sandra was thrilled to have her daughter here at long last but she didn't want any misunderstandings.

'Let's just say I had a change of heart over a few things lately. I was cross when you came over here to stay. I thought you were deserting us.' Julie took out her hanky.

'Never? Why should I do that? You're my girl and my

reminder of Paul. We just had to get away for a while. The sun and warmth have given me such strength.'

'I couldn't bear any other man to take his place and I am so sorry. It was selfish, childish and hard on you. I didn't understand how you must be feeling too,' Julie continued.

Sandra sat by her side to comfort her. 'You were only young, love, angry at the world for taking your daddy away. But life had to go on. You're my family whatever happens, and now you are making my wedding perfect just by being by my side. I'm curious to know what really changed your mind. When I left you at Christmas, you were determined not to come.'

'I did call after you, knowing I was spoiling your visit. It was childish and cruel but I couldn't help myself. I talked to the counsellor at work, knowing I needed straightening out, and then one email did just that.'

'What email?' Sandra was puzzled.

'It was from Jack, a lovely letter full of love for you. All I could think of was me, me, me. I wish I could turn back the clock and take back all the stuff I said to you over the years. Oh, and he asked me not to tell you. I know now he cares like Daddy cared. Time is precious and I nearly ruined everything.' Julie sniffed back her tears. 'I'm sorry.'

'None of that now, we've just had a fancy makeover. I don't want mascara ruining your dress. That dusky pink really suits you and tones in with mine.' Julie had made a real effort to dress for the day with sparkling shoes.

'It's only M&S but so light and sunny. I went a bit mad on the sandals though,' Julie confessed as she lifted her feet.

'That's more like it, my girl. All that matters is that you

and the family are here now and whatever happens next is for another day.'

'What do you mean?' Julie stood up in alarm at her mother's words.

'Just a bit of a setback, that's all. I'm going to need more chemo.'

'Mum, I'd no idea.'

'So…' she paused. 'Jack and I have decided to come home. I can go into the Christie hospital but there's no immediate rush. I'm not going to spoil this day or our celebrations.'

'How can you be so brave? You look so well and happy.'

'I am and that's how I'll stay. You've met Sara Loveday, she's done everything for us. The pool even has petals on it, the arch is perfect and the pot plants are gorgeous. Mel and Spiro have put on a spread like there's no tomorrow. All we have to do now is go up to St Paul's for the blessing. Will you give me away? Just take my arm as we go in. I hope Colin won't mind,' Sandra said, hoping Julie would understand how important this was to her.

'Don't be daft, I'll be proud to escort you in. This is your day and I've done enough moaning in the past. We're family and Jack is now part of us too.'

Spiro brought his taxi with white ribbons fixed to the bonnet and a bouquet of roses waiting inside. Sandra felt like a queen, a little breathless, but that was to be expected. The sun was shining, the sky ink blue. It was going to be a wonderful day, a day to savour when they returned back home. With Jack and Julie on her side she knew she could face anything the months ahead threw at her. Now was the time to live in the moment and that was enough.

*

Sara was laughing, banging a tin pan behind the bridal car as it lurched over potholes, carrying bride and groom to their reception. They were giving them some rough music as cars tooted along the route. By nightfall Spiro's mates would be letting off their guns in celebration. It was a beautiful service, simple and short, but Sally made it all full of meaning. How different from last month's debacle. Here was a couple facing a worrying future together but surrounded by love and well-wishers.

'It's couples like these who show such courage,' whispered Chloë sitting next to her. 'We must pray for Sandra and Jack and their future happiness together. Couples like them bring us up short with their courage. How lucky we are to have no such worries and battles ahead. But have you heard? Daniel's marriage is over. Dorrie and Norris have flown back to London to console him. Apparently Soraya, or her father, decided he was not the right man for her and she ditched him after their honeymoon. All that expense and fuss for nothing. Poor Dorrie is gutted. Her other son is also divorced and I'm not sure they can cope with this. Knowing their straitlaced views, they might not want to return here but selling houses right now, after the economic crash, won't be easy.'

Sara grimaced at this sad news, knowing she had no room to talk on that score. 'How's your daughter's plans?' she asked, changing the subject.

'Still on about a winter wedding before Christmas. I am so glad you are organising most of it,' Chloë whispered.

'Of course.' Sara smiled with relief. The invoice to Shelley Dorney was modest and her online business wasn't going to pick up until after Christmas when couples got around to planning their summer weddings.

'Don't worry about any local expenses, that's up to us. What Alexa and Felix do in London beforehand is up to them. I think the time of year will limit numbers but with our friends there'll still be a crowd. Blink and it will be on us.'

'Alexa and Felix are going to do all the formal stuff in a register office back home so Yannis and his dozy deputy will have to go without a fee. Talking of Yannis,' Sara confided, 'I gather they are no further in identifying the cat poisoner. Tests are inconclusive but some agricultural chemical is suspected and Griff is still hounding them for answers.'

It was Don's last night before he flew back to flog his latest paperback with a round of launches and interviews. He invited Griff and Sara to dine with him in the taverna which was almost empty as the season was drawing to its natural close. The writing courses were finished, the charter planes about to cease and St Nick's was reverting to the off season. They sat huddled by the open log fire, the only customers dining in the cool of the evening.

Sara ditched glamour for a long skirt and warm sweater. She was sorry to see Don leave as she enjoyed his company and he made her laugh. Tonight, though, he was looking strained.

'I might come back later, Griff, if there's room in the inn,' he said. 'Not done as much writing as I hoped.'

'I'm not surprised,' came the reply.

'No, this is serious. A bit stuck with this new novel,' he sighed. 'There's no spark yet.'

'Don't tell me the great Don Ford has got writer's block?' Griff teased.

'Not exactly... It's just, oh hell. I looked in my ideas cupboard and it's Mother Hubbard bare... Nothing left on the shelf that interests me. That's not happened before.'

Sara could sense his tension and concern.

'You give so much to your students on the courses, perhaps you're tired. Time for a change of scene? You could always come back alone over Christmas and join us all. Have some fun and then knuckle down to it. There would be no distractions and no excuse not to work.'

Griff smiled at her offer. 'You've had fun all summer, that's your problem, but you're more than welcome to keep me company. I'm staying on.'

'Thanks, there's some magic on this island. I can't put my finger on it but it inspires me. London won't be restful doing publicity tours so I may well take you up on the offer.'

'What offer?' Mel and Spiro joined them bringing a tray of raki glasses and chunks of baklava.

'We're trying to think up some island crime scene for Don's next book,' Sara said.

'I can think of one or two villains worth investigating round here,' Mel said. 'It's all here on Santaniki, if you know where to look.'

'Really?' Don was all ears.

'Take no notice of my wife. She knows nothing,' Spiro cut in. 'We are a crime-free island. Ask Aristides, the policeman—'

'Huh!' Mel snapped. 'That's what you think. Ask your mama, she doesn't wear horse blinkers and knows a thing or two worth hearing.'

Spiro turned away, throwing his arms in the air. 'Women, what do they know?'

Sara sensed Mel and Spiro had rowed again. There had been an atmosphere between them of late. She hoped all was well in the taverna family. 'I must get back. Thanks for a great dinner as usual,' she said, trying not to yawn.

Don rose. 'We will walk you back.'

'I'm quite safe.'

'No, Don's right,' Griff offered. 'There may be villains waiting...' How could she refuse?

'I'll settle up with Mel and catch you up,' Don said, winking at Sara. He was not going to play gooseberry. She and Griff walked down the hill in silence. The stars were out and the air was warm.

'I've never seen Don so serious,' Sara said with concern for her friend.

'Underneath all that bonhomie and bravado, he's a sensitive sort. The students adore him because he listens and gives time to them. I notice some tutors keep their writing students at a distance because they want privacy and time to work on their own project while staying here. Now tiredness has taken its toll.'

'I guess we all put our best face forward in public to hide our insecurity,' Sara added as they approached her gate.

'What have you to hide then?' Griff smiled. 'Some deadly secret worthy of a Don Ford novel?'

Sara stiffened. 'We all have stuff we'd rather not show

to the light of day, perhaps even you... Good night and thank Don again for a lovely supper.' With that she made a sharp exit.

Griff stood for a moment trying to work out what he had said that had upset her. Just as he felt her drawing close to him, she then pulled away. He had only made a joke remark but it had sent her scurrying off, taking flight from the suggestion she might have a secret herself. Blast the damn woman, what was wrong with her? Why did she seem to trust Don more than she trusted him?

30

'I really don't know why I bother!' Mel yelled at Spiro. 'You promised us a trip with the boys and now you're off with the lads to Chania. It's not fair!' There was a dance festival there and the troupe had promised to compete.

'You can come too,' he replied.

'And stand around watching all those doe-eyed girls giving you the glad eye? There's no fun in that for me.' She knew she was being unreasonable but who knew what they got up to behind their wives' backs?

'You can shop while we're on, or take the boys to the beach. It was you who persuaded me to rejoin the troupe and now every time we go off, you sulk,' Spiro snapped. 'You were keen enough to catch my eye all those years back on Chania harbour.'

'And look where it landed me... A skivvy tied to the kitchen sink while you swan off showing your moves.'

'You go out to book club, sing in the band. I'll stay, then, if it will shut you up. There's no pleasing you lately.'

'And have your friends think I wear the trousers? You go. I don't care.' Mel tossed her dark curls in a gesture of frustration.

'Don't care what?' Irini came down the stairs. 'What are you arguing about now? The whole square can hear your business.'

'Nothing, Mama. Spiro is just going to catch the ferry.'

'Then bring me the parcel of wool I ordered. You know the shop. It will be ready to collect. Don't forget,' Irini ordered as Spiro made for his taxi muttering curses into the air. 'What is it with you two? I don't like to hear you shouting.'

'I'm tired. Sara's parents came to visit and reminded me how long it is since I saw my family back in Sheffield.'

'We are your family now. You have sons to consider and my health too.'

Mel swallowed her reply. She was out of sorts and Spiro didn't understand how she felt threatened at times by his good looks, his prowess as a dancer. There was no use trying to explain how jaded and homespun she was feeling these days. Sara was always so coolly dressed, slim and full of ideas and energy. I was once like her, she sighed, but now I feel like a dogsbody. It didn't help seeing that awful Stavros smirking at her. Had he heard everything?

She nodded in his direction. 'Does that man have a wife? I've never seen one,' she asked.

Irini put down her cloth. 'No wife, not now... she left him and went back to the big island. He's a miserable bugger – his sons were at school with Spiro, such bullies.'

'So why does he come here then, tearing Griff's posters from walls and drinking? He looks so fierce and he puts the tourists off. I don't understand him when there are plenty of other *kafenions* to choose from.'

'Because I know who he is and his family. It's a small world. Stavros is one of a tribe that ruled the roost in the Apokoronas mountains of Crete. He has his reasons to live out here as an outcast.'

'From what?' Mel was curious. 'Tell me.'

'Not here, he can read my lips. He thinks he is threatening me. Come upstairs, I have something to show you.' Irini puffed up to the first floor to her living room with its walls full of sepia photographs and icons and her sofa covered in woven Cretan rugs. She pointed to one particular photograph. 'That is my grandmother, Irini Doulaki, taken before the war, a rare beauty. I am named after her. She lived with her family in the hills in the White Mountains on the big island. They were proud mountain people, fierce, warlike men who fought amongst themselves over any slight to their honour. My grandmother told me that when she was a little girl she had a special friend called Anastasia, a beautiful girl and a great wool spinner. A man named Petro Metrakis, who lived in the next village, wanted her for his bride but she loved a local boy called Manolis.

'One night, Metrakis came with his brothers and kidnapped her when she was out in the fields. Custom said she was now his bride. Manolis and his father with his brothers tracked them down to bring her home.' Irini wiped a tear from her eye. 'There was a fight with knives and guns, a terrible fight... In the morning Manolis and his family and my grandmother's dear friend lay dead, her body defiled, left on the rocks for the scavenging eagles. Such was the silence when the police came, no one dared speak for fear of retribution but vengeance was in the air.'

'That's terrible.' Mel was shocked at this story.

Irini continued, her voice choked with emotion as she wiped a tear from her eye. 'Such was the fear of the Metrakis brood, my own grandmother was sent to Rethymno on the coast, to the safety of cousins. That's where she met my grandfather, Spiro, who was a fisherman from Santaniki. They married and came here but my *yiayia* never forgot her friend and named her daughter, my mother, Anna, after her. At Anna's baptism back in her old village she heard that Papa Metrakis was found one night with his throat cut and all his brothers disappeared. Then the war came with terrible slaughter but it was rumoured that the Metrakis brothers were traitors and hanged in Chania prison but not before they had fathered sons of their own.

'Somehow, Stavros's father appeared here, bought land and olive groves, but news travelled from Crete and the Metrakis family were shunned. My grandmother made sure people knew who they were and what they had done. Vendettas are passed from generation to generation. He knows I know his history. That is why he keeps his eye on us.'

'Stavros wasn't even born then,' Mel interrupted.

'The fruit does not fall far from the tree. He's like all the others, a bad lot and a poor farmer, a bully and an outsider. Now you know, be careful. I don't trust him.'

Mel looked out the window to see him staring up at her with a lascivious grin. Irini was right. He was not to be trusted. The darker side of Irini's story was deep-seated. Mel hoped feuding and violence were things of the past but that look on Stavros's face showed they were not. Surely in this day and age there was enough bloodshed, terrorism and threats to peace, without petty slights of honour?

Sara said farewell to her parents at Chania airport. They'd had a great holiday and met all her new friends. Mel and Spiro entertained them and Sara and Griff took them round the island in Sara's old jeep. They were disappointed she would not be coming home for Christmas but understood this was her new life and business now. They were curious about Griff who she tried to explain was just a friend.

'He seems a nice chap. We'll forgive him that he'll not play cricket for Yorkshire,' Dad joked and gave her a knowing wink. Sara shook her head.

'None of that. I'm not in the market for anything more than friendships so don't be getting your best suit out of mothballs.' She was already thinking ahead about the Bartlett nuptials on St Nicholas's name day, 6 December. The community hall was to be decked with English-style decorations. Chloë wanted Mel to cater and planning lists were piling up on Sara's desk.

At least there were no local formalities this time. She shared lots of emails with Alexa to make sure it was her wishes, not Chloë's. Alexa was her mother's daughter, a well-organised woman. Olympia would be a flower girl so no bridesmaids to worry about. Felix, the groom, Griff's friend, was to wear a kilt and she wondered how Griff would react to that. This second time around wedding was much more relaxed and a pleasure to plan.

Alexa emailed, *I did all the white wedding stuff with my ex, Hugh. This time I want no fuss. Don't let Mummy bulldoze you into anything.* There was one request that puzzled Sara. *Could we have Ariadne's Christmas choir to sing in the church?*

It was Mel who explained that Ariadne Blunt had organised a group of expats into a carol singing choir. 'Not many of us left but I'll round up as many as I can and I'll ask Della to come over as well. There's Pippa and Duke, Griff... all the others are scattered abroad now and won't be back this side of Christmas.'

Before Sara could blink, it was time for the olive harvest. Soon they were all helping with the olive collection, all hands to the pump in Chloë's grove and the retreat; a seasonal marker that winter was on its way, such as winter was on a Mediterranean island. Time to focus on stripping fruit, the trek to the olive press and gallons of emerald green liquid to share around. Then came the annual ritual of harvest suppers in thanksgiving for a decent crop. It was a relief when all was safely gathered in. Sara loved being part of this annual event.

She tried to imagine herself back in Sheffield, on those cold wet windy days of November, stuck in an office, dashing to engagements. It was now a world away. Could she really be letting that safety net go? What if she couldn't make a decent living here?

Sara joined the Millars and a gang of helpers to collect drupes from the retreat. In return they were invited back into the house for a supper of moussaka, sausages and an enormous bowl of mixed shredded salad.

'Someone's been busy,' she joked to Griff, impressed by the effort he had made.

'The staff took pity on this bachelor and brought most of the dishes so I got off lightly.'

'Oh, a Jacobs join then?' she replied.

'A what?'

'It's when everyone brings a dish or two and they're piled on the table to make a feast. Some call it a faith supper... You have to have faith that there will be enough to share and there always is.'

Griff laughed, his eyes sparkling, and she felt a shiver of anticipation that this was going to be a memorable evening. She was one of the last to leave as Sparky would insist on sitting on her knee.

'Have a drink before you go,' he offered, pointing to his private sitting room.

'I shouldn't, you look done in. Perhaps just one. Do you think it will be a decent harvest this year?'

'One of the best. We'll have gallons of oil to share and you must have some too.' They sat in comfortable silence. She looked around the room with its faded grandeur. 'There's an atmosphere to this house, something special, as if...' She paused.

'So, you feel it too.' Griff edged closer. 'It's Elodie Durrante, I'm sure she haunts the place… in a nice way. Visitors comment on it. I think when someone has been happy in their home, something of their spirit lives on. I've been rereading her journal… the original, not the edited version. She describes her marriages and lovers. Poor woman was not as successful in her private life as she was in public. You must read them. I find it moving in parts, especially about the love of her life she lost. I guess we all have those episodes in the past.' Griff was very close now. 'The ones who got away but are never forgotten.'

Sara sensed he was waiting for a response. Oh, how she wished she could relax and sink back into his arms and let him kiss away all the turmoil and tension inside her, but she stiffened and sat up. 'I must go. It's late.'

'You could always stay,' he suggested, caressing her shoulder with his long fingers. 'There's no one else here.'

'No, sorry. I really must… things to do.' She felt him recoil at this reply.

'I don't understand you. I get the feeling you like my attentions and yet the minute I draw close, you shoot up like a frightened rabbit. Am I such a turn-off?'

'Not at all, Griff. It's just… I can't explain. There's a lot about me you don't know.'

'Then share with me…'

'I can't, don't push me. We're friends and I really enjoy your company. Let's leave it at that. I'm sorry.' Sara stood to leave. 'Thanks for a great supper but I have to go.'

She made for her jeep. Sparky was racing after her wanting to play. 'Back, Sparky. I don't want you run over.'

She was crying, tears of frustration and disappointment. *Why can't I let myself go? Why am I afraid to show my feelings? What the hell is wrong with me?*

December

31

Griff was making sure that the retreat was ready for wedding guests. They were going to use the guesthouse in the garden for a bridal suite. Felix and Alexa were staying on for Christmas before taking a honeymoon in the sun later.

Chloë, Simon and Sara were busy preparing for the big day and family and friends were arriving early to make the most of the recent warm weather, rumoured to last for the season. Griff had told his brother that Uncle Jolly would not be arriving until the New Year and they must find another Santa Claus.

Their Abba fundraising night would be after Christmas and there was still much to organise as well as presents, minutes and agendas for the retreat committee. He mustn't neglect his plans for next year's courses, must organise tutors and see to any more house repairs. The retreat, grand as it was, was a hungry beast and needed constant attention. Spiro and a gang of house repairers were only too happy to lend a hand as the market for building new holiday homes had dried up. It was rented properties that were in demand now.

Sara was very focused on this coming wedding; in fact, she was distant at times with a tense look on her brow. What was it that made her blow hot and cold with him? She was part of his everyday life, supporting his campaign, taking notes at meetings, volunteering to help with fundraising. Perhaps he was taking her for granted. She had her own business to run but she knew that without a decent slug of cash their new charity would be a nonstarter.

Felix's family arrived full of excitement and bearing gifts. Then business friends and wives and lastly the groom's cousin, Flissa, appeared with her new man from London. Griff was surprised this affair had lasted so long as Jace was not her usual type; muscle ripped with the thick neck of a weightlifter, making Griff feel puny and unfit.

'You met Jace in London. He's wondering if it's warm enough to swim.' Flissa looked towards the garden pool. 'Hmm… not a bad place. Stuck on that plane for four hours and then a choppy ride over here, we need to work out.'

'Sorry, pool's closed and cleaned out now. You can stretch your legs uphill though,' Griff offered but could see Flissa was unimpressed. Her eyes turned towards the house.

'You've landed yourself in some pile. That old girl in the hallway must have been loaded, building this in the middle of nowhere. Don't you think she looks like Agatha Christie? Come on, Jace, let's get changed and make the most of this gorgeous weather.' Flissa grabbed his arm. 'Let's find our room. I hope you've given us a sea view.'

How had he ever fancied that silly creature, all elbows and skinny thighs? Griff thought she couldn't hold a candle to Sara who was willowy but somehow rounded and complete.

Soon the house was filled with excited guests. He was hosting drinks and a supper supplied by Mel from his kitchen where the staff were busy preparing a vat of pork in wine and lemon sauce. Everything was laid out in the dining room and on the veranda. Elodie's home looked every bit the country house. The lamps were lit as darkness fell and Sara was coming in later to check on last-minute details.

Seeing the buzz around the rooms made Griff realise they were wasting a third of the season, closing up for winter. There could be opportunities to use the house for longer writing retreats off season; a sort of hermitage for writers and artists to find the silence and isolation needed to finish off projects or to prepare for new ones. Flights were possible, ferries did run and some artists would pay for the privacy to work in comfort. He was looking forward to Don's return for Christmas.

Sara arrived in the kitchen in her usual business wear: black trousers, white blouse, her hair scraped into a net for hygiene purposes.

'Come and meet the guests,' he ordered but she hung back.

'I'm not dressed for the dining room and Mel needs me here.'

'No, I don't,' said Mel. 'Get in there and introduce yourself.'

Sara gave Mel a thunderous look and followed Griff with reluctance. She wasn't usually so nervous round guests so he shoved a glass of fizz in her hand. 'Get that down you. This is Sara, our wedding organiser and she'll be doing sterling service with Chloë over the next few days.'

Sara smiled as she mingled and then froze suddenly, fleeing the room, pushing Griff aside as her glass crashed onto the floor.

It couldn't be… not him. She must be dreaming. But there was no mistaking his height and dark looks as he stood sipping champagne. It was him. She ran back into the kitchen. Mel caught her look of panic.

'I've got to go. I can't breathe. I'm not going back in there.' Her pulse was racing so fast she thought she was going to faint.

'Sit down. Fetch her some water,' Mel said, guiding her to a chair. 'Has someone upset you?'

'Sorry, I have to get some air,' she snapped. 'Please, let me go…'

'You're not making any sense, Sara. Calm down. This is your big break. You can't just walk out on everyone. I don't understand you.'

'How could you… you don't know the half of it. I'm off… I just can't stay here,' Sara replied just as Griff came through the door.

'Sara, you're wanted—'

'Sorry,' she called out, pushing a chair between them. 'I'm leaving.' She fled into the olive garden with Sparky chasing after her. 'Go away!' she yelled but the dog followed her to a bench, sitting in front of her and resting his nose on her thighs to comfort her. She stroked him as the tears flowed.

'Oh, Sparky, what a mess I'm making... Of all the islands in all the world, he had to turn up here. I hope he didn't recognise me.'

'Who didn't recognise you?' Mel was standing right behind her. 'Who are you afraid of in there?'

'It's none of your business...'

'But it is my business to see you running out on the job in tears. We worked hard to get this wedding. I don't want to see you throw it away. It's time you came clean. I guessed ages ago that you didn't come to Santaniki for a holiday, did you? Were you running away?' Mel held out a hanky.

Sara wiped her eyes. 'It's a long story...'

'We've got all night... the party is in full swing and the food is on the table. I'm not budging until I know what's eating you.' Then she produced a bottle of Cretan red and two glasses. 'Get that down you. You looked as if you'd seen a ghost.'

'Right on the nail, Mel; a ghost from my past standing there as bold as brass.' Sara gulped down a glass in one. 'The man I was going to marry, the man I lived with for two years who I thought loved me.'

Mel grabbed her hand. 'Do I hear a "but" coming? What went wrong. Who is he?'

'I can't bear to say his name. Let's just say he was a businessman from a local family firm who travelled all over the world for them, a man who likes all the trappings of success. Don't ask me how I caught his eye at a conference we were hosting but he swept me off my feet, charmed my parents: the white knight on a charger lifting me out of my flat on the Totley Road into his amazing apartment. I moved in, we got engaged and what a celebration that was. My diamond engagement ring was like a knuckleduster. We set a date and he left all the planning to me. There was no budget. I was to have whatever I wanted to make our day fantastic. Who would not want a dream wedding and I was in my element. Nothing was too much trouble. I put such love into the preparations, the designer dress, the hotel venue. We chose a register office, the big one in the city. He was abroad in the USA, flying back the day before our wedding, leaving it late as usual.'

Sara paused for another glass of wine.

'And then? This sounds like the plot of a movie,' Mel said, trying not to interrupt the flow.

'The night before our wedding day, I took my parents and friends out to the best Italian restaurant. It was then the phone rang. It was from Baltimore and I thought it was from him. It went dead on me... Then it rang later just as we were leaving. There was this text. "Do you really want to marry this guy?" That was all but there was an attachment... a video.'

Sara paused to take another slug of wine. 'It has played over and over in my mind ever since. He was with a woman in bed, laughing. Someone was recording them like a porn movie. I thought it was a joke but it was his bare body thrashing about. It was then he laughed and said, "I wish my girl could screw like you. You could give her some lessons." The bitch posted this to me on the eve of my wedding. I sat in the taxi trying not to believe what I had just seen.'

'I hoped you wiped it,' Mel whispered.

'I couldn't.'

'So, he ditched you like that?'

'I wish he had but no, he flew back as if nothing had happened. He had no idea, I guess, what she had done.'

'But the wedding was off?'

Sara paused again. 'I didn't want to let my parents down. I didn't know what to do.'

'You went ahead and married the bastard?'

'Not exactly... I meant to, of course, but it was too easy...'

'What happened next?' Mel asked, gulping down her wine. 'If Spiro had done that...'

'There are other ways to pay back.' Sara felt herself going cold. 'The wedding day went ahead as if nothing had happened. I did all the beauty stuff, hair, make-up, dressed myself in my oyster silk designer dress, carried my bouquet with my father and arrived at the register office. I walked down the aisle as if in a daze, as if I was floating outside my body, watching myself go through the motions. There he was in his morning suit, all smiles and charm, but when the registrar asked if there was any reason why we should not be married, I knew I must say "YES" very loudly. I pulled out my iPad from behind my bouquet and lifted it up, saying, "I think the groom might recognise this," showing those closest all the gory details. I've never seen anyone go so white and then red, or disappear so fast. I've never seen him since... until tonight. The look on my poor dad's face was one I'll never forget. No one knew where to put themselves. I had my revenge, Mel, but it didn't sit easy once my fury died away, but now...'

'You did what you had to do. I'd have taken out a gun and shot him. I hope you kept the knuckleduster ring,' Mel asked.

'What do you think funded coming here?'

'Good for you. I gather he's come with Felix's cousin, Flissa.'

'I wish her luck with him. As you guessed, instead of three weeks in the Maldives, I came here on a whim – stuck a pin into the Greek islands and Santaniki it was. There, you have the sad ballad of Sara Loveday's disastrous wedding.'

'I think you were very brave and resourceful but why on earth run a wedding business?'

'Because I want others to have what I did not get. I want to make it right somehow.'

'Then powder your nose, pin on a smile and be the great professional you are. Ignore the man. Give him no quarter.'

'But there's unfinished business between us.'

'Alexa's wedding is not the place to do it. It's her dream wedding second time around. I can cover for you up front if you need me. Who else knows… Griff?' Mel looked concerned.

'No one else knows except you – and Sally – and I'd prefer it that way for the moment. You can tell Spiro, if it helps.'

'Ah, so you've noticed too. We've been getting on each other's nerves. I get jealous, silly really, but the girls do go for him, but nothing like you've been through.'

Sara sat back. 'Thanks for listening. Better out than in, as they say, but I was so shocked to see him.'

Mel smiled. 'Have another glass. Can you tell me his name now?'

'Jason Mason Metcalfe… Jace to his friends. He doesn't like Jason. He says he sounds like a footballer. He's such a snob.' Sara found herself relaxing. In sharing her story something had shifted inside her. *You survived and made this new life for yourself. With friends like Mel on your side, anything is possible.*

'What the hell is going on?' Griff cornered Mel.

'Sorry, I must see to the clearing up.' Mel made her excuse. It was not up to her to put him in the picture.

Griff returned to his guests, confused by Sara's exit. It was Flissa who took him by the arm, leading him into a quiet corner. 'So that's the little minx who led poor Jace a merry dance, and her a wedding planner... what a joke!'

'What are you talking about? Sara is very efficient and professional.'

'You could have fooled me; no wonder she did a bunk when she saw him.' Flissa smirked, her thin lips in a tight line as if she was enjoying this revelation.

'I don't get this.' He was really confused now. 'What's she done to offend you?'

'Not me, poor Jace over there. You should watch out for her. Did you know she ditched him at the altar on their wedding day? She was off her head, accusing him of horrid lies. I hope I'm not speaking out of turn...' She paused, knowing she was doing just that.

You're relishing all this, Griff thought, but said nothing. His ex was determined to put him in the picture.

'I wouldn't want her to lead you up the garden path by that butter-wouldn't-melt-in-her-mouth look. I know I let you down at a difficult time but I'm still very fond of you.

I'd hate to see you hurt again the way I hurt you. Darling, you deserve better.' She touched his arm and kissed him on the cheek, her familiar perfume reminding him of their intimate moments. Jace marched over.

'What's this? I can't leave you for five minutes and you're on the prowl.' Flissa winked at Griff as she took Jace's arm. 'Think about it,' she whispered, leaving her host reeling from her warning. He shook his head in disbelief – surely not. After all this time Sara had said nothing. Come to think about it, she was very coy about her past, guarded even, and reluctant to let herself go with him. So that was the score. It was hard to believe she would do such a cruel thing on her wedding day. Suddenly, he felt as if he didn't know the woman at all.

Sara paced up and down the olive garden in the moonlight. She couldn't sleep, feeling sick and foolish to have fled from the party but Mel assured her she had no reason to feel ashamed. It wasn't she who'd betrayed their trust. He had let her down and she had reacted on the spur of the moment. It wasn't too late to compose herself and explain to Griff the reason she'd deserted the scene but that could wait. Her first priority now was to her clients.

Tomorrow was Chloë and Simon's special pre-wedding dinner and there was plenty there to keep her out of sight of the guests. Seeing Jace posing in that room with his new girlfriend, so much more elegant and glamorous than she was, reinforced her lack of confidence. Was she here under false pretences? She was no Shelley Dorney with her exotic clients but a mere amateur, an events planner, and yet there was more to her than that. Mel believed in her, as had Sandra and Pippa. Time to retire and sleep off her hangover.

There was a ping next morning on her phone. Mel was texting her: *RUOK? Let's go for a swim early doors.* How can I slope off when there's so much to do? she thought, but an early morning swim in cool water would wake her up and help her do her best to make the Bartlett celebrations a night to remember.

'It's not about you,' she said aloud. *All things pass, so will this*, and she found herself repeating that mantra. *You don't have to explain yourself to anyone, just get on with the day ahead and give Alexa, Felix and their families a wonderful evening.* There would be time to mull over things later.

After a leisurely swim with Mel, Sara felt she could face the day.

'Did you tell Griff why I was upset?' she asked her friend.

'No, it's not up to me. All he knows was you disappeared for no reason and I was too busy covering for you,' Mel replied. 'That Flissa woman, his ex, was all over him like a rash and your Jace was none too pleased. I think he's met his match with her, she's a piece of work.'

'A glamorous piece of work...' Sara replied, reminding herself of the slim, expensively dressed woman who would appeal to Jace's vanity.

'All legs but no tits, as my brother would say,' Mel laughed.

'Mel, wash your mouth out!' Sara chuckled.

'Good, keep that smile going, pin it tight and you'll get through today. We don't want to spoil Chloë's big do and it's going to be fantastic. Smile, ignore those two, be the pro

I know you are... *Smile when your heart is breaking*,' Mel burst into song,

'How do you stay so calm and cheerful?' Sara pushed Mel on to the sand in jest.

'Years of living with Irini have taught me some survival skills,' Mel replied, wrapping a towel round herself. 'Now, we deserve a full English breakfast. Who knows when we'll get a chance to eat again?'

Griff woke early and went for a run with Sparky, having drunk more than was good for his head last night. Helping clear up and prepare for breakfasts with Mel's staff, it was nearly dawn before he got to bed. Flissa's warning kept ringing in his brain. Had he got Sara Loveday all wrong? No wonder she blew hot and cold with him. It all made sense. She had escaped to St Nick's to start over where no one knew her sordid secret but now she was found out. All that interest in his charity, the retreat, waiting at Mel's place, was it all for show? Was she the devious little minx Flissa was suggesting? Perhaps he'd had a lucky escape because he misjudged her completely and yet... Sparky loved her and dogs never lie. Mel had befriended her and she was no pushover. How many times had he heard his mother say, 'Darling, judge someone by their friends.' It was all so confusing and he had a best man speech to perfect for the big day and a kilt to try on with all its trimmings and a bit of a stag do to organise after Chloë and Simon's dinner...

He had thought about taking the men on the ferry to Chania but it wasn't practical. Why not wild camping out in the hills with a campfire; a boys' own beer fest? They could watch the dawn with the glorious winter sun rising from the water. It was still so warm so that none of them could believe it was not summer but nights got cold. They would need blankets and sleeping bags. He had plenty of those in the retreat. At least he could keep out of Sara's way. He didn't want thoughts of her spoiling the fun. He would invite Duke and Spiro to join his merry band for a great night's jaunt, Bear Grylls style.

32

As she parked the jeep, Sara looked up at Chloë's stone house, imagining it shimmering by torchlight. There was a huge wedding wreath on the door and swags of winter greenery lining the steps to the entrance. Everything was ready for the evening's celebrations; the chimney in the outdoor fireplace was stacked ready with olive wood. It was a stroke of Mel's genius to suggest they recycle tins by filling them with dried scented herbs and little candles, covering the tables with Cretan tablecloths in scarlet, black and gold. The olive and lemon trees surrounding the patio would be full of lanterns. Light, heat and colour were important on a cool winter's night.

Chloë and Alexa found vine leaves on which each of their guests' names was handwritten in gold lettering and clipped to napkins and place settings. They made Christmassy bunting to hang around the outside that Chloë hoped she would sew into a quilt on winter nights.

Sara was envious, knowing the lengths that she'd taken to

make her own wedding reception in the hotel special. Once the news of the disaster in the wedding venue reached the hotel, tables were quickly emptied by the staff. The wedding guests disappeared into pubs and Sara returned home with her parents. These sad thoughts were interrupted by the sound of wailing as Alexa brought in Olympia in the middle of a tantrum.

'She won't wear the dress I had made for her and keeps shouting "scratchy… scratchy".'

Chloë took a closer look. 'No wonder, the underskirt is like wire netting. Who made this?' She examined the back for a label.

Alexa confessed, 'I got a friend to knock it up from an old ballgown of mine.'

'She's not going to put this on tomorrow, is she? Let me rip it out. Honestly, Alexa, couldn't you have taken her to a decent bridal shop? Poor little mite.' Mother and daughter glared at each other. Sara left them arguing. Wedding nerves were on display so she crept out of the room, only to see Jace and Flissa climbing the garden stairs. There was just time to dart into the dining room to hide. They were the last people she wanted to meet.

Simon was sitting in a corner mulling over his iPad for news. 'You are escaping too?' He smiled over his specs. 'It's bedlam in the kitchen and Olympia's screaming blue murder. I'm afraid I'm keeping out of the way. I do hope it will be okay. Chloë has put her heart and soul into this evening.'

'And it shows, tonight will be special and the meal will be delicious with lots of courses. The taverna team will do her proud, so don't worry.'

'Have you heard the latest? The boys are going camping overnight into the hills for a sort of stag do. Griff's organised it.'

It was the first Sara had heard of the plan. 'Is that wise? You never know what can happen. I recall one event in Sheffield when a coachload of guests decided to hit the bright lights of London for the stag night. Forty chaps went out... only three came back the next morning for a wedding at three o'clock. They'd gone into Soho and the rest you can imagine...' she said, recalling the mayhem that followed.

'The groom?'

'Dragged almost unconscious onto the coach by the best man and a mate, thank goodness.'

'Ah, the perils of demon drink,' Simon laughed. 'I'm certain Griff will make sure they are back first thing. If not, we'll send a posse out to fetch them. He's a sensible man. They invited me to go but I'd rather sleep in my own bed than on a damp outcrop of rock.'

Sara was relieved that this meant Griff wouldn't linger after the dinner and she would be busy clearing up in the kitchen. It would be all hands to the pump to make sure everything was ready for Alexa's big day.

By the evening, the party was in full swing. Alexa was wearing a slinky purple velvet sheath, Chloë in a black evening dress. The expats and neighbours of the village were all dolled up to the nines in party gear and Olympia was running around in a pink tutu with sparkling tights. The lanterns flickered and Pippa whispered in her ear, 'Don't you think women over forty look wonderful by candlelight?'

Sara had to agree. 'It adds mystery and allure to our

faces but you still have a year or more before you hit that milestone. I have only a few months to go,' she replied, nudging her. 'Can't say I'm looking forward to it. The weather's being so kind to us tonight, when you think of poor Dorrie's do.'

'She's here in full warpaint. I'm glad she's got over the… er, better not say,' she whispered as Dorrie approached in a silvery brocade trouser suit.

'You've hit the mark once again, Sara. Though it was a pity no one turned up for the St Nicholas Eve service at St Paul's, or at the chapel on the rock. It is such a special day for the Greeks. We should honour St Nicholas too, not reduce him to Santa Claus.'

'I know Irini and her friend went to church. I'm afraid most of us were very busy here but thank you for reminding us of the omission,' Sara retorted. 'That woman!'

'Shush, she'll hear you,' Pippa warned, seeing Dorrie within ear shot.

'Let her, I don't care. You'd think after I did her a favour…'

'Dorrie can't help seeing herself as the guardian of our moral conduct. She still looks down on Duke and me and can't bring herself to call Harmony anything other than "Baby", bless her. She'll be as jealous as hell of Chloë's success.'

'Who's babysitting for you tonight?' Sara asked.

'She's down at the tavern with Irini. I'll not be staying too long.'

'No rest for the wicked. I'd better see what's happening in the kitchen.'

'Want a hand?'

'No thanks, you're a guest so find that handsome husband of yours and get the music going.'

Griff took the men up towards the caves. He'd found head torches for everyone but the path was steep to where they laid a firepit out of stones and rocks like the shepherds made in the hills. It was a fitting end to a great evening. Everyone was full of delicious dinner and wine. Simon had made a brief speech and welcomed everyone. The girls dressed up for the occasion. He looked for Sara but she was keeping out of the way, no doubt ashamed. What a hypocrite she was planning weddings when… He didn't want to think about her. Spiro and Duke joined the gang, plus a new Dutch couple, Wim and Dirk, friends of local residents who were on a cruise. They had helped him prepare the camp in advance.

Felix was on form, leading them in a chorus of dubious rugby chants. Any sheep or goats fled at the strange cacophony of noise echoing around the rock. They'd brought midnight snacks in rucksacks with blankets and jackets from the reserves in the retreat. When it grew chilly, they roasted village sausages and souvlaki sticks over the fire like boy scouts. There was a case of Mythos beer chilling in the caves. Spiro brought a guitar and began to sing some ancient local songs. Everyone sat around chatting under a canopy of stars. 'Here's to the bride and groom, *chronia polla*, many years,' he toasted and they clinked mugs. Spiro joined Griff to light up a cigarette. 'Who wants one?'

'Thanks, no, if I have one, I'll want the packet,' Griff confessed. 'What a fine night for December,' he added.

'Ah, the snow will come then and the storms. Two years ago, there was a family living here,' Spiro said, pointing into the cave.

'Yes, Mel told me… Where are they now?'

'On the mainland. That was quite a winter but tomorrow will be fine. We will dance for the couple and you will all join us. In Greece, the man dances and the women watch. We dance like peacocks showing who is the strongest and most virile. You Brits dance like penguins. How can you take a woman like Sara in your arms and just shuffle around in circles? I know you like her.'

Griff needed to put Spiro straight. 'That's her ex-fiancé over there, the muscleman, Jace,' he whispered. 'She dumped him on their wedding day; a woman like that is not to be trusted.'

'Is that so? Who told you that?' Spiro said, staring across at the man in question.

'Felix's cousin, she warned me.'

'The one who eats you with her eyes. I wonder why?'

'Is it not true then?' Griff felt confused.

'Oh yes, Melodia told me a little but it was not as you were told.'

Griff sat up. 'What happened then?'

'It is not for me to repeat but do not trust that man.' Spiro pointed to Jace who looked up, seeing them staring at him.

'What's up, mate?'

'*Tipota*... nothing, just telling my friend how you screwed up your wedding. You tell Kyria Felicia another story, I think.'

Jace shot up at this insult. 'Now you listen here... you don't know the half of it...'

'You forget, my friend, my wife knows everything.'

Jace rushed forward. 'She's a liar then.'

'You call my wife a liar... You are the liar.' Spiro jumped up, punching Jace in the jaw, knocking him back. Griff then sprung up between them, caught in the crossfire as Jace was launching a fist towards Spiro but not before Griff landed a blow to Jace's nose. There was a crack as bone hit bone. Felix was on his feet, ready to enter into the fray.

'You broke my bloody nose, you maniac.' Jace lashed out to fell Griff. Felix pounced but Wim and Dirk held him back. 'Think, what Alexa will say if you turn up with half a face?'

Duke stood up. 'Cool it... This is supposed to be a fun night, not a punch-up.'

Felix brushed his jacket. 'If my cousin has spread a lie, it is because she was told one, matey. She must have believed what you said to be the truth. I won't hear another word said against her.'

Jace was holding his nose but got no sympathy from the onlookers. He was going to have a shiner in the morning but he was stuck on the rocky outcrop knowing it was too dark for him to retreat down the track alone.

Griff gathered himself. 'I'm sorry, Felix. Let no one say a word about this in the morning. We don't want anything to spoil Alexa's day.'

The fight had silenced everyone. They retired into their sleeping bags but a wild and chilly wind brought them, one by one, into the shelter of the cave. The evening had turned sour. Griff couldn't sleep. His ribs were aching and his head spinning. This had not been a good idea and he was confused. What had happened between this man and Sara? Who was telling the truth?

'I don't know what happened last night but I hear Griff's got a black eye and Jace's nose is facing sideways. Spiro is not saying a word,' Mel said as they were finishing off decorating the community hall. 'Flissa's fella had to see Dr Makaris to put it straight. Stag nights usually end up in a ruck,' she laughed. 'Felix was down first thing to the pharmacy for arnica. No one will say what the punch-up was about.'

Sara was too busy decorating the tables to show much interest. They had a red, white and green theme to the tables, with red gingham tablecloths, jars full of red carnations with sprays of silvered twigs, swags of green foliage from pine trees, scenting the room better than any spray, candles in pretty red holders that would flicker in the dark. The stage was lined with pot plants ready for the band and the dancers, sound systems checked, heating ready if it got cold.

Alexa wanted Cretan rugs as wall hangings as it was the very saint's day of the island and pictures of St Nicholas lined the window ledges. It ended up as a sort of mixture of Greek and English themes but very colourful. She had chosen a melange of hot dishes, warm fresh tomato soup with basil, roast lamb chops with mint and rosemary, vegetarian risotto with pine nuts and sultanas and spices, bowls of fruit, cheeses and a traditional English wedding cake iced with holly leaves and berries.

Their blessing service was a private affair with just close family and friends who filled the little church. Olympia was the flower girl in her frilly dress with no scratchy lining.

Sara kept her head down, avoiding any of the ceremonial, feeling a bit like the hired help, knowing that was her place to stay in the background until required. She took pictures of Alexa in her beautiful red velvet cloak shimmering in the sunlight over a simple gold silk shift. The bride carried stems of white lilies, her hair caught up in a ripple of curls. Chloë stood behind her in an ankle-length dress of emerald green slub satin and for a moment Sara felt a stab of envy.

Why did men in kilts look so distinguished, so masculine and handsome? she thought, as she watched from a safe distance. Griff was no exception in his black velvet jacket.

Perhaps this was as good as she could hope for here. Was it time she returned to the UK and put into practice all she had learned? Not in Sheffield or Yorkshire but in pastures new? Somewhere in a county town where she could work online and find wonderful venues for local weddings.

St Nick's had been her healing place with a chance to develop new skills and an understanding that each generation needed to marry in its own unique style.

She thought of the wonderful Cretan wedding of the doctor's son and new wife now starting out together in their twenties; Pippa and Duke wanting a different day to celebrate their union; Sandra and Jack, second time around, celebrating with their family, as were Alexa and Felix. She had helped them all fulfil their dreams. Money wasn't everything in making a wedding day special. Poor Daniel and Soraya, so mismatched, who found that out too late, and lastly her own ghastly wedding fiasco. She had so much experience to offer clients now.

She loved living here, making new friends and experiencing all the four seasons on this magical island with its distinctive culture. Was a chapter of her life really coming to an end? The thought of going back home with her tail between her legs like Sparky when he got told off held no joy. Sara felt her spirits plummeting into a deep gloom and it wouldn't do. People were depending on her to be in control, smile and welcome guests and make the evening festivities go with a bang.

'You've been standing over that vase in a trance... cheer up, missus.' Mel smacked her on the bum. 'Penny for them... we'd better crack on. The bride and groom are on their way.'

33

Griff sat in the church clutching the rings. He was feeling self-conscious about his black eye and being the butt of jokes and winks. Ariadne's depleted choir sang their favourite carol 'Love Came Down at Christmas'. It was all rather magical and Sally the vicar gave everyone a warm welcome.

Jace didn't show at the service with Flissa. He was nursing his wounded pride out of sight somewhere down by the harbour, by all accounts. Flissa caught Griff's arm coming out of the church. 'What happened last night? Jace is furious. Felix was being very coy… something to do with that Sara.'

'I think your beau owes you an apology.'

'For what?' She looked puzzled.

'Let's put it this way: he's been economical with the truth about the wedding that never was. There's more to it than his version of events. Let's leave it at that but I don't think he's one of life's keepers, Fliss.' Griff didn't want to discuss the matter further but Flissa was insistent.

'Now you've got me worried. Sorry if I got things wrong but Jace was very cut up seeing her here.' She paused, her cheeks flushed, gabbling on trying to gain his interest. 'You did right to begin a new life after the Bannerman affair and I was no help, was I?'

'You can do better than Metcalfe.' Griff felt some pity for her.

'I did but I let him go, didn't I?' She gave him one of her puppy looks but Griff was immune to her obvious flirting.

'That's past history. If I've learned anything here, it's that you can find new challenges, forgive yourself for past failures and move on. It's not impossible. Don't waste time looking for love that doesn't last. Remember you're only as rich as your friends. When the chips were down for me, I found out just who they were and you weren't one of them.' He knew he was hurting her with this comment but he wanted no misunderstandings. 'I've been rereading Elodie's memoir. She had relationships sussed. Trust your instincts even if they let you down now and then. But I must go...' Griff made to escape.

'We can still be friends.' Flissa held out her hand.

'Of course, must dash,' he replied. Poor Flissa would learn the hard way that tanned muscle and good looks were only skin deep. She had abandoned Griff in his darkest hour when his confidence was at rock bottom and now he was confused himself, misjudging Sara's own tragic experience with Jace as being all her fault. They were two of a kind, both had suffered humiliation but had found fresh starts here on Santaniki.

Sara was orchestrating these great wedding events and he was creating fresh impetus to the retreat. He hoped Elodie was looking down on his effort with approval. He had found her jottings inspirational, honest and revealing. She had got her priorities right, ditching her two husbands to live her own life. He would have loved to have met her in person but she was there on the page and her words would live on.

There was just time to nip back home to check on tonight's guest accommodation, sheets and towels changed, bathrooms cleaned, give Sparky his dinner, and bathe his swollen eye. Then he remembered he was best man and his speech was still on his bedside table. He would need to push on or Felix would be panicking that he had done a bunk.

As he reached the drive, Katya and the cleaners were finishing off. 'Where's Sparky?' he asked while the girls smiled at their boss in a skirt.

'Out in the bushes, somewhere in the garden.'

'Spartacus!' he yelled, but the disobedient little mutt didn't come to greet him. There was no time to fuss over him. When he was hungry, he would find his bowl. Griff grabbed his speech and ran down the hill to the *plateia* where everyone was lingering over drinks while the photographer was posing guests in groups.

'Where've you been?' Felix rushed to his side.

'I forgot my speech.'

'No time for that, we need some location shots and you are included.'

Griff was soon swallowed up in the crowd, ushered towards the statutory beach scenario. The locals stared at the men in tartan as their pleats swirled behind them. His own grandmother was a McFarlane so he could wear the tartan with pride. Griff was glad his calves were strong enough to look good in traditional socks.

There was a procession of guests and onlookers as they walked up the hill to the hall by the square. The reception party greeted the bride and groom with cheers, the tables looked bright and his speech went down well enough. Spiro translated to some of the Greek guests but he was relieved when it was all over and he could relax.

Simon's father of the bride speech was brilliant and Alexa got up to put her side of the story. Griff kept a lookout for Sara but she had disappeared into the kitchen with Mel, and he sensed she was avoiding him.

The bride and groom did the customary first dance, unrehearsed and relaxed as the floor filled with guests until Spiro's troupe burst into the space and displayed their moves. Then they got everyone up to link up and try some simple steps to 'Zorba's Dance'. Olympia had fallen asleep on Chloë's knee and still Sara made no appearance. He knew she would be somewhere and he was desperate to explain.

'Time the boys went home, *Yiayia*. Look, they're snaffling sugared almonds off the tables. They'll be sick,' said Mel as she grabbed them both. She needed eyes in the back of her head when those two were getting into mischief. The food was going down well and Spiro's group had got guests onto the floor. Sara was still hiding in the back thinking everyone now knew her secret but that wasn't so.

She and Spiro had talked long into the night about her sad story and how Jason betrayed her. It was good to feel closer to her husband once more when he told her how he had defended her honour. She was relieved there were no knives or guns involved.

Once the boys were dragged away, she began to clear away dishes while the men were dancing when Flissa leaned over and pointed to Spiro. 'Who is that? I'd like to take him home with me. He's sex on legs,' she whispered.

Mel bent over with a gravy boat hovering ever closer to Flissa's scarlet lacy dress and cleavage. 'If you do, lady, I will have to kill you. That's my husband.' The look on Flissa's face was a treat. 'I should look a bit closer to home, if I were you,' she continued. 'Your partner has a roving eye. Or has he not told you about his conquests in Baltimore? You should see the video…'

'What are you talking about?' Flissa replied.

'Nothing, I thought you knew…'

'About what?' Flissa flashed a venomous glare in Mel's direction as she walked away smiling. That should set the cat among the pigeons.

It was late and the Cretan musicians played on until the small hours. Griff escorted some of the oldies back to the retreat. The music rang out across St Nick's. It was time to escort the bride and groom to the guesthouse for the night, lovingly decorated in their honour with rose petals and favours on the bed, candles lit. Horns hooted, guns rattled. No one would be getting any sleep that night.

It had been a fabulous day. When Griff finally staggered back into the retreat kitchen, he saw that Sparky's bowl was still untouched. 'Sparky!' he yelled into the garden but his dog didn't greet him. Perhaps he had hidden from the gunshots. Griff was too tired to explore further, assuming that in the morning Sparky would be at the door waiting.

Sara slept in, exhausted from all the backroom preparations that had made Alexa's wedding such a success. Chloë presented her with a huge bouquet of flowers and a bottle of champagne as a thank you. It was all too hectic to worry about Griff and Flissa or Jace. She caught a glimpse of him with his black eye and had to laugh. At least Felix had arrived unscathed from the stag night punch-up.

Bits of the fracas were leaked among the kitchen staff and Jace was somewhere in the centre of it with his broken nose. Flissa wasn't telling anyone why he didn't show up at the wedding or reception. Trust him to bunk off like he did with her. For all his muscle he was a spineless coward. How had she ever thought he was the man for her?

The guests were out on a tour of the island while the newlyweds slept on. Both sets of parents had clubbed together to give them a week on the famous luxury ship *Hebridean Princess*, touring round the Scottish islands so Felix could touch base with his ancestral home on Skye, seat of Clan MacLeod.

Olympia would have 'Gampy and Ganima' all to herself. No one was budging until after Christmas and Sara had no plans since there was the SPARKY fundraiser to organise.

Posters and invites had gone out, asking for fancy dress materials. They had the post-Christmas lull to recuperate and prepare for the event. She hoped people would be enthused and ready to party. Part of her wanted to back out, feeling awkward around Griff.

When she roused herself out of a stupor of self-doubt and made for the minimarket, she was met by Pippa with Harmony strapped to her chest.

'Have you heard? Spartacus is missing. No one has seen him in the town or around the square. He doesn't stray far as a rule. Griff is distraught in case he's been poisoned, though there's not been any incidents of late. He's out searching with Duke. I do hope the little dog is okay.'

'He's tough and streetwise,' Sara said but worried all the same. Sparky was their poster boy. The children in school had watched the vet showing them how to examine a dog for mange and fleas. 'He'll turn up. There may be a bitch on heat… Oops, he's no longer entire, is he?'

'He may be trapped somewhere out by the rocks.' Pippa waved goodbye and headed uphill.

Sara wanted to help look, knowing how much Sparky meant to Griff and to their campaign. It was not like him to wander far from his master. Perhaps Mel might know more.

In the taverna, Irini was knitting furiously like Madame Defarge and smiling for once. 'It was a good night for everyone. My son was a star.'

Mel was at work in the kitchen stirring the beans with

Katya, business as usual for them. Spiro was out taxiing guests around the coast and the villages at the other end of the island.

'Sparky is missing,' Mel greeted her.

'I know. No one seems to know exactly when he disappeared. I guess while we were all at the wedding.'

'Dogs vanish, they have a will of their own,' Irini contributed, not looking up from her needles.

'He's no ordinary dog,' Mel shouted back. 'He's special, rescued, restored back to health and Griff's companion and our poster boy.'

'Poof! You English make such a fuss of them. Pets are for children.' Irini had spoken but Mel was having none of it.

'You saw the pictures of him, unrecognisable, barely alive and ill-treated by someone.'

'He reminds me of Maria's little pooch. She was very fond of him.'

'Maria who? Perhaps he's gone back to her.'

'I doubt it, she left years ago. Poor Maria, such a martyr...' Irini sighed, shaking her head.

'But which Maria? There are many Marias in this town.'

'Maria Metrakis, Stavros's wife... the one who got away.'

'Didn't Sparky come from that area?' Sara asked. Mel put down her cloth and they both gathered round Irini to question her.

'It's not him... I never saw it again after she left. Perhaps she took it with her. Stavros would have shot it a long time ago.'

'That's the same man who tore down our posters, the one who sits on the square twiddling his beads, dressed like a tramp?' Sara said. 'Do you think Sparky isn't lost but taken?'

'Whatever for, a useless dog to be fed and watered?' Irini carried on counting her stitches.

Mel looked at Sara and rolled her eyes in exasperation. 'Shouldn't we tell Griff? Why didn't you mention this before? You've seen Griff's dog plenty of times under the table in the taverna.'

'As I said, Melodia, all little dogs look alike to me. If you venture up there, take Aristides, the policeman. Stavros and his boys will not be challenged on their own property and you must find proof before you go making accusations against the Metrakis clan. I will pray to St Phanourios.'

'Why would he take little Sparky? It doesn't make sense,' Sara said.

'Who knows what goes on in that madman's head?' Irini looked up. 'This is man's work, not for you. The police have had a bellyful of those brothers over the years. Aristides will know what to do.'

34

It was the book club's Christmas supper and Sara knew what she was going to take. If St Phanourios had any clout then she must make a Lost and Found cake to share among the group so Sparky would be found quickly, safe and well, not lying somewhere poisoned like poor Orpheus. His poisoner had never been detected.

She chose a recipe online, and placed her statue of the saint where he could oversee the proceedings and bless her efforts. She gathered the ingredients together on the table; flour, water, sugar, olive oil, chopped walnuts, cinnamon, baking powder and a lemon from the garden. Mixing everything in a bowl, she poured the thick batter into a baking dish to cook for an hour.

Hovering over the oven, afraid it might burn, she prayed it would rise and not flop back. Looking up to the wooden statue she smiled. 'Now it's up to you.'

Sandra had invited the club to her big house by the shore where she had gone to much trouble decorating it with fairy lights and bits of greenery. 'I've just heard about Griff's little dog. I hope they find him soon.'

'Don't worry, St Phanourios is on the case,' Sara laughed, handing out slices of her cake with pride. 'Irini says he finds all sorts of strays and even finds a girl a husband. Perhaps he'll add me to his list.'

Dorrie Thorner looked down at the plate. 'This all sounds pagan to me.' Mel gave her a look that said shut up. 'Still, this does look tasty, Sara, and not too dry. But you can't beat an Aga for making moist cakes.'

'Where would you find an Aga on Santaniki?' Chloë replied. 'This is delicious. I shall make a wish for the poor dog to come home. Now who is going to kick the evening off with a seasonal reading?'

'Just before we do,' Sandra looked around, 'I want to tell you all that Jack and I are going back soon for good. Julie has invited us for New Year. We've had a wonderful stay, thanks to all of you, with so many happy memories to cherish. When I'm lying under a scanner with my eyes clammed shut, I shall take along my Cretan music CD to relive that wonderful night, dancing under the stars on my wedding night.'

Everyone clapped and wished her well. 'You will come back. I just know it.' Mel gave Sandra a hug. 'There will always be a welcome for you here.'

They settled down to read out their chosen poems and stories as darkness enveloped them and firelight flickered, letting them imagine they were back in Britain on a winter's night.

How could I leave all this? Sara thought. Sandra and

Jack were going back to family. Much as she loved her parents, there was nothing else waiting for her in Sheffield. Here she felt stronger, in control of her future. She had faced the worst in seeing Jason again but knew there was one more thing she must do, if she was to banish him from her life once and for all.

Griff had searched all day, down by Sunset Beach where they often walked, up to the rock cave in case he'd followed his scent, around the cafés on the harbour in case he was scrounging for food. He must be starving by now. He feared the worst outcome. Hot and flustered, he trudged on, looking in alleyways, asking locals with no result.

Sparky was part of his life on the island and if he returned to England, Sparky would be coming with him. Duke and Wim had gone in opposite directions to him but all to no avail.

It was nearly two days since he went missing and Griff prepared himself for bad news. Had he been in some accident that no one had thought to report, or was he trapped down some gully?

It was Mel who poured him a stiff whisky when he arrived tired and dishevelled at the taverna. 'Any news?' she asked but he shook his head and slumped over the table.

'We've lost him,' he replied. His cheeks were sunken with tiredness, his forehead burnt by the sun.

'Not necessarily,' Mel replied. 'Irini told us an interesting thing. Sparky reminded her of Maria Metrakis' pet, the one who may have been left behind on the farm.'

'Not with that crew!'

'It's a thought worth pursuing,' she added, seeing the hope in his eyes.

'Just wait until I get up there.' Griff jumped up but she pushed him back in his chair.

'Caution is needed here. Don't go alone. Irini says take Aristides. It could get ugly. Spiro will drive you up there with Duke and Wim. Wait here. If you rush in who knows what might happen. We don't know that he is there.'

'If they've harmed him… I'll…' Griff was beside himself with fury. It was then that Irini, overhearing the plan, came downstairs slowly and banged her hand on the table.

'You stay away, Kyrie Griff. This is between our people. Yannis, the mayor, the policeman and Spiro will take care of this matter and I will go with them. I have words to say.'

'Mama, no!' Mel shouted. 'It could be dangerous.'

'He will not touch me… I know too much. Please, Kyrie Griff, let us do this our way.'

'I have to come then Sparky will know it's me.' Griff was not going to be left behind like some timid onlooker.

'Stay in the pickup then,' Irini ordered, her face stern, her hawk eyes like slits. 'We must take them by surprise.' The fierce look she gave him was reassuring in some strange way. They meant business and if some local had shamed their friendliness to strangers, then honour must be restored. 'Go back to your guests. Bring them here. Mel and Katya will give them supper. What we do, we do in silence…'

'She's right,' Mel whispered. 'Keep schtum and let us take care of things.'

*

Sara found Jason Metcalfe sitting slumped over his Mythos waiting for the ferry. Felix told her where he was hiding. 'Flissa blew him out and flew back yesterday without telling him.'

Sara stood over her ex until he looked up. 'There you are. I want a word with you. How could you tell lies about what happened between us? It's time things were cleared up once and for all.' She ordered a frappé and sat down. Her heart was pumping but she continued.

'You did me a great wrong, cheating on me. Well let me tell you, you are no Michelin star in the bedroom. How dare you complain about me to that whore? You're just a wham, bam, thank you, ma'am, a burger and chips, not fine cuisine. It was always about you, not me. You may be the body beautiful but that doesn't make up for tenderness or imagination. I am so over you and, I guess, so is your latest squeeze.'

'Have you finished?' Jason snapped. 'You're doing my head in—'

'No, I have not. You made a big mistake thinking I would put up with your antics. You let me think it was all my fault for not being good enough but let's face it, you've a lot to learn about pleasuring a woman. A sorry wouldn't go amiss.'

'Sorry for what? It was you who shamed me in front of my parents and mates. You could've warned me.'

'And find myself alone at the altar while you did a runner? No, I think what I did was just right. It's taken me months to come to terms with our fiasco of a wedding day.

You cheated on me because you didn't really care. I was just another trophy for your cupboard. You would've ditched me sooner or later if someone better came along but I got in there first. Grow up, Jason, learn from your mistakes like I've had to do or you'll go on making them.'

'You can cut out all that psychology crap, leave it off.' He looked up. 'Thank God, here comes the ferry. I can't wait to get off this scabby island. I wish you luck.'

Sara watched him roll his case towards the ship, walking out of her life for ever. He would never learn and for the first time since her wedding day, she felt a tinge of pity for the man.

As she turned to return home there was a shout.

'Sara! You've come to meet me, how kind.' It was Don Ford lugging his bag, waving to her. He had kept his promise to return in the off season. How glad she was to see him.

It was nearly midnight, dark and chilly as they rattled up the track to the Metrakis farm, a ramshackle collection of stone cube-shaped sheds, rusting farm equipment and old vans cluttering the entrance. Griff could smell the wood smoke rising from a small chimney in the house. An oil lamp flickered in a window. It was then their dogs barked, announcing their arrival. The door opened. Stavros stood bleary-eyed in a long shirt over his belly, his bare white legs thin and hairy. 'What the hell is this?' he yelled.

Irini got out of the car seat, dressed in black, wrapped in a shawl, her headscarf covering her hair. 'Kyria Maria Metrakis, do you have her dog?'

'What bloody dog? Is this some joke?' The torches of the policeman, the mayor and the men shone into his face.

'You know the one, the poor beast Maria left behind.'

'What are you talking about, woman?'

Aristides stepped forward in his uniform. 'We have reason to believe this is the wretched creature Kyrie Griff found starving, beaten and left by a track not far from here. He had crawled to find shelter from the sun.'

'Nothing to do with me,' Stavros argued but Irini was not finished.

'Maria, your wife, came to me the night she left with bruises on her cheeks and arms. She told me how you abused her. It was unspeakable. The doctor came out to dress her wounds. You tried to break her spirit but she left by ferry, crying that she was unable to go back for her pet because you chained it over there.' Irini pointed to a post.

'Rubbish! I never touched her,' Stavros argued, but he looked vulnerable now, half naked, surrounded by local men and this avenging angel in black.

'So, maybe you punished her little dog instead, chained it, threw it some grain now and then and kicked it out to die?'

'This woman is mad but what do you expect from a Papadaki troublemaker?'

Spiro leapt forward, about to thump him, but the men held him back. 'You don't talk to my mama like that. The Papadakis know all about your family.'

'We want to search your premises.' Aristides stepped forward, his hand holding his holster. 'If the dog is not here, we will leave you in peace.'

'Do what you want, you'll find nothing here.'

Griff couldn't wait any longer and jumped out of the pickup; he called out for his dog but there was not a sound. Perhaps they were barking up the wrong tree after all but his instinct was on alert. He was sure Metrakis was holding something back.

As they were searching with torches, Spiro tripped over something. 'What's this?' He lifted a tin to the light. It was a tin of rat poison… 'Is this what I think it is?' He called the others to examine it more closely. There were fresh grains inside.

'We do have details of the exact poison used to kill cats and strays in St Nick's and Kyria Ariadne's cat, Orpheus. If this tin matches our sample…' Aristides threatened.

'It's never been out of this shed,' Stavros said without conviction. He looked nervous.

'Then what's it doing out here half open?'

'You have no right to search my property or remove my goods.'

Irini was having none of it. 'You Metrakis are mountain thugs. Your name is mud on Crete. There are many who still recall the murder of Anastasia and her family. Memories are long. Is that why you hide out here? I know what your family is capable of and you are cut from the same cloth, a bully, a thief and now a poisoner. When Santaniki knows this, there will be no hiding place for you on this island. Save your face and tell us where that dog is, or else I curse you to hell and back!'

For a second there was silence then Stavros stuttered,

'He's my dog, it belongs to me. It got lost and the foreigner stole it. He owes me compensation.'

They all sneered at this volte-face. 'Pull the other leg, Metrakis. You saw how it recovered and blossomed into a fine dog that is heading the campaign to rescue strays. You waited until everyone was at the wedding and took him, lured him into your van. I bet he did not come willingly. Were you going to sell him online, given half the chance? Where is he?'

'How can I steal what is my property?' Stavros shuffled from one foot to the other, his two sons peering behind him.

'Don't tell them, Papa.'

'Shut up, you fool,' came the reply.

Griff had heard enough of these excuses and wandered off with his torch. Stavros was not stupid enough to put the dog in his yard. He was a sly one. Perhaps he wanted to hold him for ransom, the crazy man.

Having jogged around this area enough, Griff knew all the farms had shepherds' huts where they milked their sheep and goats for *myzithra* cheese. They were usually a distance away but not too far. He kept on whistling, calling out, hoping against hope in the silence. Only a bell owl answered his call.

He was about to turn back but called one last time. A bark replied, a bark he would recognise anywhere. Sparky was calling out to him and all he had to do was follow the sound blindly, trusting his instinct until he came to a round stone hut, the barking and whimpering reaching a frenzy. 'Sparky, I'm here, coming to rescue you, old boy!'

*

Mel sat with Sara and Don in the small hours after the last of the wedding guests staggered back to the retreat. 'Welcome back, you're just in time to see the drama unfold,' Mel said as they filled Don in with the latest developments. He stoked up the fire while they made a pile of zucchini fritters, braised chicken pieces in red wine, a mountain of Greek salad with tomatoes, cheese, greens, finishing off with large slices of baklava. They were keeping themselves busy, trying not to think about what was going on up in the hills.

'Irini has taken a new lease of life over this business. She dressed all in black like an avenging widow. I've never seen her look so fierce. Those Cretan genes were calling out for vengeance but I hope she's not tired herself out and done something foolish.'

Sara refused to go home until they returned. Earlier, she had stood before her carved statue of St Phanourios, hoping all the prayers offered to him to find things were true and not just a legend. 'Do your stuff and I'll bake another cake in your honour,' she whispered. Thank goodness no one in Sheffield could hear her pleas. They would think she'd gone doolally.

What if the Metrakis men got out their guns? Surely the mayor, policeman and Spiro were a match for any threats. As for Griff, now she knew how the men had defended her honour and given Jace a thumping, with black eyes and bruises for their trouble, all fears for her own reputation were forgotten in her concern for his safety.

They drank endless cups of Greek coffee, tidied up,

swept and mopped, cleared the tables and still they didn't return. Mel was beginning to panic. 'Should I call for reinforcements?' she asked, just as the sound of wheels brought them to their feet with relief. 'Spiro, Mama!' Mel shot out of the door to greet them. 'Jesus, Mary and Joseph, you're back in one piece. I was so worried. Is Mama safe?'

Spiro kissed her with passion. 'All's well and look who we have here.' He pointed to Griff cradling Sparky in his arms. There was the little dog, none the worse for his adventure. 'The warriors return,' he said. 'Mama was magnificent. That place is a hovel. They won't be troubling anyone for a while.' Spiro stood proud, sniffing the air. 'What can I smell? I'm starving. My magnificent Melodia thinks of everything.'

Irini beamed with pride at her son's words. 'I tore a strip off that man, threatened him with curses and exposure and he crumpled like the coward he is,' she said.

Griff was stroking the dog's head. 'I found Sparky chained up in a milking hut with water and some kibble, thank God, no harm done.'

Aristides chipped in. 'We think we have found the source of the poison on Stavros's farm. If it is tested and found to be a match, then the Metrakis men are in for a grilling and substantial fine. They will pay compensation for the trouble they have caused but without Irini softening them up with her threats, I doubt they would have admitted anything to us. What a night!'

Sara caught Griff's eye and smiled. 'So glad you're all back safely,' she offered and to her relief he smiled back with warmth. St Phanourios must have been watching overhead as they brought the supper to the table and everyone wolfed it down.

'Don't forget the meeting for the SPARKS night tomorrow, Sara,' Griff said. 'This little chap and me are heading for bed... what's left of the night. You should all do the same and thank you once again for all your help. I dread to think what might have happened to Sparky if we hadn't found him. Come along, Don, I think we can find you a bed. There's a good crime story here, don't you think?'

Sara nodded to them both, relieved they were all home safe, men and dog, and that she and Griff were still friends. Aristides escorted her back towards Ariadne's villa. 'A good night's work, Kyria Sara.'

Sara thanked him, knowing more things had shifted than what happened at the farm. Jason had left with his tail between his legs and it was as if a weight was shifted from her shoulders. Giving him the hard word had released all that hateful venom out of her system. Now she could relax and enjoy her first Christmas among friends.

Christmas

35

Sara never experienced such a festive season like this before. Everyone joined together in preparing decorations to sell at the traditional Christmas market in the *plateia*. Griff organised a stall for SPARKS. Together they made leaflets of information and adverts for the Abba tribute night. Chloë and the book club ladies baked mince pies by the dozen alongside a vat of Christmas punch, full of fruit and spices heated on a primus stove. St Nick's was festooned with lighted boats in windows in honour of St Nikolas, patron saint of all things nautical. Christmas trees, artificial or made from pine branches, brightened up the square.

In a decorated tent Griff was cajoled into his Uncle Jolly role as Santa himself. Sara was amused to see Duke carrying in little Harmony to meet him. He came out with a howling toddler. The weather was cool and seasonal but no snow was forecast as was the case two years before.

Spiro and Mel grilled chicken souvlaki on sticks and

the taverna was lit with lanterns and wreaths. Local artists displayed their work, jewellers, patchwork, weaving, olive wood sculpting, soaps, creams and cosmetics and candles scenting the air. Over the island there was a wealth of talent beavering away at their crafts.

Then there was the carol singing in the community hall and a Nativity play by the school children with a feast of Christmas biscuits and breads, cake and sweets. Sara had never seen such goodies and ate far too much.

Later she walked down to the beach with Don. 'It's great to have you back. You're my ally. I missed you,' she confessed.

'Ally against who?' he replied. 'Griff? What is it between you both?'

'I don't know… You heard about Jason arriving, the man I should have married? It floored me at first. It was such a disastrous experience.'

'Are you saying you will never trust another man again?'

'Something like that. I was on the harbour giving my ex a piece of my mind when you arrived. Since his departure I do feel different. I admire Griff, who wouldn't, but you know…' She hesitated. 'Not sure where it would lead. Why am I telling you all this?' she asked as they found a bench to watch the gunmetal waves crashing onto the shoreline.

'Because we're friends,' Don said, patting her hand.

'Why did you return so early? I thought you were home for Christmas. Isn't there family?' She hoped she wasn't prying.

'Writing can be a lonely occupation. You get caught up in your own little world, in the bubble of edits, deadlines, launch tours. I had a wife. She was understanding at first and put up with my absences and schedules but I left her too long and she found someone else. I never blamed her. I can be a selfish old buffer when the work isn't going well. I didn't read the signs, too engrossed in being successful, pleasing audiences, acting the clown. It took its toll.'

'I'm sorry, Don. I had no idea. You always seem so cheerful.' Sara sighed, knowing now how everyone tried to hide their sorrows by a mask of bravado.

'Oh yes, good old Don who likes a tipple, flirts with the girls. It's a well-honed act, my dear, and hard to keep up of late. Here on the island I can relax and no one wants a piece of me. To be truthful my latest book is a stinker. It has no legs and that's scary for an author... Last night when I got back to the retreat, it felt like coming home and I had the strangest dream. I thought I saw someone standing over me, smiling, holding out a sheet of paper. I woke and a new idea just popped into my head. I was so excited, I shot out of bed, banging my toe and started writing. That doesn't happen to the likes of me but it has now, much to my surprise.'

'How wonderful. So you will stay on?' Sara was so pleased for him.

'Oh yes, I have to catch this story while it falls. Sound weird to you?'

'Not at all. It was a dream that brought me back here to work, a wedding at sunset on a beach.'

'Then I think this calls for a drink or two.' Don hugged her. 'If I were twenty years younger, Griff would have some competition, young lady.'

'Don't be daft. I think Griff has had enough of me blowing hot and cold. Come on, we need to get you organised for the tribute night. You have to look the part, it's your era after all,' Sara laughed.

'Don't rub it in, you're as young as you feel, and as a matter of fact, I've come prepared.'

Chloë and Simon opened their home for a Christmas Eve supper, a chance to dress up, exchange gifts and catch up on any gossip. The Papadakises insisted Griff, Sara, Don, Pippa and Duke share their Christmas Day.

No one knew that Sara, Mel and Pippa were rehearsing a secret routine and Irini was sewing them costumes from old curtain remnants. Their confrontation with the Metrakis family was the talk of the neighbourhood. Irini held her head high as she recalled each detail, suitably embellished into a battle royal. Mel and Spiro sat back smiling but Markos drank in every word. '*Yiayia*, did you really fight them?' he asked.

'She fought them with words, mightier than any sword. Mama faced them with the truth and made them feel shame,' Spiro replied. 'That is a victory without guns, my son.'

It had been a wonderful day. Sara gave Griff a little picture of the retreat made by a jaded artist who had been on one of the courses there and found his mojo again. For Mel, she brought a beautiful lacy shawl knitted to order by an old villager in Sternes village. Sparky got one of those bright cotton neckerchiefs. She gave the boys books and for Irini, a bottle of organic hand cream in the pocket of a pretty pinafore. Spiro, Duke and Don got bottles of whisky, and Pippa a scented candle and a smocked dress for Harmony. She had tried to give local gifts to everyone and shared a parcel from her parents, full of her favourite Turkish Delight, iced Christmas cake, chocolates and the latest book by Pat Barker to discuss at the book group.

She'd promised her parents that she'd come home for a visit in the New Year. Now that there were three more enquiries for summer weddings to follow up and prospects of other bookings to come, she wanted to stay longer on the island. They were also busy drumming up support for the Abba night which was taking shape. Griff was foisting tickets on everyone he could catch. They wanted decent raffle prizes and, miracle of miracles, Simon used his contacts, explained the charity and got a signed T-shirt from some of the stars of *Mamma Mia*. It was going to be auctioned along with cases of Manousakis's best wine from Chania. Don brought signed books from his best-selling author friends and those famous Yorkshire vets sent them signed copies and wished them well.

Griff and Sara carried on as normal under Don's watchful eye. This was not the time to discuss the Jace and Flissa affair. There was too much to do and Sara felt exhausted with weddings, parties, meetings and returning hospitality as best she could. She hadn't realised Christmas could be so tiring. No wonder mothers took to the bottle as they prepared for the onslaught of guests, relatives and fractious children. Then she caught a stinking cold, retiring to bed to sleep it off.

Three days later, feeling washed out but excited, she

helped as they set up the hall for the Abba event with posters of the film and a sound system to play tracks. Sara hoped everyone would get into the spirit of the party. Griff was going to give a short presentation about the SPARKS charity and plans for an online appeal on social media. He was asking for volunteers to foster dogs until they were rehomed.

As the lights were dimmed, in trouped partygoers in all sorts of fancy dress, mostly flared trousers and home-made kipper ties with fedora hats and frilled shirts. Chloë wore a magnificent maxidress with dangling beads. Dorrie did her best with a long skirt and a velvet bandana round her head. Norris managed a scarlet shirt and a false moustache. Sally wore a fringed skirt with cowboy boots and hat. Greek and expats were vying for the most flamboyant costumes with sequins and velvet waistcoats dug out of old trunks in cupboards, hidden away for decades, reminding everyone of misspent youths, all a little tight in the chest and on the thighs.

Pippa was dressed up as Donna in denim dungarees and a cotton shirt. Dark-haired Mel wore long flared pantaloons, sunglasses and a floppy hat while Sara wore a jumpsuit and a string of beads, a bandana round her hair.

Duke wore the most outrageous frilled shirt, open to the waist with a huge medallion hanging over his hairy chest, velvet hipsters and kinky boots with wedges. How he had found these showstoppers, no one knew. Everyone was clapping and whistling, ready to dance as the music blared out. Then Don appeared and everyone cheered. He was wearing a gold lamé jumpsuit with huge frilled flares on his trousers and on the sleeves. He had a long-haired wig and platform boots, waving what looked like a spliff of wacky baccy in one hand, gesturing a peace V-sign in the other. There was no doubt he was the outright winner.

Griff hid behind the stage causing a roar as he appeared in jeans, sleeveless T-shirt, a leather cap and black moustache as one of the "village people" to present the prize to Don. He made his small presentation with Sparky on a lead wearing a spotted bow tie. When supper was announced there was a rush for the seventies-style buffet: pineapple and cheese on sticks, a selection of dips, finger foods, sausages, trifles, black forest gateaux, cheesecakes with fruit toppings.

Then it was time for the girls to step up on stage and Mel let rip with 'Take A Chance On Me' while Pippa and Sara were trying to mimic the film choreography as best they could. Sara had no voice to join in the chorus, just a husky croak, but they let their hair down and the audience clapped them on. Then Mel sang 'One of Us'. Spiro and the boys watched, once more enthralled and proud of her amazing talent.

Afterwards, the music got louder, the dancing went on late into the night but not before the auctions, raffle and tickets raised nearly a thousand euros. It was a triumph, enough to set the charity up on a serious footing. By this time Sara was on her knees with exhilaration and exhaustion. Her voice was a mere husk and her head thumping with tiredness.

Chloë and Simon, seeing the state of her, offered to drive her home and she didn't refuse. The headache grew worse, her bones aching, and she felt a feverish heat in her body; too little sleep for days, too much to drink, not enough to eat but she recognised this was no cold but the dreaded flu. She could hardly peel off her jumpsuit and collapsed on the pillow, her throat burning. The room was spinning above her. She was going nowhere from this bed.

Mel called into Ariadne Villa to return some dishes. The door was unlocked, curtains still closed. 'Sara! Only me...' There was no answer, so she yelled up the stairs to find her friend burning up with fever and coughing in a chesty way.

'Sorry, can't seem to get my head off the pillow. Don't come near, I don't want you to catch anything.'

Mel smiled, knowing it might be a bit too late. 'I'm calling the doctor, I don't like the sound of your chest, you look awful.'

Sara was too sick to protest. When Dr Makaris came, he listened to her chest and prescribed antibiotics for the infection there. 'Lots of water, aspirin, *malotira* tea, just rest,' he ordered. 'It's a virus with a little complication. She's strong but her chest is tight. She can't be left alone though,' he said.

'Don't worry, I'll ring round, we can see to things for her.'

'She's not the only one with this virus; she's the fifth I've seen this week. Don't get too close until the fever's broken and don't let Irini near her.'

Mel smiled. Irini was still basking in her role as saviour of Spartacus and prosecutor of Stavros Metrakis who had abandoned their taverna, thank goodness. The doctor's warning wouldn't stop her mother-in-law sending Sara every Cretan remedy known to man. All their faith was in the mountain tea which would restore her immune system, relieve fever, restore sleep: the cure-all of cure-alls.

Dorrie Thorner promised to do any shopping and collect prescriptions. Sara's effort to make Daniel's wedding happen was not forgotten. Chloë became head nurse, wearing a mask as precaution. Now that Alexa, Felix and Olympia had returned to London, she was feeling the gap. Katya took sheets and towels to be laundered. The book club came to the rescue too, keeping an eye on the patient, feeding her gossip, magazines and soup. It was a team effort from all her friends on the island. Sara couldn't thank them enough.

36

Griff was pleased to see Don beavering away in what was once Elodie Durrante's study. Since his return, he was the model of industry, typing away like a man possessed. Don looked up. 'You've heard about poor Sara. She's got the flu... been doing far too much running around for you and got little thanks for it.'

'What do you mean? Every time I went to thank her, she dashed off on some urgent task.' Griff hadn't heard about the sickness. He'd presumed she was avoiding him.

'There's no danger of you catching the bug then.' Don took off his glasses. 'Sit down. I have something to say. Isn't it about time you made a serious move in her direction or are you scared she might turn you down? I've never known a couple dither so much.'

Griff felt himself blushing. 'It's none of your damn business.'

'Yes, it is... you're well suited and I'm very fond of you both. I'd hate to see things drift. You should talk about how you feel to her. It's the only way to find out where you stand.'

'I never took you for a marriage counsellor,' Griff replied. Don meant kindly enough but this was a personal and private matter.

'Believe me, I've learned the hard way. If you don't talk things out, misunderstandings get in the way. I lost my wife because I was too busy being Don Ford, crime writer par excellence, too busy to notice we were drifting apart until it was too late. Now my ex-wife has a new husband and grandkids. My family consists of a line of books on a shelf. They don't keep you warm at night.

'Miss Durrante entrusted this house so it could ring with creative life. I've found friendship, inspiration and hope here but a woman by your side would add so much more to the place. Think on... "I shall say zeece only once." Now let me get back to the murder scene.'

Griff felt guilty not to have heard Sara was ill. He was so wrapped up in the SPARKS idea, he was losing sight of the plight of others. He went to see Mel, offering to sit in at the villa, but she was concerned not to spread the virus. He collected lemons and tried to concoct a lemonade cordial laced with herbs but, distracted by a phone call, he burnt the pan. They still hadn't talked about the Flissa and Jace episode. Did Sara know how he had doubted her?

He missed her visits, admiring her go-to enthusiasm and courage in making this whole new life for herself here. She'd worked her socks off for the Abba tribute night and it had clearly worn her down.

All he could do was send flowers and a copy of Elodie's

journal; the one Ariadne had discovered in Elodie's little study. This was the unedited original version, far fruitier than the one they edited and put out as an e-book. He wrote a get-well card saying they were going ahead with charity status. SPARKS hit the *Chania News* with a picture of Sparky and an appeal for foster homes. The Souda Animal Shelter came to offer advice on the best way forward. Metrakis got off with a fine, a caution and a threatened inspection of his own animals' welfare. Banned from Irini's café, he slunk off to a seedy *kafenion* close to the harbour, out of sight. Griff knew enough about human nature to know that a man like that would never change his grudge against the world but Irini pointed her finger at him and he knew he was a marked man.

Sandra stood among the line of suitcases, staring out over the infinity pool to the sea beyond, shimmering in a silvery light. It was time to leave this house set on the cliff top. Would they ever return to Santaniki? It had been a glorious nine months, topped by their wedding and Julie's visit. It felt too much at times. Christmas had been a whirl of invitations and now there was the New Year to look forward to back home with Julie.

She said farewell to Mel, Irini and the book club but Sara was still sick and she couldn't risk an assault on her immune system. She needed to be strong for the trials ahead but coming to rest up here was worth every penny. Sara's thoughtful touches to their wedding day would stay with her for ever. She wanted to leave a gift and a card.

They made one last trip to Rethymno and among the cobbled ancient streets she found a perfumery which sold the very scent Mel suggested Sara might like; something that smelt of roses with vanilla tones. They boxed it in gorgeous gift wrapping. There was such pleasure in giving a thank you, she thought. They lunched in the shade of their favourite restaurant, the Pigadi, then bought gifts to take home for Julie's family.

Now the sun would be replaced by grey skies and winter chills but she was ready to leave Paradise. Their days in the sun would live in her memory to be revisited when the going was tough. Dusty, their rescue dog, would travel back with them on the same plane. He would be a good companion for Jack if the worst should happen. Best to leave the party on a high note while she was still well enough to travel without aid. There was always the hope they might return.

It took over ten days before Sara began to feel human again, able to taste all the little dishes Irini sent over to get her back on her feet. Chloë came most days to check on her progress and brought pictures of their wedding, thrilled it had gone so well.

'We were able to get shots of the best man so his black eye didn't show. Felix told us all about the infamous camping trip and we were so sorry to hear of your own dealings with Jason Metcalfe. I gather Flissa sent him packing. Perhaps she'll choose better next time. Poor Dorrie's back to form. I thought she'd turned a corner, in fact, but at last week's book club she was ranting about our reading list choice of novels once more. It was a relief in a way. St Dorinda didn't sit well on her.'

'She's been kind to me though.' Sara had to defend Dorrie's efforts to help out. 'I can't thank you enough, all of you, for keeping me afloat. I don't know how I'd have coped alone. How on earth did I catch this lurgy?'

'You were run down, racing about making people's dreams come true. Perhaps it's time you found a dream of your own.'

'But I have, Chloë. Coming here has been the best thing, making a living in such a beautiful place is a joy.'

'It's not so beautiful now, chucking it down, a month's worth of rain in a week.'

Sara hadn't noticed the weather, sheltered as she was by the fireside in her dressing gown. 'I must get myself dressed, I feel a fraud.'

'You take it easy. Viruses return if you overdo things.' Chloë produced a parcel. 'It's from Sandra and Jack. They've gone back to Manchester for good. We couldn't let her come to say goodbye but I hope they will come back next year, all being well, and fingers crossed for her treatments.'

Sara opened the box, finding inside a large bottle of her favourite perfume. 'How did she know? Was it Mel? She's seen what I use.' Chloë nodded. 'I must have their address to write and thank them. It's the real McCoy, pure essence, how generous. I feel so pampered. It's time to get up and doing. I've been reading Elodie's journal, what a woman she was. Simon and the committee have done a great job getting it in print.'

'Simon enjoyed getting back into publishing circles

again. They had to edit out some of the more libellous extracts. Look, I must go. Wonderful to see you back in the land of the living.' Chloë blew a kiss and departed.

Sara took a shower and found her jeans hanging off her hips. She looked gaunt and her cheeks sunken. 'Not the best look, Miss Loveday,' she said. 'But better than the alternative.'

Three days later, she felt her limbs no longer wobbling and took herself down the path into the garden, battered by the rain, but it still looked welcoming and comforting in its own way. Then she forced herself back to her laptop, panicking at what she may face there. Was there any business among the stream of emails? What was the state of her bank balance? Her head still felt like cotton wool, a bit waffy and out of focus. She slammed the lid shut. I'll face that tomorrow, she thought, dousing herself in the rich perfume. It felt so luxurious and extravagant. They couldn't have given her a more thoughtful gift. Sinking back onto the sofa, she heard the doorbell ring. 'Come in,' she shouted. 'It's not locked.' Who needed to lock their doors on this island?

Turning around she saw Sparky bounding in. 'We've come to see the invalid at long last. How are you?' Griff was standing in the doorway with a bunch of flowers. She waved her hand.

'Sit down... coffee?'

'No, I've brought wine, some cheeses and a box of baklava. Rumour has it that you need fattening up after your ordeal.'

Sparky was nuzzling at her knees, his tail wagging. 'You see, we're both delighted to see you up. Where's the glasses?'

'I'll get them,' Sara offered.

'No, stay there and be waited on for once,' he ordered. 'You and I need to talk,' he went on, pouring two glasses of deep red wine. 'Hope you like this. My brother sent me a case.'

'I don't think I'm supposed to drink yet but what the hell, one glass won't harm me.' Sara paused, seeing the look on Griff's face, an intense gaze. 'What needs saying?' She sat back, waiting for his answer.

'Just that we missed you, that I believed Jason's lies about you and for a moment I doubted your integrity but in my gut I knew it couldn't be true and yet...' He looked away.

Sara sat back, relieved that things were out in the open at last. 'I was hurt, thinking everyone might know what had happened between us in Sheffield. Mel was very discreet but Spiro came to my rescue, I gather. Perhaps what I did was OTT. You have no idea how gutted and furious I was. I had to get away.'

'Oh, yes, I think I do. Max Bannerman, my ex-business partner, ruined our success, bankrupted me, kicked me in the balls and buggered off to the Cayman Islands with his fortune intact, so I know only too well what it is to be betrayed, to have your trust destroyed and be taken for a fool. I was so ashamed. That's what brought me here in the first place, to hide away, blaming myself for being far too trusting...'

'I'm sorry, I had no idea. You kept things private as I tried to do.' Sara leaned forward, facing him with a sigh. 'I hadn't a clue... I knew Jason was a control freak but I just went along with his suggestions; cut your hair shorter, no clutter in the flat, lose some weight. It's a hard lesson to learn that he wanted to create an image that just wasn't me at all, to look good on his arm. We're two of a kind, you and me, landing up here on our beam ends to find new careers and new friends. How strange is that?' Griff took her hands in his, his deep blue eyes smiling with relief. She covered his hand with her own. 'Do you think fate brought us here?' she asked.

'I don't believe in fate, we make our own destiny by the choices we make,' he replied.

'Synchronicity, isn't that the buzz word for when you take your courage in hand, take a risk and then something good happens?' Sara sensed him closing in, her heart racing.

'And you smell delicious, by the way,' he said, before kissing her gently. 'We've been orbiting around each other for months, coxing and boxing. I knew there was something in your past. There were moments when I sensed you wanted me but then...'

'I know, but that was then, this is now.' Sara kissed him, this time withholding nothing. Sparky jumped up, barking, not wanting to be left out. 'We might have to finish this in private,' Griff laughed.

'No time like the present then,' Sara replied, pointing to the stairs, hoping she had made her bed.

'Sparky... stay, stay here, good boy,' Griff ordered as the little dog watched them retire to her bedroom, his head on his paws, looking forlorn, sensing it was going to be a long wait.

Three months later

'What are you doing for your birthday next week?' Mel asked as they were sitting on the terrace of the retreat sipping iced lemonade.

'I'm trying to forget it. Who wants to admit to the big four-oh?'

'Nonsense, it's the new thirty. Has Griff made any plans to celebrate with you?'

Sara had moved into the retreat with him after the New Year and Don Ford was now renting Ariadne Villa. She was keeping quiet about the date. 'He's had to go back for his niece's confirmation. She's his goddaughter.' They had made a brief visit to the ancestral home in the Shropshire hills where Sara was greeted like a long-lost sister. 'He did ask me to come but knew that Mum and Dad had emailed to say they would like to visit to celebrate with me. We'll be staying on Crete for a few days to explore the island. They were insistent I joined them. I'm really not bothered about it. I find birthdays depressing, another year older and all that.'

'We celebrate our name days here but I don't think there's a St Melodia yet. My baptismal name is Maria so I get plenty of cake and flowers then. Have you a second name?'

'Catherine... after my gran. I always think it a waste of a good name. It never gets used except on a passport or at a wedding.'

'I must say you look so happy. I can see it's going well with Griff. I'm sure he'll bring you something back from his visit. Any more wedding bookings?' Mel was always interested in her business. She was becoming a dear friend.

'Three confirmed bookings for May and June so I'm glad of this quiet break now.'

Later, Sara took Sparky for a walk onto the stony track. Spring was in full blossom with roadsides a riot of wild flowers, poppies, daisies and tulips.

How could she explain to Mel her new life with Griff? He was everything she could wish for, tender, passionate and considerate. What had she done to deserve such a change of fortune? She didn't mind her birthday being low key. It was good of her parents to make the long journey here but she would take the ferry and meet them at the airport.

It would be a packed few days visiting the museums and the botanical gardens of Crete, a trip onto the Omalos plain to see the wild orchids and tulips. They were going to stay at a bijou hotel behind the harbour in Chania, returning to St Nick's on her actual birthday. It was a shame Griff wouldn't be there to greet her, Mel would be busy and even Don had returned to London for some publisher's bash. She was trying not to feel a little deserted but it seemed everyone was otherwise engaged. They had taken her at her word that she didn't want a fuss.

Sara loved waiting at Chania airport to meet her visitors and brides-to-be. Dad hugged her. 'It'll be good to have you all to ourselves for a bit,' he said. 'I remember holding your mum's hand trying not to faint as she pushed you out into the world. It seems like only yesterday.'

Sara smiled, sensing this was going to be a quiet but loving birthday to remember.

Mel was up a ladder fixing lanterns to the olive trees. 'How does this look?' she shouted to Spiro who with Duke and Simon was trying to erect an arch of foliage and flowers by the entrance to the garden of the retreat. 'Has Natalie brought the cake yet? Thank goodness she's back from her travels.'

Nat was a founder member of the book club alongside Chloë and Ariadne Blunt. She was their star baker. Her cakes were to die for. Chloë was busy filling vases for the table filled with roses and blossoms while Dorrie and Sally were helping Don put up a big banner by the entrance to the drive.

'Are you sure she'll want the whole town to know she's forty? I would hate it,' Dorrie said.

'Why not?' Don replied. 'Anyway, we're only putting *Chronia polla* on the street lamps. She'll think it's for someone else.'

It was all hands to the pump that morning, roping in everyone who knew Sara – even Irini was busy preparing dishes for the feast. Mel was not going to let her friend get away scot-free from this landmark birthday. What were a few porky pies when it came to giving Sara this surprise?

Griff was on hand supervising. He had returned yesterday with Don. Little did his lover know to what lengths her friends were going to keep this a secret. There were helium balloons to tie up and the big dining table extended for the dinner.

Allan and Josie, Sara's parents, were in on the deception and had a tight schedule to fill so that they returned to the island after all the other guests were assembled. Even Sparky would have his role to play but that was for later. Everyone was entering into the spirit of the event.

Irini had to keep them in the taverna long enough with cake and name day treats. Mel ordered a little icon of St Katerina from the monastery at Agia Triada on the Akrotiri peninsula. Irini would give this to her from the family. Allan and Josie knew to string things along until the signal to come up was texted. The party was being planned like a military campaign.

The one drawback was how to get Sara out of her usual jeans and T-shirt into something partified without arousing suspicion, but Josie came up with the perfect solution. Mel was so excited for her friend. She, who planned so many happy events, was going to get a celebration all of her own.

*

When her mum had finished unpacking her case, she brought a parcel into Sara's room. 'These are for you from us.' Sara opened the box to find a string of creamy pearls. 'How lovely! I've always admired yours…'

'I've kept these for years, they're natural ones. My aunt left them to me. She's the one who lived in Hong Kong, never married but everything she bought was genuine. I think every woman of a certain age should wear pearls, fake or real. Try them on.'

Sara sat by the mirror to admire their effect around her tanned neck. 'Thank you.'

'And there's something else from her too. I thought it might be useful on a model for one of your online wedding blogs.' She opened a package wrapped in tissue paper and lifted out a full-length ivory satin wedding dress. 'This was Hilda's. It was never worn. Her fiancé died in Burma during the war. I found it folded in a cupboard. How could I part with it? It's beautiful, cut on the bias. She was tall like you. I thought you might like it.'

Sara fingered it with care. There was a scent of rosemary and lavender, not mothballs. 'It's perfect, vintage and expensive by the feel of the satin. I've been thinking about a vintage angle for when I do another wedding fair. Mum, it's too good to have sticky fingers touching it. I'd wear it myself…' Sara laughed, seeing her mum's face. 'Don't go giving me ideas.'

'Dad and I are so proud of you, making a new life out here, much as we miss you, and now you've got Griff. The first time I met him I had a feeling he was right for you. It's a pity he'll be away on your birthday, love.'

'Don't worry, we'll be back and forth. I need to be seen at some wedding fairs, if only to give Paradise Tours a run for their money.'

'Don't overdo it. What with the artists' courses, a big house to run and a business of your own...'

Sara smiled. Trust Mum to fuss. *I might be forty in a few days but there's life in the old girl yet.*

'Oughtn't we to be getting back to the retreat?' Sara said as she sat in the taverna sipping village wine and wondering how she would eat the enormous slice of chocolate cake Irini had baked specially. Her parents sat back, in no hurry. 'Thank you so much for this icon. It will sit in my office.'

'It's St Katerina in honour of your own second name,' she explained. Mel must have tipped her the wink when she had asked about her middle name.

'I really think I should be getting back now.' She was surprised Mel wasn't there to greet them. 'Where's Mel?' she asked, but Irini shrugged her shoulders. 'On the beach with the boys, I think.'

Sara stood to make a move and then her mother nudged her, throwing half a large glass of red wine over her jeans, soaking right through to her legs with a blood-red stain.

'Oh, how clumsy of me,' her mum cried.

'No worries, I'll change when I get back.' Irini rushed over with a damp cloth, only making things worse.

'You can't walk through town like that on your name

day. You have a case of clothes right here. Change into something. I will wash your jeans,' she ordered, pointing to the toilet. 'There's no one in… It is too hot for trousers.'

Her mother was rooting through her bag. 'Here, put this on.' She held up a floral printed sundress they had chosen in Chania, and the pearls. 'I'd like to see the effect.'

'I'm only going up the road in the jeep.' Sara was feeling pressurised into complying. She didn't see Dad winking at Irini. She tried not to feel annoyed as she peeled off her shirt and wet jeans, stepped into the floral dress and ran a comb through her tousled hair. The sea crossing had done it no favours. She fixed the pearls and shook her head. What a fuss about nothing. It was not like Mum and Dad to dawdle when there was a swimming pool to cool down in. They climbed into her old jeep that was parked in the harbour to take them back.

'Oh, look,' said her mother. 'What does that sign say?'

'Many years, their version of happy returns,' Sara answered, noticing there were posters all up the road on the lamp-posts. She'd never seen that before. It was then she saw the helium balloons by the entrance to the retreat. What was going on? Had someone booked the garden without her consent? She turned her back for a few days and someone had taken liberties. Then she saw the banner on top of the huge arch. What was going on? 'Happy Birthday, Sara!'

Then all hell was let loose as friends were popping out of bushes, waving and smiling: 'Welcome back.' How had they managed all this behind her back? She turned around to see her parents grinning.

WEDDING IN THE OLIVE GARDEN

A WEDDING IN THE OLIVE GARDEN

'You knew about this?'

'You didn't think we were going to let you celebrate your big birthday with a pizza and a pint?' Dad replied.

'Now I get all that pantomime in Irini's was done to get me changed...'

Sara walked slowly up the drive to greet her friends who were all done up to the nines in party gear. There were bottles of fizz and bouquets, cards and kisses. It was all too much to take in. Such a pity Griff wasn't here to enjoy it with her. Then Don appeared from nowhere. 'You are supposed to be in London,' she said with her hands on her hips in mock rebuke.

'So I was, but not for long. Happy birthday, my dear Sara. This is for you.' He produced a parcel wrapped in foil. 'Open it later.'

She spied Simon and Chloë, Dorrie and Norris, Pippa and Duke, Sally and her husband. 'I never expected this.' Her eyes were filling up. 'Is this all your doing?' She pointed to Mel and Spiro who were arm in arm together, laughing.

'Not exactly.' A familiar shape stepped out of the trees. 'Happy birthday, darling!'

Sara spun round in surprise and ran into his arms. 'You deceitful devils. Here's me thinking nobody knew or cared. Thank you, everybody.' She could hardly speak for crying.

Griff led her to the veranda where the feast was being laid out and in the middle was a gorgeous iced cake piped with roses and ivy leaves. It was too beautiful to cut. There were pictures taken, corks popping, glasses clinking but she had eyes for only one man as the local musicians began to tune up for dancing. Sara could hardly breathe or eat for excitement. 'When did you get back?' She nudged Griff.

'After you'd gone. Look who are over there.' A couple were waving to her. It was Griff's brother Rufus and Serena, his wife.

'They came all the way out here for me?'

'I thought it was about time they came to see where we live and work. They are mighty impressed.' Griff turned to Sara. 'It's going to be quite a night.'

Griff could see the delight on Sara's face. She looked radiant as they tucked into her favourite dish; rooster, oven roasted in red wine with a side salad of greens and Nat's home baked rolls. The house had never looked so festive. Looking up, he saw a shadow flitting across the top window as if someone was looking down on them. Was Elodie giving them her blessing? She would approve, he was sure, for the novelist had known real love in her lifetime. Now there was one more task he must perform before they danced the night away.

Taking his leave, he found Sparky snuffling for leftovers under the table and took him inside to put on his special pouch. 'Come on, old boy, you can do the honours.' Leading the dog to the table, Griff banged his spoon on the table to gain attention.

'Ladies and gentlemen, thank you for giving so generously of your time and effort to make this a memorable night. Mel and I could not have done this without you. As you may recall, Sara and I did not get off to the best of starts. She thought me a burglar and I thought her one of those annoying tourists, but over time we have become the dearest of friends. She is working tirelessly for our dog rescue charity which I am happy to announce can now begin to rehome strays across Europe. Tonight, though, is not about all this good work.

'Tonight is about wishing Sara, here, a happy birthday and all the very best success for the future. She has made herself part of this community, building up her business, bringing welcome income into our tourist economy. It is only right that Sparky and I give her something from us to add to this splendid celebration.' Griff motioned Sara to stand up and Sparky jumped onto the chair.

Sara saw Sparky was carrying something in a little pouch around his neck. 'What's this, for me?'

Griff nodded. 'Open it,' he said as she released his present from the collar. 'I hope you like it.'

Sara unwrapped the paper to find a small leather box and lifted the lid. Inside was a ring; a half hoop of diamonds with a large emerald in the middle. She was speechless, looking to Griff in surprise. 'It was my grandmother's,' he whispered as he placed it on her finger. 'Marry me, Sara Loveday, please, and soon...'

There was silence as their guests waited for her answer. Sara grinned. 'Of course... but only if I can book the olive garden.' There were cheers and a roar of congratulations. She looked across to her mother who was wiping her eyes with tears of joy. What a night to remember, she thought, as she looked down at the lanterns flickering, the candles in jars, the scent of white jasmine. Here was the perfect wedding venue and Aunt Hilda's dress was waiting to be worn at last, but most of all, here was the best man in the world beside her. If this was what forty was going to be like, bring it on.

Recipe

LOST AND FOUND CAKE
(*Phanouropita*)

500g self-raising flour
250ml water
250g sugar
200g olive oil
250g chopped walnuts
250g raisins
2tsp baking powder
1tsp ground cinnamon
Zest and juice of 1 orange

Heat oven to 150°C.

Put all the above in a bowl and mix well. Pour the batter into a 25cm diameter baking tin. Bake for one hour.

Traditionally shared into forty pieces!

It is said it will help unmarried girls find a husband; others bake this cake to help people find the right path or to help farmers find stolen animals.

Acknowledgements

Without some helpful anecdotes and experiences from my dear friends, Trisha and Mike Scott, and the professional expertise of wedding planner, Elizabeth Cradick (elizabeth@weddingsincrete.co.uk), my heroine would have failed on all fronts. Any mistakes are therefore my own.

Spartacus bounced unplanned into my story, inspired by my own rescue dog, Mr Beau. I am grateful to my friend Heather Welham for information on the dedicated work of ARIA (Animal Rescue In Apokoronas) and their rehoming services.

Many thanks once more to my agent, Judith Murdoch, editor Rosie de Courcy and copy editor Liz Hatherell for their excellent editorial advice, and the team at Head of Zeus for their encouragement.

For David and I, falling in love with the island of Crete all those years ago has been a great source of inspiration and joy. As for St Phanourios and his powers, he has not let me down yet in finding anything mislaid.

Leah Fleming

About the Author

Leah Fleming found her true calling as a storyteller after careers in teaching, catering, running a market stall, stress management courses in the NHS, as well as being a mother of four. She lives in the beautiful Yorkshire Dales but spends part of the year marinating her next tale from an olive grove on her favourite island of Crete.

leahfleming.co.uk
@LeahleFleming